Praise for
YANKEE INVASION

"IGNACIO SOLARES has written a superb novel set in one of the most dramatic moments in our history: the Mexican-American War of 1846–48. Our country was shaken to its very core by this invasion and military subjection, which culminated with the episode on which the book centers: the hoisting of the United States flag in the main square of Mexico City. It is impossible to understand Mexico or the past, present and future of its bilateral relationship with the United States without a thorough knowledge of this war and its aftermath, and now *Yankee Invasion* provides readers with a wonderful opportunity to become acquainted with this crucial moment in the shared history of Mexico and the US."

Arturo Sarukhan, Mexican Ambassador to the United States

"This is a riveting historical novel of the invasion and occupation of Mexico City by US forces during the Mexican War but more important, *Yankee Invasion* is an unusual, highly original, and most welcome detectivesque testimony of the nightmarish history we don't seem to be able to wake up from."

Irene Vilar, author of *The Ladies' Gallery: A Memoir of Family Secrets* and *Impossible Motherhood*

"Hungry to understand the roots of anti-Americanism? Want to know what national greed and the overreaching of American foreign policy resulted in in the mid-19th century? Read Ignacio Solares' novel. You'll realize why it's common knowledge that America's best friend around the world is the escape goat."

Ilan Stavans, author of *The Hispanic Condition* and *Mr. Spic Goes to Washington*

"Imagination, memory, and history come together in Ignacio Solares's story 'rendering an accounting' of love, awkwardness, fear, shame, and horror at the impending US invasion of Mexico City in 1847. Masterfully crafted, the novel, like a punctum, cuts through and rips open the smooth surface of the official history and exposes the raw matter of Abelardo's memories buried deep but still haunted by the witnessing of the killing of an American soldier trying to raise the flag over the capitol on September 14, 1847—the memory of that event brings forth the private passions and indiscretions of yester-year, the daily life of the people in the times of General Santa Anna, the glorious and that less glorious past of the nation, as well as the insights into the trauma of the shared history of Mexico and the United States. A singular tour de force in a lucid translation by Timothy G. Compton."

Professor Michal Kobialka, University of Minnesota

"*Bienvenido* to this translation of a searing work by an out-standing Mexican writer."

C.M. Mayo, author of *The Last Prince of the Mexican Empire*

"In a period when Mexico has to choose between being a just and progressive country or one still tied to corruption and injustice, *La invasión* is a call to sense and responsibility."

Salvador Elías Venegas Andraca, mindsofmexico.org (Mexico)

"If life is a dream, Solares seems to say, then history is a night-mare ... The novel opens with an ominous symbol—the gro-tesque image of the US flag flying over the Zócalo."

Mauricio Molina, *Letras Libres* (Mexico)

"Centering on September 14, 1847, the day on which the US flag was raised in the heart of Mexico City, *La invasión* presents facts, reflections, and debates relevant to today."

Javier Valenzuela, *El País* (Spain)

"The most important political and military battle in Mexican history is precisely the US invasion ... here is a chronicle of the moment when that nation was on the verge of disappearing."

Oscar Velasco, gaceta.cicese.mx (Mexico)

"The collective biography of the Mexico that lived through the trauma of the US invasion ..."

Alejandro Estivill, *Hoja por Hoja* (Mexico)

"Solares, an award-winning Mexican novelist and playwright, presents a wonderfully written book about the invasion and occupation of Mexico City by US forces during the Mexican War (1846–47). As an elderly upper-class gentleman reflects on his youth more than fifty years earlier, readers learn about the fear, shame, and embarrassment that this dark period in Mexican history brought to its people."

On *La invasión*, named one of "Best Adult Books of 2005,"
Críticas (United States)

Yankee Invasion
A Novel of Mexico City

YANKEE INVASION

A NOVEL of MEXICO CITY

~

Ignacio Solares

TRANSLATED *by* TIMOTHY G. COMPTON

~ Introduction by Carlos Fuentes ~

SCARLETTA
PRESS
co-published with ALIFORM 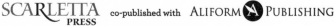PUBLISHING

MINNEAPOLIS

Scarletta Press
10 South Fifth Street, Suite 1105
Minneapolis, MN 55402, USA
www.scarlettapress.com

Co-published with
Aliform Publishing
117 Warwick Street SE
Minneapolis, MN 55414, USA
www.aliformgroup.com

Discussion questions are available on
both websites.

Library of Congress Cataloging-in-
Publication Data

Solares, Ignacio, 1945–
  [Invasión. English]
  Yankee invasion : a novel of Mexico City
/ Ignacio Solares ; translated by Timothy
G. Compton ; introduction by Carlos
Fuentes. — 1st ed.
      p.   cm.
  "Co-published with Aliform Publishing."
  Originally published as La invasión,
2005.
  ISBN 978-0-9798249-4-4
  1. Mexican War, 1846-1848—Fiction.
  2. Mexico City (Mexico)—History—
American occupation, 1847-1848—
Fiction. I. Compton, Timothy G.,
1960– II. Title.
  PQ7298.29.O4415813 2009
  863'.64--dc22
                              2009001476

La presente traducción fue realizada con
sustento del Programa de Apoyo a la Traducción de Obras Mexicanas en Lenguas
Extranjeras (ProTrad).

This translation was made possible with
support from Mexico's Programa de
Apoyo a la Traducción de Obras Mexicanas en Lenguas Extranjeras (ProTrad).

Book design by Mighty Media Inc.,
Minneapolis, MN
Cover: Anders Hanson
Interior: Chris Long

First edition

10 9 8 7 6 5 4 3 2 1

Printed in Canada

This book has a dedication.

∾

We went on forming the new face of the city with knife stabs.
MANUEL PAYNO

CONTENTS

INTRODUCTION

by CARLOS FUENTES

IGNACIO SOLARES, the prominent Mexican novelist, play-wright, critic and cultural one-man-show, comes from the border state of Chihuahua. Perhaps this explains, to a certain point, his fascination with northern Mexico and, especially, the universe—for it is such—of the border between Mexico and the United States.

Mexico has had a highly centralized cultural and political history. Since the reign of the Aztecs (to 1521) and then the Colonial (1521–1810) and independent (1810–present) periods Mexico City has been the crown and magnet of Mexican life. A nation isolated within itself by a geography of volcanoes, mountain ranges, deserts and jungles, Mexico has always found a semblance of unity in the capital city, today a vast metropolis of twenty million people, reflecting the jump in the country's population from fifteen million in 1920.

The majority of Mexico's writers, whatever their regional origins, end up in Mexico City: government, art, education, politics are all centered in what was previously known as "la región más transparente"—where the air is clear. This does not mean that provincial Mexico has not had great works of fiction. Whether in the wake of the vast revolutionary movements (Azuela, Guzmán, Muñoz), or in the abiding truth of isolation, religion and death (Rulfo, Yáñez and the State of Jalisco) Mexico has seen itself in movement within Mexico, very rarely in its relationship with the world. The most outstanding novel of Mexico in the world is Fernando Del Paso's *Noticias del*

Imperio, the tragic tale of the failed empire of Maximilian and Carlota, told by the latter in a dream sequence of memory and madness.

The northern frontier and our relations with the United States have had few literary explorers. Solares is notable in this. Francisco Madero, the scion of the northern aristocracy and initiator of the Mexican Revolution, has attracted Solares both as fiction and theater. Pancho Villa, the bandit and revolutionary chieftain from Chihuahua, is central to Solares' tale—*Columbus*—of Villa's brief incursion into that New Mexico town in 1916.

But now, Solares takes on a major event, mostly ignored by Mexican literature: the invasion of Mexico by United States forces in 1847, obeying the unwritten law of territorial expansion from the Atlantic to the Pacific. The young and disorganized Mexican Republic was in the way and had to be dealt with in the name of "manifest destiny." The opposition to "President Polk's war" by figures such as Abraham Lincoln and Henry David Thoreau was useless. First Texas achieved independence, then was admitted into the Union. But to reach California and the west, Mexico had to be defeated.

Yankee Invasion is the tale of this dramatic conflict. It is easy to write it with a simplistic view of the powerful USA overcoming the weak Mexican Republic: Goliath beating David. It lends itself, thus, to a Manichean tale of "Good Guys" and "Bad Guys"—but who were the "Good," and who the "Bad"? For as soon as we ponder the goodness and evil of the situation, we are obliged to shed some light on the latter, while withholding the shadows of the former.

This is the great merit of *Yankee Invasion*. Solares plays with light and shadows, effects and defects. He does this through a remarkable narrative structure. The narrator, Abelardo, is telling the story that he lived as a young man several decades later, when he is old, sick, cared for by his wife and his doctors but lucid in his memory of the dramatic days of his city, Mexico, occupied by the forces of General Winfield Scott, the stars and stripes flying over the National Palace and the contradictions that Solares does not shy from. The American army brings a semblance of order to the defeated city. Yet the defeated themselves will not stay put. A famous contemporary print shows the Zócalo, Mexico City's central square, occupied by the US army and the US soldiers being harassed by an unforgiving population. Stones are about to be thrown and sooner than later, the Americans understand that they cannot control a city as populous as Mexico and a country with such a strong sense of identity, language, religion, sex and cuisine, even if its politics are a sham, a rickety post-colonial structure that only the new revolution will fortify.

So it was. The United States left Mexico south of the Rio Grande to its own devices and took over the vast Southwest from Texas to California. And Mexico, chastened, fought its own civil war between liberals and conservatives. The latter lost: they betrayed the country asking for foreign-armed intervention, the France of Napoleon III. The liberals won. Led by Benito Juárez, they re-founded the Republic and let us find our own way.

Written from the precarious vantage point of the future immediate to the novel, yet written by an author, Solares, contemporaneous to ourselves, *Yankee Invasion* holds a tacit invitation to see and be seen as subjects of history passing through the sieve of fiction. Solares thus gives us a very rich tale of history relived, the past as present, the wholeness of experience as an act of the imagination directed not only at the past, but also at the future of the final warrior, the reader.

CARLOS FUENTES
Mexico City, 2009

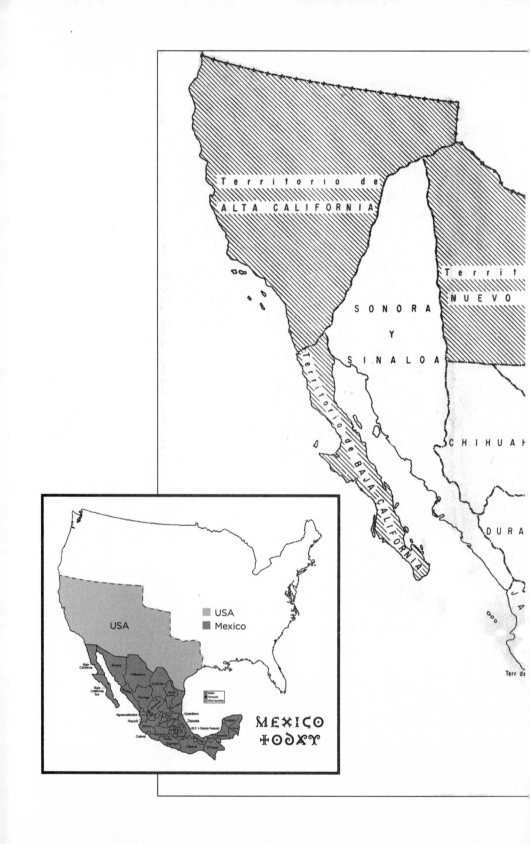

Territorio de **ALTA CALIFORNIA**

T e r r i t ...

NUEVO

S O N O R A
Y
S I N A L O A

Territorio de BAJA CALIFORNIA

C H I H U A H ...

D U R A ...

Terr de ...

USA

USA
Mexico

MEXICO TODAY

UNITED STATES TERRITORY

o r i o   d e

MEXICO

COAHUILA Y TEJAS

UA

NUEVO
LEON

NGO

MEXICO 1824

ZACATECAS

SAN LUIS POTOSI

TAMAULIPAS

LISCO

GUANAJUATO

QRO.

VERACRUZ

YUCATAN

COLIMA

TLAX.

MICHOACAN

MEXICO

PUEBLA

TABASCO

OAXACA

CHIAPAS

SOCONUSCO

TIMELINE OF MEXICO
1838-1848

1838–39. War of the Pastries (Guerra de los Pasteles). War between France and Mexico erupts, ostensibly caused by the destruction of a French-owned bakery in Mexico City.

December 1838. General Antonio López de Santa Anna (president of Mexico 1833, 1834–35, 1839, 1841–42, 1844, 1846–47) loses his left foot while attacking French forces in Veracruz.

February 1839. Santa Anna becomes interim president of Mexico.

March 1839. Mexico signs a peace treaty with France.

October 1842. Mistakenly believing Texas and Mexico are at war, US Commodore Thomas Jones seizes and occupies the port of Monterrey, Alta California, for one day.

November 1844. James K. Polk is elected president of the United States in part on an expansionist platform that includes the proposed annexation of Mexican territory.

July 4, 1845. The United States annexes Texas.

October 1845. President Polk orders the US consul in Monterrey, California, to develop plans for the peaceful annexation of California.

1846–1848. US–Mexican War.

January 1846. General Zachary Taylor leaves Corpus Christi, Texas, to begin the US invasion of northeast Mexico.

May 1846. After a skirmish between US and Mexican troops, President Polk sends a message to Congress that "American blood has been spilled on American soil" and declares war on Mexico.

September 1846. Mexican residents of Los Angeles, California, begin an uprising against US occupation.

September 1846. President Polk replaces General Taylor with General Winfield Scott as commanding officer of US troops in Mexico.

August 1846. The United States occupies Santa Fe and declares New Mexico to be part of the United States. Towards the end of 1846, former Mexican governor of Alta California Manuel Armijo mounts a rebellion against the US occupation, which is quickly put down.

November 1846. The United States occupies the port of Tampico after General Santa Anna orders its evacuation.

December 1846. Santa Anna is named president of Mexico.

January 1847. The United States annexes the Mexican provinces of Nuevo Mexico and Alta California.

March 1847. General Scott begins the siege of Veracruz, Mexico's most important port.

April 1847. President Santa Anna names himself also commander-in-chief of the Mexican army, a position he holds through the end of the war with the United States.

April 1847. General Santa Anna loses the decisive Battle of Cerro Gordo, near Jalapa, Veracruz.

May 1847. The US Army occupies the city of Puebla.

August 1847. The United States defeats the Mexican army at the Battle of Churrubusco, which opens the way for the invasion of the nation's capital, Mexico City.

September 1847. The United States defeats the Mexican army at the Battle of Molino del Rey.

September 1847. General Santa Anna orders the retreat of his forces from Mexico City and heads to the provincial capital of Querétaro.

September 1847. The United States defeats Mexico at the Battle of Chapultpec, where six young Mexican soldiers die in battle trying to defend the Castle of Chapultepec, going down in history as the Niños Héroes (the Boy Heroes or Heroic Cadets). Among the US troops engaged in this battle are Ulysses S. Grant and Robert E. Lee.

September 14, 1847. The American occupation of Mexico City begins.

September 15, 1847. The United States raises its flag over the National Palace in Mexico City.

September 1847. Santa Anna resigns the Mexican presidency.

February 2, 1848. Mexico and the United States sign the Treaty of Guadalupe Hidalgo, which recognizes the Río Bravo (the Río Grande) as the southern border of Texas and further cedes New Mexico and Alta California to the United States for $15 million.

June 1848. Mexican government officials return to the capital to take power, putting an end to the US occupation.

PART
ONE

I

The Yankee who attempted to raise his flag over the National Palace on the day the Americans arrived was killed by a bullet, but despite police efforts, they failed to discover the identity of the killer. The barbaric torments they planned to inflict upon the assassin were frightening.

GUILLERMO PRIETO

THE CATHEDRAL BELLS rang out like golden bubbles in the intense air on that morning of September 14, 1847, welcoming the Yankees who had just invaded our city. Since the Church had become such a cowardly bureaucracy, what else were we to expect? Christ seemed to have left it altogether. The indignation of the people exploded when a Yankee soldier started to raise his flag over the National Palace. Our hearts skipped a beat—the entire world skipped a beat. Enraged shouting and nasty insults mixed with muffled moans and sobs, although plenty of people chose to put their heads in the sand and not look at all. There it was in the clear morning air— what we had feared so much for months—the fluttering Stars and Stripes, symbol of the despicable power which intended to subjugate all nations and cultures of the nineteenth century.

Ironically, we inhabitants of the city were witnessing this fateful scene in the main plaza, where four years earlier Santa Anna had ordered a grand monument to our independence to be erected, of which only the base was now constructed.

However, the Yankee soldier who was raising the flag failed to complete his task, because a very accurate bullet coming from a nearby rooftop cut him down. When they saw his body collapse like a marionette whose strings have been cut, and the American flag barely at half mast, the multitude let out a

3

prolonged howl and attacked the Yankee soldiers who were on both foot and horseback near the doors of the Palace. Their weapons couldn't protect them for long because the masses fell upon them in growing waves, however much they managed to shoot down some of us.

"Death to the Yankees!"

My entire being was filled with uncertainty. Fear overcame me and I started running to get out of the plaza, bent over, out of joint, my head in a fog, thinking as if in a trance that one of those bullets which I heard intermittently was destined for me, that I was running right toward it and could do nothing about it. Or that one of those glimmering knives or bayonets was waiting to put an end to my shameful actions. Many times I tripped, slipped, was pushed, fell, got up and caught my balance. I felt keenly ridiculous to flee that way, so clumsy and unable to stay on my feet.

One time when I fell I managed to see—inside a cloud of dust—a group of women scratching, biting, stripping and spitting on a Yankee soldier, who seemed in shock and writhed as if in convulsions.

Another soldier seemed already dead. A sticky white substance oozed between the curls of his blond hair, and his face— a brutal face which death had not yet altered—was covered in blood. A pair of poor wretched people stared at him in fascination, as if he were still warm prey. They nudged him with their feet again and again, a bit fearful he might come back to life and arise.

Everything was happening as if in a dream. The struggles, the fighting between adversaries, the shouts, the gunshots and the scattered corpses were all real images, belonging to the world of real reality, so to speak, but they hovered in a kind of fog.

I was about to leave the plaza when a claw-like hand grabbed my ankle. I fell to the side of a wounded Yankee foaming at the mouth and flailing desperately with his hands in every direction, even though he could barely move the rest of his body. His fist smashed into my face, causing a sharp pain and a torrent of blinding colors. Without really thinking I took my knife from its sheath and buried the blade into his heaving chest. The Yankee opened his enormous eyes, which gleamed one last time just for me, and words—I assume insults—moved convulsively behind his teeth, but were swallowed up by his bleeding mouth.

The worst thing about suffering, and particularly the suffering of agony, is that you experience it alone, and that poor Yankee—who may not have even known for sure why he had come to our city—must have felt truly alone at that moment. But I had to stab him one more time. The problem was getting the knife out, since it was buried to the hilt. I did so with unnecessary force, and in the process I pulled something in my shoulder, then I stabbed him again through his filthy blue jacket, which became more and more soaked with blood. His eyes turned white, he took one last mouthful of air and then his jaw dropped, releasing a torrent of blood-tinged foam. His hands, quite pale and covered with freckles, came to rest at his sides. I stayed with him until his eyes retreated completely into the deepest part of himself. I watched how his facial features became sharper, like the edges of a rock. I saw how his skin took on an opaque clay tone, cold like moist earth and silent like a mineral. I could clearly see the moment when that man's soul departed from his vanquished body. I killed him, without a doubt. Or at the very least I finished him off. I wept and an infinite pity invaded my being. It was as if I could see in the misery of that man my own misery and that of everyone in the plaza. I believe I very nearly embraced him, which would have been ridiculous under such circumstances, or even dangerous, since surely someone would have thought I was in favor of the Yankees, and who knows what would have happened then. I left him there, with my knife imbedded in his lifeless chest— as if to confirm that it was I who had crucified him. I stood and ran from the plaza. The pain of the blow to my cheek had diminished, leaving a mere echo of pain, and I could feel with my tongue a gash in my gums. The taste of the salty blood I had to swallow turned my stomach.

"Death to the Yankees!"

It wasn't the Stars and Stripes the Americans raised over the National Palace, but death itself.

One night Father Jarauta, hiding in my house, told me:

"The opposite of death is not transcendence, or even immortality. The opposite of death is fraternity. We need to think of the Crucifixion as a mere act of fraternity."

II

Delight, Mexicans, in the significant and rich place which
is yours in the workings of the Universe.

GUADALUPE VICTORIA

AROUND THAT TIME, during my episodes of melancholy
I would frequently see—or catch glimpses of—flames
flickering in the sky. They would come and go, dance about,
and sometimes descend and alight upon, for instance, the
tower of a church—they loved churches, especially baroque
ones—or appear in the middle of an empty street, above a dry
well, near the twisted roots of an old tree, among the ruins of
a razed house. Sometimes all I had to do was blink or rub my
eyes to make them disappear. Other times they would linger
quite a while, filling me with anguish, because typically they
were a prelude to an intense headache.

Concerned, I asked Dr. Urruchúa about it. At first glance
his explanations didn't seem to me very scientific:

"They may be souls of the dead, bound to the earth for now
by a powerful love or loathing, that float randomly as if some
implacable wind were shaking them, but will vanish into the
air as soon as you say the Lord's Prayer. Do that, Abelardo, my
friend, and you will see how quickly you calm down."

An expert in the art of seeing through the soul's tangled
veils, he fastened his penetrating, fierce pupils onto me.

"Furthermore, I don't think you can dismiss the idea that
those flames in the sky might be ominous signs of disasters
looming over the places where they appear. It would only make
sense given the grim circumstances our poor city currently
faces. In either case, the Lord's Prayer wouldn't hurt." He listened to my heart, looked in my eyes, checked the color of my
tongue, and took my pulse, all the while seeming like an ento-

mologist fascinated by a rare species. "Of course, it could just be simple phosphenes produced by mechanical stimulation of the retina or some type of pressure on the eyeball. Try to sleep better, my friend. Drink the lime tea and valerian I prescribed for you, as well as ten drops of rye ergot for your nausea, and take a bath in rose water half an hour before going to bed. Insomnia as serious as yours can induce all sorts of hallucinations."

I never did follow his advice about the Lord's Prayer, preferring instead to relativize the event, rub my eyes hard or simply wait for the flames to wander off on their own. As the *Zohar* states: "Secrets preserve the world."

But the flames in the sky returned fifty years later when I opened again my house in Tacubaya, to the extent that I had to limit my visits there.

The worst thing was that at times the flames would turn into lightning bolts which would appear for just a moment like fish surfacing the water. My memory brought back what I most feared, and my head felt like it was about to explode.

Time seemed to be doing continual somersaults, and I was no longer *here* and *now*, but *there* and *then*. I spent hours in the vacant rooms of the house taking in the aromas of the past, which played havoc with my soul. Sometimes I would close my eyes, and the flames would enter into me. I'd leave the house like a blind man, clinging to the walls, and my coachman would have to help me to the carriage. I became afraid that the entire sky would light up and I would go completely, irrevocably, crazy. Some lights are unbearable.

Magdalena, my wife, knows I spend many mornings in the supposedly cathartic labor of writing something, anything—especially if the writing has no particular purpose, with neither the pretension nor intention of being published. Reading over my shoulder, she asked me:

"Did it really affect you so profoundly to go back to the house in Tacubaya? I told you to get it cleaned first. No doubt you're allergic to the dust. And there must be rats living there, too. You should have sprinkled oregano water throughout the house, covered your face with a scarf and taken a double dose of potassium bromide before going in."

Of all the medications I have taken during my lifetime—and I run from them like the plague—I remain faithful to potassium bromide because it alone has helped me with my bouts of sadness. My wife, by contrast, spends all her time seeing doctors. When she gets up she starts the day by faithfully chewing a clove of garlic and absinthe petals for stomach pains, then magnesium sulfate for tapeworms, followed by salyscilic pills for pains in the bones, some other pill for her chronic constipation, and mouthwash with myrrh tincture after every meal to strengthen her gums. She ends the day by taking belladonna to help her sleep, which is ludicrous because ever since I have known her she has slept like a log whether she takes anything or not. Since what she likes more than anything else is to read and read, she is terrified of anything happening to her eyes, so she washes them two or even three times a day with chamomile tea and applies eye drops to keep her vision clear.

She has a strong preference for the real and therapeutic. She says that unused moral energy turns into neurasthenic neurosis, hence her advice:

"Why don't you take advantage of the lights in the sky returning and once and for all finish that chronicle you've left dangling—the one about the Yankee invasion of Mexico City in 1847? Don't publish it if you don't want to, but finish it. Tell in the first few pages how you stabbed that poor Yankee soldier. That will do you some good, a sort of public confession. I'm afraid that before long cerebral arteriosclerosis will keep you from writing anything about anything."

"I would have to go into details, and I would rather have arteriosclerosis just help me forget the whole thing."

"It's also a public memory which belongs to this city."

"Right, but it's a humiliating memory."

"It seems to me that's the most important kind for reflecting upon the human condition. Humiliating memories and droll memories. Didn't you want to write a retrospective on all the droll episodes contained in our history, up at least to Maximilian and Carlota? What happened with that?"

"I started from the end and worked backward but got bogged down. I never got past the episode in which the

Mexican firing squad shot out one of Maximilian's eyes. The embalmer couldn't find a single artificial blue eye in Querétaro, so the black eye from a local statue was finally inserted into the socket of the executed emperor. From his Hapsburg crypt in Vienna, Maximilian stares at death with one blue Austrian eye and one black indigenous eye. Think of it! I wrote so much philosophical commentary on that episode alone that the text was becoming muddled and had lost its humor, so I decided to stop writing and take it up again later. Which is what has happened with almost everything that I've tried to do in my now lengthy life."

"You should decide once and for all to finish something. I'll help you." Her hazel eyes, with their lovely flecks of green and yellow, smiled ironically.

Under her mask of wrinkles, which she has accepted with the same resignation as she has so many other things, those beautiful eyes still have the mysterious depth and serenity as when I first met her, and they are only stirred by anger or certain moments of excitement. When I met her she was living in Querétaro, the daughter of a prestigious lawyer from whom she inherited her love of learning and good literature. They had a library which was the envy of the city: it had shelves with glass doors all the way up its high walls that held some two thousand books bound in calfskin with his initials in gold on their spines. Magdalena was twenty-four, with wheat-colored hair and peach-colored skin, as well as slight premature furrows in her brow, the result of a personality skilled in switching brusquely from extreme tension to a long and pleasant ironic relaxation, or from ebullient enthusiasm to a stubborn, harsh expression, all of which reflects a domineering desire to impose her opinion and convictions.

She is an avid reader of everything published in Mexico as well as new works she has a contact send her from Paris. She is intensely involved in the literary world of the city. One afternoon I found her sobbing inconsolably because she had just read in the newspaper *El Siglo XIX* that Manuel Acuña had committed suicide.

"Imitating him is the least his readers could do to honor him," she said, but I still don't know whether she was kidding or not.

Or she flies into a rage because Lerdo de Tejada recently wrote that in our city "a cowardly feminization alters and subjugates our most privileged natures. Gangrene is wrapped up in diaphanous tulle and the fruit of feminine venality results in increased bureaucracy." She threw the newspaper in the air, threatened to send a scorching letter, which she's never done, and declared something along the lines of "the twentieth century will be feminine or it simply will not be."

She has nearly doubled the number of books she inherited from her father. They are scattered in disorderly piles throughout the house, inspiring silence and giving off the air of an abbey, which no doubt influenced our children to flee from home as soon as they could. Despite her voracious appetite for reading, Magdalena has chosen to keep her distance from academic and literary circles. Nevertheless, if she is on the street and bumps into someone like Guillermo Prieto—wearing his indispensable wide-brimmed straw hat—she greets him with exaggerated enthusiasm and brings up his most recent article. But that's it. She says you have to be wary of writers, never getting to know them too well, and rather just be satisfied with reading them. I think she's right.

As the years have gone by she has developed a dangerous tendency to say things for their shock value. Maybe this comes from her literary tastes—she reads too much Charles Fourier, one of her favorite French authors. Thus I have to take a great deal of care in choosing the social events we occasionally attend. Not long ago, at a dinner in the home of government minister Chávez Torres, she said the most outlandish thing— that if we want to save the country, in the not too distant future women will need to participate in politics as fully as men. And it got worse. She said that prostitutes are social victims and she looked forward to their vindication, along with that of the poor, the peasants and servants. This caused several guests to drop their monocles, and the minister's wife, a woman always dressed in black who exudes an air of virtue, refused to acknowledge my wife the next time their paths crossed at the Lady Baltimore Café.

Confidentially, my wife has gotten even worse. During a Sunday dinner with one of our sons and his wife, she mentioned Charles Fourier—whose name alone makes our hair stand on end—who says that "when it comes to love, all fantasies are good, especially for young lovers," and that "all couples have a right to their own idiosyncrasies in love, since love is at its very essence the best part of us: the irrational." My son nearly choked on dessert and his response caused my wife such consternation that it almost lit up the table: "Part of the proper upbringing of women should be to forbid them to read novels—novels of any kind." My wife threw down her napkin in disgust and said, "Yes, right, let's return women to the time when Spanish inquisitors prohibited the publication or importation of novels in the colonies, saying that those senseless and absurd books could damage the spiritual health of the Indians. Did you know that's why the inhabitants of Spanish America read only contraband fiction for three hundred years and the first novel published here had to wait until after Independence, until 1816? Did you know that, son? But how would you know, since despite all the efforts your father and I made you never managed to finish a book, not even one filled with tales of adventure? On the other hand, I do recognize that you have managed to dedicate every ounce of your physical and spiritual life to business and making money." The tension in the air could hardly have been thicker—my daughter-in-law didn't lift her eyes from her plate—so I awkwardly changed the subject and told them about an elephant that had escaped from the circus and crushed a drunkard who had been wandering around at night. "Can you imagine the poor man screaming at the elephant: 'You don't exist! You don't exist! You're a figment of my imagination!' a moment before feeling the blow which sent him into the next life?" Later that evening when we were alone, I scolded Magdalena for bringing up Fourier. I asked how it ever could have occurred to her to mention such things in front of our son and his wife, who are so circumspect and reserved. Of course people will think we're crazy. They'll probably never come back, as resistant to change as they are. I told her she had done nothing more than poison our dinner. She replied furiously, "Oh, so it's more important to have a good meal than open our children's eyes? The worst blind are those who refuse to see. Is that what you want for our children—hearts where things only settle to curdle or clot? If you hadn't interrupted me with that idiocy about the elephant and the drunkard, I would have liked to mention that Fourier also speaks about a future ideal, a happy society which will include 'noble orgies' and 'collective amorous connections,' and masturbation and homosexuality will not be repressed but rather encouraged, so that everyone will be able to find his or her soul mate and be happy whatever their personal preference. Of course, no one will hurt anyone else, because everyone will make their own choices."

When Magdalena waxes eloquent on those topics, her gleaming, devoted eyes fill with a fiery ecstasy. Eyes alluding to a secret triumph, difficult to communicate.

Compared to her ideas, my comment on doubts about finishing my account of the United States invasion of our city in 1847 must have sounded downright reactionary.

"Apart from the personal and the historical, to say the least, what if I included a little about the two women I fell madly in love with back then?"

"Who?"

"I've mentioned them a thousand times. They were named Isabel, both the mother and the daughter."

"Do you see why I always say that at our age we forget things so easily?"

"Even if I don't publish it, someone could discover the manuscript when we die. The first thing family members do is look for exactly that kind of dirt among the papers of the deceased, especially when they have reputations for eccentricity the way you and I do. Plus, they could go look for the family of those women. Just imagine what a gift that would be to our grandchildren, knowing that their grandfather was a pervert who fell in love with a mother and her daughter. And what would they think of you, my wife and their grandmother?"

"Honestly, they can think whatever they want about me. Besides, I highly doubt they would read it, even in the remote case of finding it. You can always state in the first few pages that you are writing a sort of historical fiction, something you *imagined* when you were twenty-five. And since you aren't a historian, all you did was *imagine* your version of the Yankee invasion." A smile of triumph swept her face.

"That might be the answer. The other day I saw with great clarity the ghost of Isabel in the house in Tacubaya. Her face was a little dark and she had a yellow glow around her silhouette."

Magdalena has grown accustomed to my visions and hears about them with the same resignation as people listening to falling rain.

"If you really loved those women so much, it will be a nice distraction for you to write about them, rest assured. Recreate the scenes, add some details, do some inventing. In the meantime, I assume you'll give me some well deserved rest," she said, opening one of my desk drawers, something she knows bothers me to death. "Here's a pile of notes which, you can be certain, will go straight into the trash after you die. I'll be sure of that! Why have you kept them all these years if you're not going to use them? Just look at how much space they take up," and she began to look through the drawer without any consideration. "Besides, the most important reason to write it is because you're still as anti-American as you were back in those days."

"More so. And as long as you have that drawer open, let me show you what I recently read. I have a clipping right over here."

"If the Díaz government ever found those clippings, Mexico would most certainly declare war on the United States."

"Listen to this: 'We have received word that in Los Angeles, California, in 1854, there has been a homicide per day, with the majority of victims Mexicans ... In the 1860s, the lynching of

Mexicans was such a common occurrence in the region that newspapers didn't bother to report the details ... Research has shown that the number of Mexicans lynched between 1849 and 1890 is calculated at ...' Did you hear that? That's less than ten years ago! Listen: 'Even today, almost every crime committed in Los Angeles is immediately blamed on a Mexican, and lynching is a very common punishment, especially when the supposedly guilty party is a Mexican.' How does that hit you? The death of a Mexican at the hands of an Anglo-American is not worth the consideration of the authorities who are supposed to carry out justice. And it doesn't even merit a glance from the press because it's so humdrum and ordinary. My God!"

"What better argument do you need if the Yankees still treat us the same way they did when they invaded, and I don't imagine things will change anytime soon. Sit down to write and you'll see your mood improve. Stop following me around all day long and you might even stop seeing lights in the sky."

"What if I just publish all my notes, with a prologue?" I asked, looking into the drawer filled with yellowed newspaper clippings, now in an even bigger mess thanks to Magdalena. "That way they wouldn't get lost. I could assemble a kind of anthology or something. I would simply compile them."

"You're trying to run away from writing about your guilt and hallucinations, which are insufferable for the people who live with you. Plus, you probably traumatized those poor women."

"Perhaps."

"Even the mother?"

"I lavished the sweetest words on her, I admit, but always from a respectable distance."

"I am well aware of your respectable distance. That is why it's easier for a woman to control a man from nearby than at a distance. If you don't write your story now, all those images will haunt you at the moment of your death, which would be much worse, I assure you. And might not the city itself need you to remember and write, so just like you it can purge its own guilt?" she asked, taking some new notes out of the drawer and studying them closely.

"What the city wants is to forget that entire episode.

Haven't you seen the looks on people's faces when the subject surfaces?"

"I'm talking about the city, not just the people living in it. Everyone knows that a group is much more than the sum of its parts. That's why Chateaubriand says that when he writes he likes to go somewhere like a hilltop, so he can observe whether the amphibious human lizard he is contemplating responds to more than just fate in its constitution and dissolution, or is rather just a magical figure capable of moving about, under specific circumstances, in more essential and transcendental spheres. For example, this city during the Yankee invasion of 1847. Do I make myself clear?"

"As a bell."

"Then get to work and start to empty that drawer." Her lips curved into a conciliatory grimace.

I tried to get back to writing my chronicle, but the moment I would step into my vacant house in Tacubaya, I would see the lights in the sky and my migraine would glare menacingly at me through the cracks in the walls.

What if those little lights in the sky were once again, as Dr. Urruchúa interpreted them more than fifty years earlier, ominous signs of imminent disasters hovering over a place? I shudder to think about that. It makes me look skeptically at the political situation—so stable on the surface—that our country enjoys at the end of this century.

When people live through an earthquake they simply want—above all else—for the ground to stop shaking, and at my age I really don't want to go through another earthquake. That's another reason it's so hard for me to write about those years. After all, from the time of my birth until I was almost thirty, from 1821 to 1850, in addition to the traumatic wars and foreign invasions, we suffered through no less than *fifty* changes of government, almost all the result of armed uprisings. As if that weren't enough, eleven times we were governed by the inimitable General Santa Anna. Our ill-fated political life was at the mercy of squabbling Masonic lodges, political parties constantly at loggerheads, ambitious military leaders and killers and fearless outlaws. Who wants to spend their time remembering such things, no matter what my wife says?

Although I don't leave my house much, an occasional brief walk through the city with one of my children is enough to let me breathe deeply the diaphanous air of peace and social stability—which is very apparent—and what they call "progress," a word with French overtones in recent years.

"Imagine this city occupied by Americans," I tell my son as I look around. "Imagine a Yankee police officer posted on every corner staring with visible disgust as you go by, that is if he's not stopping you to ask with gestures where you're going, or spitting right in your face because he doesn't understand you, and when he doesn't understand you he'll scream at you in a thick English which you don't understand, or he arrests you and takes you to the Plaza de Santo Domingo for a flogging to help you learn to express yourself."

"What about the French?"

"My God, boy, the French are the essence of chivalry compared to the beasts we have as northern neighbors."

We walk down Espírito Santo Street toward Plateros and rest for a moment in the blackened leather booths in the Concordia Café. I savor a glass of sherry, thinking that everything is fine and I am in the place where I always should have been. Where did I leave that young man of twenty-five who flirted with suicide and had mystical experiences? What would I possibly complain about now, besides arthritis and the fact that my legs fail me? At least I sleep better, I don't feel as though my heart will stop at any moment, and the needle-like headaches stay under control as long as I don't seek out spirits and lights in the sky.

At times I simply rub my eyelids and allow my eyes to accept the tenuous morning light filtered through the curtains, recognize the calm world, and then tranquilly I go back to sleep, sinking down into the softness of my pillow.

Who would have thought that sometimes even Magdalena's snoring lulls me to sleep? The gurgling rise and fall of her breathing, the whistling, the intermittent volcanic eruptions, the holes she rips into the air all help me come to terms with the world and the night. And to think that at one point I cushioned my entire bedroom to keep the tiniest outside noise from entering.

Perhaps, like for so many "decent" folk today, my main concern ought to be the extension of the boulevard Paseo de la Reforma. Manuel Gutiérrez Nájera wrote not long ago:

City government has to consider further beautifying this city of palaces in which we live. We mustn't be satisfied with what we have. The Paseo de la Reforma urgently needs work. On festival days carriages cannot circulate comfortably and horses are very limited in their gait. Pedestrians need more room and, finally, this beautiful boulevard should be extended all the way to the forest of Chapultepec. Isn't that possible?

The truth is I can't reconcile myself to the calm surrounding Mexico as we come to the end of this century. There is a total neglect of matters of the soul, as my wife would say. We neglect matters of the soul and beggars proliferate on every street corner, parading their wounds, waving their stumps, putting their starving children on display, asking for alms in loud voices or simply moaning in a falsetto tone. A situation that could swallow up the present and the future, like the sea swallows shipwreck victims.

"Deep down," I say, looking around, "we understand the deception in all this, don't we, son?"

"I don't understand."

"That we need to relativize our point of view about the things that surround us, as your mother says."

"Ah."

"It seems we can only understand reality from the point of view we find ourselves in at the moment." My son's eyes wander lost on the ceiling, which always happens when I start to wax philosophical. "We believe there is a verifiable reality here in which you and I are seated at this booth in the Concordia Café, having a glass of sherry, and we know that in an hour or so we will return home where our wives and children await us.

All this offers us a mental and ontological orientation, if you will allow me to use such a pedantic term. We feel very confident in ourselves, very assured of ourselves and all that surrounds us. Our clothing and gold watches don't reveal to other people who we really are—just look around at them. But if at the same time we had the gift of mental ubiquity and could contemplate this same reality from another perspective, like that of our waiter, considering everything he is and has been—look at the skill with which he handles that tray, at the courtesy he shows his clientele, at the way he has fully adopted the role of waiter—we would then see that our shoddy self-centeredness keeps us from fully perceiving any valid, concrete reality. Our beliefs are founded on self-interest, on the value of our watches, on the delicious flavor of the sherry, and on a need to affirm our identity so that we don't fall into a labyrinth of doubt. If we ask ourselves useless but nagging questions about why the devil we came to this poor planet and why so many people are starving to death on the streets, do you think we'd ever find our way out of the labyrinth?"

"Let's go," says my son, standing up. "The waiter heard you talking about him, and you've made him nervous."

III

There is an inexplicable tragic aspect to the history of Mexico which crushes the capable and honorable, to the benefit of the inept and thieving.

FRANCISCO ZARCO

WHAT CANNOT BE DISPUTED is that a dark feeling of anguish, but also of intimate and joyful desecration, has enveloped me ever since I turned the key in the lock of the house in Tacubaya, the door creaking as it swung on its hinges.

I lived in that house during my youth, and as an only child ended up in charge of it when my parents, Mexicans by birth, got fed up with Santa Anna and went to Spain, homeland of their parents.

They supported our movement for independence and always drilled into me the idea that Mexico should consist of and be for Mexicans. They put up with plenty: Iturbide's farce, constant military takeovers and conspiracies, the "Pastry War," confrontations between the exalted, the pure, and the moderates, and between centrists and federalists, the economic crisis (counterfeit copper coins became so common that the treasury took seven hundred of them out of circulation and determined that only nine were legitimate), and tax increases courtesy of Santa Anna (a *real* for each carriage wheel, a *real* for each dog, a *real* for each window facing the street, a *real* for each roof spout that channeled rain water toward the street ...). But they did not put up with, in fact it was entirely impossible for them to endure, an event that took place in January 1846: Santa Anna's foot, which had been severed by shrapnel in Veracruz, was unearthed and a procession of ministers, governors, military officers, cadets from the Military Academy, students and people from every social class transported it to the Santa

Paula Cemetery, where the distinguished poet Ignacio Sierra y Rosso delivered an exalted speech prophesying that the name of Santa Anna—not his severed foot—would endure until the day the sun stopped shining and all stars and planets returned to their original state of chaos; the president of Congress placed the urn containing the remains of his foot into a cenotaph crowned by the coat of arms of the Mexican Republic; an aria from *Semíramis*, Santa Anna's favorite opera, was performed; the masses gathering outside the cemetery erupted in cheers and applause; and Santa Anna wept profusely and kissed the pavilion covering the urn. My parents refused to put up with that, and my father, seething with indignation, threw into the air the newspaper with the article about the event and started preparing to depart.

Besides, ever since Santa Anna rose to power for the first time, I think that understanding his relationship with *his* people is fundamental to understanding the phenomenon of "Mexicanicity," which at that time we put so much effort and care into trying to construct.

"What did that man possess which caused the popular masses to see him as a Messiah?" Justo Sierra asked years later.

For starters, he was an actor in the most theatrical sense of the word, performing in a monumental farce.

He supported the movement for independence, he proclaimed the Republic, he helped Vicente Guerrero become president, he declared himself a federalist, he vanquished the Spanish in Tampico, he spoke of the need to liberate Cuba, he was a staunch defender of the legitimate government of Guerrero, and then suddenly he did a 180-degree turn and associated himself with the Conservative Party, which he would champion. He repealed the Constitution of 1824 and established a centralized government. His conduct was always arbitrary, capricious and of course very theatrical. He passed legislation on a whim, with no particular plan or method. It seems deep down that he looked down on *his* beloved people. With each turn that he took he exacerbated an existing hateful resentment or created a new one. He ended up at odds with the federalists, the centrists, the clergy, the poor, the working class, government employees and capitalists (from whom he was constantly demanding money). For example, he fired all government employees who did not adhere to the Jalisco Plan and the Principles of Tacubaya—triggering an unprecedented rate of unemployment—and he ordered a draft of fifteen thousand men, which he implemented by sending soldiers at night to grab the poor, the drunk and the confused and put them in the army. Legions of so-called new soldiers would arrive, followed by their starving women and children, scrawny specters marching as if sleepwalking. Santa Anna also chose twelve hundred men to create a grenadier force which he dressed in the finest uniforms, complete with luxurious fabric, leather belts and hats lined with bear fur twenty inches high. He lost a foot, but maintained an iron fist, issuing arrest warrants for any individual, class notwithstanding, who threatened public order in word or deed. Newspapers railed against him "with scorpion poison" and he closed *El Cosmopolita, El Restaurador, El Voto Nacional* and others. (Regarding his sensitivity to the press, years later Guillermo Prieto recounted how he was summoned from *El Monitor* along with Eufemio Romero from *El Calavera* by His Serene Highness: "Seeing us in his presence, he brandished an article at Romero, thundering at him in a voice mute with anger, 'Tell me who wrote this damned article so I can rip his tongue out!'")

Despite all that—his multiple falls from grace, his public disgrace, the harsh jokes of which he was the butt, the bitter curses breathed against him—each time the hero returned to power, a new triumphal entry was organized for him in the capital that everyone attended; clearly people love pageantry, but "decent folks" also anxiously cherish the thought of a protector. In contrast to my parents' disgust, I didn't miss a single one of those celebrations, my mouth watering in anticipation every time.

At the head of the battalions, a band would perform an anthem recently composed in Santa Anna's honor. The military would parade, starting with the artillery regiments, then grenadiers, sharpshooters, and finally the southern cavalry decked out in yellow suede, followed by a line of floats, twenty-one-gun salutes, triumphal wreaths and colorful fireworks.

I remember most vividly the entry into the capital when the mutilated savior of the homeland, reclining languidly on a sumptuous sofa, smiling and overcome with emotion, brazenly displayed his empty pant leg, his limb having been shortened by a French cannon. As he passed by, the people would heave emotional "ahhh's." (Later on Santa Anna decided that his peg leg wasn't stylish enough, so he switched to a magnificent prosthetic decorated with a shiny leather Napoleonic boot.)

The Cathedral bells would ring out. The pigeons, momentarily scattered by the bronze peals, would return to the campanile like fragments of a restored peace.

Everyone and everything would contribute to the homage.

Together the shouts and acclamations would stir up the wind and ruffle the trees, yanking from them copper-colored leaves that soared in the air and eventually fell to the ground like lifeless wings.

The truth is that the wealthy loved the ostentation which Santa Anna impressed upon official life, despite the constant financial downturns. Banquets, ceremonies and soirées took place one after the other without interruption. Carriages imported from Europe and extravagant clothing filled the streets. Women wearing jewelry, feathered hats and airy muslin dresses would preen at the cock fights in San Agustín de las Cuevas. Each day military officers would parade in their dress uniforms bearing all of their showy decorations. *Charros* on horseback were dazzling in their sombreros adorned with elaborate hatbands and pants with silver filigreed buttons that ran down their legs like two streams of silver. An Italian company launched the Santa Anna Theater with its most exclusive opera repertory. Men in tuxedos accompanied by ladies wearing gloves reaching to their elbows applauded madly. The owner of the theater, Francisco Arbeu, stated in an interview published in *El Siglo XIX*: "I have completed my vow to have the inauguration of the theater on exactly the same day as the installation of the Supreme Constitutional Government.

More than just a debt of gratitude, I was paying homage to the Supreme Head of the Republic, to whom we owe everything and who gives us everything."

But perhaps nothing seemed so significant to me regarding his relationship with *his* people as what happened after an earthquake which occurred in the capital in April 1845 when, symptomatically, Santa Anna had fallen into one of his moments of greatest disgrace.

I remember that the Cathedral clock proclaimed four thirty in the afternoon. People were passing down the streets as usual, coming and going from businesses and restaurants, attending church services, and doing their office work. A vendor offered his wares on some street corner. Suddenly everything stopped; or more accurately, everything started to move because the earth started to tremble violently. Anguish drained the color from the faces of people who started to shout and cry, and the tremors continued so long that women fell to their knees on the sidewalks, lifting their arms into the form of a cross and imploring heaven to cease its wrath. The flagstones in the atrium of the Cathedral cracked. Carriage horses rose up on their hind legs and whinnied, the coachmen lashing their whips to no effect. I started to pray in a quiet voice, moved away from the swaying buildings and pressed into the multitude in the middle of the plaza.

The city was seriously impacted: the Tezontlale bridge collapsed, San Lorenzo Hospital was destroyed and the chapel of Santa Teresa la Antigua ceased to exist. Numerous structures collapsed on La Misericordia, El Sapo, San Lorenzo, Tompeate and Victoria Streets, resulting in countless deaths and injuries.

In the ensuing days the city suffered aftershocks and the government turned to religious authorities to make public appeals for peace and calm (from the population as well as the earth). The interior minister hurriedly sent for the Virgin of the Sanctuary of Remedios, who was thought to have miraculous powers in such matters.

But most surprising of all was the rumor that started to circulate throughout the city, as much among the poor as the rich, that the earthquakes were happening because Santa Anna, Benefactor of the Fatherland, the very Soul of Mexico, was in jail and about to be executed!

The heavens were lodging their protest through the earth.

Just in case there might be an ounce of truth to the rumor, Congress, recognizing the value of acquiescing to the beliefs of the masses, hurried to draft an amnesty law which commuted his sentence to a simple ten-year exile (which, of course, didn't last that long). And then the earthquakes stopped.

I better understood the essence of Santa Anna—and how he took advantage of the need we Mexicans have for a strong and charismatic figure, and even more importantly, a melodramatic and sensitive one—when some time later I learned of a letter which Sam Houston sent in August of 1836 to Andrew Jackson, President of the United States:

Mexico is a country possessing enormous natural resources which could be exploited under a responsible and honest government. In its ranks there are first-rate politicians, but they are relegated to secondary roles by the insatiable ambition of military leaders. If any one of them manages to bring the country stability, Mexico may have the strength to reclaim by military force the territory of which it has been stripped. We should, therefore, foster civil discord by any means we may have, and to this end General Antonio López de Santa Anna, who during the last decade has headed numerous military coups, can be very useful to us. Against conventional wisdom, which would dictate his capture, I recommend that we set the predator free. I would ask that you reconsider your position and allow him to meet with you in Washington. Such a meeting would have no particular benefit other than to serve as an excuse to give him some breathing room and facilitate his return to his country, where he will be our best subversive agent. With his unruly genius agitating the political arena, no government will possibly be able to right the ship of state and Mexico will continue in its chaos, where it is to our advantage that she stay for a long time, so that her weak military will be unable to impede our future annexation of Arizona, Colorado and both Californias.

IV

Our Mexico, our homeland, was a virgin sleeping on her chaste bed of flowers until the filthy arm of the invader grabbed her like a whore, and celebrated her dishonor as a triumph.

MANUEL PAYNO

DESPITE MY PARENTS' PLEAS, I decided to stay in Mexico: the social and political turbulence which engulfed us seemed the ideal setting for my literary and journalistic aspirations, however nascent they may have been.

I had no financial difficulties and although on the surface my way of life had not changed—meals at regular hours, reading, meeting with friends, minor health problems and long periods of insomnia—at the beginning of that year, 1847, my nervous ailments started to become more pronounced and I sensed beforehand the intrusion of a new and troubling outside force: the United States army's invasion of Mexico City.

From the moment that possibility became apparent, as tangible as one of those little flames in the sky which I saw, I joined up with a group of friends in the Progreso Café. Much more than religious beliefs or political convictions, which are so confusing and shifting, what united us was a fervent anti-Americanism, and that was the focus of our meetings.

"We already gave them Texas. What's next?"

"We obviously haven't managed to stabilize our independence."

"Our government hasn't figured out how to create a national identity here."

"We will never truly be independent with the United States right on top of us. It's a fool's dream."

"The problem is the mental colonialism we continue to suffer."

"The Spanish left Mexico in ruins."

"It's the fault of the purists."

"The moderates."

"The conservatives."

"Santa Anna sold us out to stay in power."

"Only the Jesuits could have managed to keep Texas from falling into the hands of the Protestants."

"They'll use the knife on us the same way they did the Apaches."

"I've heard they spit on Indians."

"Only a Spanish emperor can rescue us. The Spanish conquered us, but they stayed to give us religion, to educate us, to mix with the women, to found a nation; the Americans will only come here to exterminate us, you'll see."

"The republican system was not imitated by Mexico nor adopted as a form of subordination to the United States. Whoever thinks that is swine. Our republic was created here as a result of our own Mexican political struggles—just take a look at it. Only through representative systems were national demands brought to the forefront. A comparison between American institutions and those of our country is sufficient to see that the fruits of the 1824 Congress came from a full understanding of Mexico's reality—gathering the ideas of the insurgents, but also of the representatives of Chilpancingo and the principles of Cádiz in 1808."

"Imagine if the United States had decided to kill or expel from their territory every British-born inhabitant the way we did with people born in Spain. Would they be as powerful as they now are?"

"Exactly! I've been telling you this for years: we would be better off seeking protection from a power like the British—endowed, serene and steadfast."

"Establishing the British army on Mexican land—in Chihuahua and Sonora, for instance—would prevent future American aggression, since the United States would never dare give up its peace with England. It knows whom to fight."

"José María Luis Mora recently wrote: 'Would Mexico not benefit by selling part of its territory to England? This would protect the rest of the country. Otherwise we risk losing it in subsequent American invasions, perhaps eventually losing our national independence.'"

"But Mora also said: 'We possess an intrinsic goodness which could provide stability in Mexico, give us reconciliation, allow us to create the necessary institutions. This intrinsic goodness exists in our country, but to develop it we need time. Time, time! Meanwhile, we run the risk that the United States, using one treaty after another, will overrun our weak borders and appropriate everything.' "

In the midst of that chaos some of us, like Dr. Urruchúa and I, felt the need to reaffirm our identity as Mexicans and stabilize our independence—in which education and art would be a determining factor—through man's unfettered freedom from authority and tyranny, through the honesty of public servants elected democratically, not leaving aside the grave needs of the indigent for justice and equity. Who or what party could represent us if even the liberals—with whom we sympathized—spent all their energy quarreling with each other? For that reason, at least for the time being, until better political breezes began to blow, we were undoubtedly and openly anti-American.

The masses set the example and dragged us along without regard to social class. I even shared a gun with my coachman during that conflict.

That is why the following needs to be stated emphatically: Only the indignation of the poorest of the poor in response to the Yankee presence, so brutal and crushing, managed to unite those inhabitants of the nation's capital who still believed in a free and sovereign Mexico. It turned *us* into the principal actor of the war, without regard to social status, political leanings or religious beliefs. It happened despite the fact that a large portion of the population—especially, and predictably, the filthy rich and foreigners doing business in Mexico—holed up in their houses or hurried to show their support for the invaders by flying the foreign flag from their balconies or at their businesses, and even throwing flowers in their path.

Guillermo Prieto wrote: "Those long rows of men, wearing no uniform, not cut from a mold, not moving mechanically like puppets, but bearing the dignity of common men, were the family which fought in the defense of our larger home which we call Mexico."

I confess that I am a skeptic in things political. I believe that only a spiritual rebirth and allowing the *other* into our daily lives will change the world some day. But those events in 1847 spurred me on to an active and defiant participation which I would never have imagined nor desired, given my steadfast pacifism and emotional hypersensitivity.

Fear (which so easily becomes hate), along with the confusion which surrounded us—no one knew what to believe, no one knew what anyone believed, and it seemed like we were all against each other—were the juices in which our desperate actions had stewed. It is true that Mexico City had become accustomed to a routine of military coups and plots. The routine involved domestic matters which seemed to end like a common cold and then after a time came another and then another, none of which was serious. The threat of invasion by the Yankee army was another matter altogether and took us all by surprise. Oh, we were naïve—to the very end we assumed that Santa Anna and his army would arrive to save the city. As General Winfield Scott saw from the very beginning, his best allies were none other than the Mexican generals, each one fighting against the other, accustomed to military uprisings, and each believing that he possessed the requisite attributes to occupy the presidential throne.

When I returned to my abandoned home in Tacubaya—I had rented it out for several years and later simply resisted going back to visit it—I relived all that with the splendor and terror of those foolish flames.

Despite that anguish, I seemed to be drawn back there on my weary legs, trembling with the old and powerful desire to remember and write, which I thought had forever left my system. In this, as with everything, I had to put myself in my wife's hands.

ɤ

Due to their enormity, there are crimes that border on the sublime. Taking control of Texas, accomplished by our compatriots, qualifies for this honor. Modern times offer no other example of robbery on so great a scale.

HENRY CLAY

BUT HOW COULD I avoid sentimentality and be more objective if the moment I turned the key in the keyhole of the main door, which creaked as it swung on its hinges, the little dancing flames in the sky returned and time did a sudden backwards somersault? As I walked down the hallway, I passed by large flower pots with parched dirt empty of plants and flowers, then the large gallery of pillars leading to the dark dining room with its humid beams and red *tezontle* floor, then the old and withered bedrooms with large windows which were either broken or so dirty that barely any light could enter. I went up to the moth-eaten attic, with its beat-up armoires, wobbly chairs, and tarnished, ghostly mirrors. That's where we hid Father Celedonio Domeco de Jarauta, a Jesuit and Spaniard who organized the guerrilla movement in Veracruz and cut down with one expertly aimed bullet the Yankee who tried to raise his flag over the National Palace, and then commanded a great part of our insurrection against the invaders.

Perhaps things actually aren't the way we live them but the way we remember them. When I sat down once again at the marble table on the patio next to the large stone cross under the poplars, my memories could well have come from even further back, much further back. For example, I remembered the precise instant when my mother took out a fringed red tablecloth and placed it on that very table, next to some jasmines long since gone. Someone lit the wick of a lantern and I heard—and I hear it again as I mention this—the clinking of silverware and plates on a tray. Conversations, whispers and laughter come from the kitchen. That kitchen transports me to the past—fertile with aromas, purified by time, overflowing with essences and alloys of herbs and spices. The unique flavor of "those" *tamales*, the rich variety of sweetbreads spread out on lace doilies, and the thick, frothy hot chocolate. I can feel the warm humidity of a summer evening after the rain. I once again smell the wet earth—"that" wet earth—the eager jasmines long since gone, the azaleas covered with transparent drops of water which multiply the yellow light of the lantern for children with eyes eager to see such things. To see such things and then relive, so many years later, the luminous smile of my mother at the exact moment when dinner was served on the patio—because it was a special occasion, because my father was absent, because at the slightest excuse my mother would have us eat outside—and at that exact moment the lantern's light burned out and a dog on a neighboring patio behind our house suddenly barked as a big moon began to rise. The jasmines, long since gone, seem to tremble, and everything revives again inside me, so much so that I didn't even realize that silent tears are streaming down my cheeks.

VI

It is the most unjust war that history can conjure up, motivated by the ambition, not of an absolute monarchy, but of a Republic—the North American Republic—which aspires to be at the forefront of civilization in the 19th century.

LUCAS ALAMÁN

I THINK THAT I started to suffer from insomnia as a very young child. As time went by it got worse, plaguing my adolescence. And with the Yankees threatening to invade our city, it almost drove me crazy.

I was deathly tired, but when I would lie down and shut my eyelids in desperation, I would simply feel a shifting within my skull, signaling my entry into a second level of darkness which only accompanies insomnia. My head seemed to fill with vivid images swirling in every direction.

Dr. Urruchúa was visibly concerned about me and, I suspect, didn't quite know how to help. He would say with his soft, high-pitched voice, almost a purr:

"For starters, my friend, aside from your illness, you are using this potential Yankee invasion, which may never even happen, as an excuse to exhume your most secret, shameless obsessions."

"Are they only *my* obsessions, doctor?"

"I understand. I think you may be right—quite probably they are also the obsessions and shameless dreams of your parents, your distant ancestors and even a good number of people you've seen in the street. It is well known that thoughts act as lightning rods, and all you have to do is concentrate on a particular topic or event and all analogous thoughts and events jump the fence to come near. Be careful."

Dr. Urruchúa's attitude regarding that "potential" Yankee invasion was desperate resignation. At times he even seemed to infer that it had already happened and he would contemplate it not as an event he needed to confront, but as a memory, a story, a picture framed and hanging in his living room.

He was very short and as thin as a branch of a quince tree, but on one occasion I took him by the arm and recognized the energy he concentrated into his movements, the resilience of his bones and the magnetism of his skin.

With their metal rims, his glasses hid a look of serene detachment, like water beneath the moon.

As he used to say, perhaps it was precisely the marked difference between our tastes and temperaments which made us such good friends. I ran to him the moment I perceived any unusual pain or had a strange dream, requiring him to demonstrate his brilliant patience. From the first moment I met him at the Progreso Café, I felt we had a unique bond, played out in a friendly game of increasing mimicry in which even the most obvious oppositions revolve within a context which binds and situates them.

A perfect symmetry ruled our relationship, because he also passed through confessional stages. How I've needed him since his death. How tightly woven was our friendship, no matter how we kept it exposed to a double wind, to alternating pressures.

Apart from that, the period during which I lived alone in the house in Tacubaya was marked by anticipation (although certainly, before the Yankee invasion I was not exactly sure what I was anticipating), infertility and confusion. Just like the rest of the city. There was confusion everywhere—everything had the same value, identical proportions, equivalent meaning, because everything actually had been stripped of any importance, and somehow things were happening outside of regular time and real reality, so to speak. Repeated gestures and anticipation (although, I reiterate, I really didn't know the anticipation of what) seemed to vibrate outside of me, in the air as well as in objects I would find trembling in my idle hands. Whether my eyes were open or closed, I experienced the same obstinate image of anticipation (of what, I asked, of what?), followed or preceded by the same acid stench, the same dirty fatigue of my privileged social class, the same vestiges of interminable groaning which began in utter darkness who knows how many years or centuries before, which I inherited.

"If you would look for a steady job, with a regular schedule, you would cut your problems in half," Dr. Urruchúa counseled me shortly after we met. He even personally helped me get a job with a newspaper published by a friend of his. I gathered and edited articles, staying until late into the night with the pressmen—but I only lasted two months. I didn't even collect my pay—I donated it to the cause and welfare of the newspaper, which was named *El eco del otro mundo, The Echo from the Other World,* and was openly Christian and spiritualist, without being Catholic. Very anti-American, that's for sure.

Perhaps—despite the accompanying agony—I simply preferred to live in absolute idleness, immersed in my obsessions, my visions and my secret appalling dreams. Even time became jumbled and confused in my unrelenting, tiresome, tense anticipation, combined with nights during which even if I did manage to doze for a few hours near dawn—in that stage of sleep which really isn't yet sleep, but simply blurs the line between consciousness and sleep—I would awake violently, plagued by truncated images, shredded voices, pounding light cutting through the darkness, creaking furniture, the psalmody of wind coming through gaps in the windows, and the first sounds of the city would fill me with anguish (had they finally arrived?), as if my nerves, extending beyond my skin, had branched out through all of Mexico City to gather its most intimate vibrations.

I tried everything to get to sleep, following Dr. Urruchúa's orders: light dinners, infusions of valerian and lime, rose petal baths, skull massages, permanganate enemas when feeling heaviness in the stomach, and bromide and potassium pills. I even tried the advice of a folk healer from Portal de las Flores: lie down in a lateral position oriented toward the Earth's magnetic pole, always toward the Earth's magnetic pole.

Nothing helped. Nights would burn like black oil and devour my poor astonished eyes.

I could well have said, like Othello:

Not poppy, nor mandragora,
Nor all the drowsy syrups of the world,
Shall ever medicine thee to that sweet sleep.

Neither could I avoid taking my worries to bed with me, striving to decipher the indecipherable. I imagined the city, its streets, the people's faces and the air itself as they would be when the Americans were here among us, imposing themselves on us with their large, brutal, light-skinned presence, almost like embodied ghosts.

Sometimes it was worse to actually fall asleep, because my dreams would make me feel even more anguished when I woke, and before getting up from bed I would have to elucidate and then rebuild the world—my unique world—with the same painstaking exactness as doing a puzzle. I spent hours and hours studying the first rays of the sun on the ceiling and the walls, hearing the torturous marching of time in the city clocks. The early morning hours stretched outside and inside of me. If I ever managed to capture a dream—or sometimes simply the idea or an image of a dream—a heartrending hoped-for jubilation would envelop me, as if every dream were a premonition, which of course they're not.

"That's it!" I'd exclaim, snapping my fingers, and I would jump out of bed and go down to the kitchen for a cup of hot chocolate, or if it was later in the day out to the street for a newspaper.

I would breathe in the new morning air and relish the first rays of the sun.

But my jubilation was unfailingly fleeting, because all I had to do was glance at the front page of the newspaper for the long shadow of anguishing anticipation to envelop me once again.

Even before the enemy landed on the beaches of Veracruz, families had begun to evacuate, taking refuge in the nearby towns and villages if they lacked the resources to go and hide in safer places like Orizaba or Jalapa. Those who bravely decided to stay crowded into the city's highest sites with their binoculars trained toward the coast. Didn't they sense that as soon as the Americans initiated their cannon attacks the city would be filled with death? Even children joined the fateful spectacle. People are aware that not far beyond Vigas, to the left of the main thoroughfare leading to the capital city on the way to Perote, there are places from which they can gaze on the sea in its marvelous grandeur. Some saw everything—from the furthest point at which the waves mix with the sky, to the milky waters of the Ulúa fortress, to a point not far from the capital where, glimmering in the sun, the sinister Yankee vessels were visible.

"Didn't they sense that soon their city would be filled with death?" The question marks of the questions seemed to reverberate within me for quite a while. Of course invasions have been rather common in the existence of men throughout time, but they are difficult to grasp when they are about to affect you. "This can't be happening to me!" is the most frequent expression of such people. There have been myriad invasions and wars in the world, but invasions and wars always catch people by surprise. "This can't last—it's too illogical to last." Undoubtedly invasions and wars are indeed illogical, but that doesn't keep them from happening. Invasions and wars aren't for the "decent" people of large cities like ours—those things aren't real, they happen elsewhere, in rural areas, in the provinces— they are just bad dreams and all you need to do is wake up as soon as possible. But you don't always wake up from them, and the bad dreams don't end, especially for good-willed people who are never prepared.

I stopped by the hospital to see Dr. Urruchúa and told him about my most recent thoughts and reflections.

"They'll be here soon enough, that's for sure. Don't be so desperate, my friend. They'll be here soon enough," he answered in a tone somewhere between ironic and indifferent which, I would imagine, is only learned when one works every day with frustration and human suffering. "You'd be better off thinking about something else, even if, as you say, the invasion catches you unprepared. Heavens! By fearing them so much you're going to bring them before their time! Concentrate on the 'here and now,' on this beautiful night we have overhead, for example." He smiled, making a broad gesture with his hands as if he were fencing.

We walked down Espíritu Santo Street and turned onto Coliseo heading to the Progreso Café, where we used to join that small group of friends with whom we dissented on a lot of things—like any group of friends gathering in the city—but with whom we shared a relentless anti-Americanism: anecdotes, concerns, worries, possible solutions and, above all else, the most recent news regarding the war Mexico was waging against the United States. (As I write this years later, the expression, "the war Mexico was waging against the United States," brings back a familiar bitter taste and triggers the same familiar sensation I felt back then—frightening serpents slithering down my spine. How could we Mexicans have possibly waged a war *against* the United States?)

And, sure enough, as the doctor had mentioned, on high was a night as pure as a violet.

Carriages were starting to arrive at the Teatro Principal, which was only separated from the Progreso Café by a narrow passageway. Some of the carriages were quite elegant, while other rented ones were drawn by plodding mules with bags under their eyes. Obviously desperate, one driver, wrapped up in a hooded riding cape that covered all but his eyes, lashed his mule with a whistling whip. On the street corner, an Indian woman hawked her merchandise in a loud voice, "Roasted chestnuts, almond candy!"

Before entering the café, I insisted with a stubbornness bordering on impertinence, practically whispering in the doctor's ear:

"Sometimes ... sometimes I dream they've already arrived, that they're already here, and I wake up ... how can I describe it? I feel like someone who has been buried alive and finally opens his eyes to his fate, with the advantage of finally having accepted it. At such moments I think that no fate is better or worse than any other as long as you can accept it. At least that's what I think."

"With your dreams and visions, my friend, you are purging who knows how many inhabitants of this city of their guilt. But stop worrying. As long as it's a double, your first drink will free you from anguish for a while—you'll see," said the doctor, and he slapped me on the back and waited for me to enter the café.

We sat down at a marble table in the corner, just to the side of the entrance to the billiard room. Marcos Negrete, dean of the group, had been holding the table for half an hour. We always found him anxiously devouring some newspaper. He held his venerable bald head high, with ruddy cheeks and small metal-rimmed glasses riding dangerously on the tip of his long nose. His stiff collar and black bow tie almost strangled him. He always greeted us cheerfully and would start to comment on something he was reading, but Dr. Urruchúa would stop him with an imperious hand in the air.

"Not yet, Don Marcos, please, not yet."

Although the topics of war with the Yankees and the outrages of Santa Anna inevitably became part of the conversation, the good doctor tried to postpone them as long as possible and would lecture us on things that had nothing at all to do with the topic, such as the difference between "impeded pus," "well-cultured pus" and "laudable pus." Which would naturally beg the question he used to ask himself—why the devil did more women die of puerperal fever in hospitals than did out of them while cared for by their friends? Might it not be possible, as he had begun to suspect recently, that physicians caring for birthing patients were not washing their hands after performing autopsies on cadavers?

Someone would inevitably ask, "How can you think about physicians washing their hands before a birth when this city is on the brink of being leveled by the Yankees, doctor? Does anyone even care about that?"

The truth was that the poisons circulating under our skin that day—and every one of those days—making us ill, was the new and alarming news:

"I read that a group of young people from Veracruz is 'raising money to set up a provisional blood bank' by putting on theater performances, and that women 'are sewing small sacks and putting together cannon pouches, as well as preparing sheets and bandages to take care of the wounded.' And the number of eligible men joining the national guard is impressive."

The next night, someone else added this new information:

"The most powerful naval force ever assembled in the Americas is now approaching Veracruz, with over seventy ships."

Later came more news that sent shivers down our spines:

"General Winfield Scott has given the final orders to launch barges full of soldiers onto select Mexican beaches. His 'only fear,' they say, was the fortress of San Juan de Ulúa, and because he was unsure of the reach of the artillery from the fortress, he sent a small squad which, having been fired upon by the military there, let him know what little danger he faced from the Ulúa batteries. Assured that he would not expose his men to danger, he had them land on the island of Sacrificios at two in the afternoon on March 9."

"Word had it that Ulúa had four hundred cannons. The truth was there were only two hundred twenty-four, of which less than half could manage more than two shots because lack of maintenance had left them in awful condition."

"Everything in this country is in terrible condition. How could we possibly wage a war against anybody?"

"Six thousand projectiles rained down on the city of Veracruz."

"They say eighty soldiers are dead along with some four hundred civilians, mostly women and children."

"General Juan Morales fled in a ship accompanied by the presiding officer of the National Guard, leaving Veracruz to its own fate. Supposedly it was so he wouldn't have to formally surrender and salute the American flag, but in reality he was scared out of his wits."

"Look at this," Félix María Ortega said one night, showing us a drawing he had just made on a napkin. "Without Texas, our country will have the shape of a horn of plenty, don't you think? Except that the opening of the horn faces the United States! Perhaps that explains what is happening. Who can resist having at their feet a horn of plenty without taking from it and enjoying it? Can anyone?" His full-moon smile made his ruddy cheeks and blond sideburns expand even further.

The murmur of conversations and laughter blended with the sound of billiard balls in the next room and the clinking of glasses. Cigar smoke wafted aloft, creating on the ceiling the appearance of ships loaded with foliage. People going to the Teatro Principal stood out in their apparel, the women wearing billowy dresses and the men tails and white vests with gold buttons.

"As a matter of fact," I interjected, "*El eco del otro mundo* just launched a section featuring letters from people who want to share their impressions, their inquiries and even their dreams. One woman stated that for the last five years she has been dreaming that a giant blond Yankee entered her home and stabbed the entire family."

"Our dreams will include more and more Yankees. There's nothing we can do about it," Dr. Urruchúa said, looking sternly at me. His eyes fluttered behind his glasses like fish in a fishbowl.

The truly terrifying thing—being buried alive and opening your eyes to your fate—was to have them so close while the city was in absolute chaos.

"Jalapa has now fallen as well."

"I've been told there are no longer street lights in Jalapa, and that in the darkness you hear shouts and cries from the fugitives of Cerro Gordo, and you hear about the stores and houses of the people who fled being looted. Early in the morning the American cavalry entered the city in a brutal manner, first gathering in the main plaza, then fanning out through the city."

"La Joya has also fallen, so get ready."

"And Perote."

"The fortress of Perote fell into the hands of the enemy with its forty pieces of brand new artillery, five mortars, and everything in its store: ammunition, food, money, military uniforms. It's a complete embarrassment."

"Las Vigas has also fallen."

"And Puebla is on the verge of falling."

"How horrible," exclaimed Martínez del Campo, thin, elegant, educated, refined, his hands trembling uncontrollably.

Every member of our group took his personal sufferings and fears, worked them into a lather, forced them to grow, and then saw to it that they would contribute to the overall fear of the group, that enormous black cloud which was going to come out of the sky and cover the entire city.

Who will protect us? The Virgin Mary? The Archangel Michael? What saint will rush to our aid? Will Santa Anna? "Horrors!" exclaimed Martínez del Campo as he cleared his throat like an actor about to appear on stage.

At least in my case, I came to recognize rather quickly that the impending horror had very little to do with a fear of death. On the contrary—what really caused me horror was the idea of living with a Yankee on top of me. As Dr. Urruchúa explained, fear always has a visible aspect, a defined form in time and space—fear of an animal, or of a physical assault, or of a threatening face. By contrast, horror is anguish: vague, beyond our grasp, almost supernatural. That's why when someone—I think it was Juan Gamboa—said half in jest and half in earnest that the Yankees are the incarnation of Evil on Earth, many of us shivered ever so slightly—I'm sure many of us felt it. Dr. Urruchúa, naturally, did not, because he immediately made an ill-timed remark:

"For the sake of argument, let's say that the Yankees *are* Evil. So what?" The corners of his mouth relaxed into a sarcastic smirk.

"So what?" Gamboa queried in a tone an octave higher than his regular voice. His double chin rested on his bow tie.

As he frequently did, the doctor made use of a literary quote.

"I believe that in the end, and please hear me out, Evil does not belong to any one nation or race. Even if it were to belong to the United States, they would be doing us a favor by bringing it to our country. Remember the response of Dante Alighieri during the Venetian carnival, when the Count of Medici sent his servants out to find him among the masses of masks and costumes, armed with the question, 'Who knows Goodness?' Dante was the only one to answer, 'He who knows Goodness is he who knows Evil.' When the Count of Medici learned of the response, he exclaimed: 'That was Dante! Summon him. I won the bet! Is he irritated that we found him out?' However, Dante's smile, half evil and half victorious, betrayed the fact that he was not bothered at all."

The doctor's words must have seemed too fancy and cultured to Polo García Venegas, his stubby white hands playing nervously with the embroidered little lion on his dark vest, and so he tried to simplify:

"To know Evil, all Mexicans have to do is get to know Santa Anna. How could anyone do any better than that?"

"But that is lower case evil. In any event, he is more stupid than evil," the doctor insisted stubbornly.

"Therefore, doctor, in your opinion Mexicans need to endure a Yankee invasion to later appreciate more fully the advantages of liberty and independence?" Gamboa continued incredulously, his voice rising in tone until it became harsh. He put out his cigar in the ashtray with far more physical force than necessary.

"Quite possibly," responded Dr. Urruchúa, looking at the palms of his hands.

"Doctor, I'm afraid this confirms that you only come here to make fun of us. You have no right to do so. This is a place for friends," Gamboa asserted smartly, wrinkling up his nose as if a stench had suddenly assaulted him.

"On the subject of Evil, listen to what I just read in *El Monitor*," Marcos Negrete interrupted. He always interrupted when he sensed the least bit of confrontation in the group, and this one was really serious. "It reports that Sam Houston said, 'The matter of the African slave trade is not unconnected to the political forces in our country. The thought persists that thousands of Africans have recently been imported to Cuba with the intent to transfer a large portion of them to Texas.' Bear in mind that in the 1830s the price of slaves, thanks to a law from Louisiana, dropped considerably. To raise the price they had to take control of Texas. Vast regions to populate with new slaves. What minds the Yankees have!"

But Gamboa wasn't about to let go, although he softened his tone when he asked, "Doctor, what do you think about that type of evil, whether it be upper case or lower?"

A resigned, sweet smile made its way onto the doctor's lips.

"At this point, I would merely say, as did Horace: 'If you are seeking peace, prepare for war.'"

I returned home in Marcos Negrete's carriage. We arrived with an unmistakable jolt. I was about to get out when his arm stopped me, his hand like a claw. Although the carriage had stopped moving, his metal-rimmed glasses continued to ride dangerously on the tip of his nose.

"Level with me, Abelardo, my friend. Don't you believe that the best thing that could happen to the inhabitants of this city is for the Americans to invade?"

I freed myself with a brusque movement. He must have felt that my gaze bore holes right through him.

"How can you even think ...?"

"I think about my children and the children of my children. And about the children you will have. Think about it. Some people even want to become part of the United States in order to achieve peace and prosperity instead of the poverty and chaos we have today. Others think a war would be the way to free ourselves from Santa Anna and break down the hegemony of the old Carlist army and the dominance of the capital over the states. I am a man of principles, as you well know, and have come to the conclusion ..." His neck seemed particularly gorged, throbbing and quite red. Despite the indignation his words were causing me, I almost asked him to unbutton the neck of his shirt and loosen his tie.

"Please, Don Marcos, don't ask such a delicate question when you know ahead of time that we won't agree, that we can't possibly agree. It almost seems as though you don't know me, that you haven't listened to all I have said and repeated in the group regarding my convictions in this matter."

"A word please. I'm telling you this ... because I know how we both share the same fear."

"You seem to offend me more deeply with each sentence."

"Pardon me for saying this to you, for daring to say this to you, perhaps because I had a couple of absinthes too many, but fears open us up, unite us, give us solidarity." He cleared his throat, then added in the same tone: "Fear determines our relationships in love as much as our political views. And today, at this moment, I confess in absolute sincerity that I am scared to death. I'm petrified with fear, which is what they say about three thousand of our soldiers at Cerro Gordo and about Captain Morales when he fled Veracruz scared to death. Do you understand?"

I felt that my only option at that point was to be completely frank with Don Marcos, for whom I had nothing but respect and sympathy.

"The difference is that I am always deathly afraid because *they* are going to come. I simply can't bear the thought of it."

"I understand. But let's look at things a bit differently. We are afraid they will come, agreed, but what will happen to us if we keep them from coming?"

"I don't understand."

"It's simple. I think we've already lost the war and shedding more blood is pointless. But in the unlikely event that we should triumph, what would we accomplish by beating Scott and his army, by keeping them from invading the city? How do you think the United States would react to that?"

"By going home. By leaving us in peace."

Now it was his turn to ratchet his harshest and most incisive eyes onto me.

"Don't be naïve, Abelardo my friend. They would not have started this war with such an attitude. Didn't you see the drawing Ortega made of the horn of plenty, with its inviting opening just across from Texas? They're not going to finish until they've devoured the entire horn, and all in one sitting. They would send thousands and thousands of American soldiers to reinforce Scott—as many as it took to finish the job. The blood-shed could last for months or even years, believe me."

His words, which were not void of logic, just made me dig in my heels deeper.

"I understand what you are saying, Don Marcos, but I am going to confess something related to that fear which you mention. I have become convinced that my fear isn't so much of death, as of having a Yankee on top of me."

"On top of you?"

"So to speak. We are all afraid of death, but some of us are even more afraid, much more afraid, of crises of anguish, of shaking and having cold sweats because of a certain nearby presence. Knowing that presence is out there, lurking in the shadows and headed our direction. A repugnant, intolerable face. A sense of rejection which resides more in our guts than in our minds. Now do you understand me?"

He didn't say a word. As he said goodbye he lowered his somber gaze, twisted his lips kindly, but in a way that couldn't quite be called a smile, and patted the same arm which moments earlier he had gripped with unnecessary force.

It would soon become clear that many more people thought like Negrete than I'd supposed.

VII

May all Mexicans finally embrace each other,
May all mothers cease their crying,
And may all arms become silent.
Immortal God, forgive my brethren!

MANUEL CARPIO

"AND WHAT ABOUT these pages? Who wrote them?" my wife asked when she discovered handwriting that wasn't mine, her nostrils quivering with curiosity. As she rifled through the papers and clippings I keep on my desk, she was turning them into chaos.

She insists that she wants nothing more in life than for me to leave her alone, but she has never been able to resist poking her nose into my business whenever she has the chance.

"Those are notes from Dr. Urruchúa, whom I have told you so much about. He gave them to me not long before he died because some of them refer to me and my nervous maladies. They also include his notes about the problems he faced as a physician when the Yankees invaded and filled the city with dead and wounded."

"What does he say about you?"

"Listen to this, for example: 'In his *Anatomy of Melancholy*, Burton assures that severe cases of sadness can "paralyze muscles, impede speech, and cause negative visions." Yet it may be that not all of these visions are so "negative," and some of them may even have a bearing on reality, on *another* reality. Might it not be within the realm of possibility that, in some cases, the victim of melancholy becomes a visionary? Regarding the little flames my friend Abelardo sometimes sees in the sky, undoubtedly they are related to his nervous illness, but they also caused me to remember a passage from the Bible which can shed light on the phenomenon: *Nation shall rise against nation, and kingdom against kingdom. And great earthquakes shall be in divers places, and famines, and pestilences and fearful sights and great signs shall there be from heaven, for those who can see them.* Could it not be that victims of melancholy discover warnings in the heavens which we—poor normal beings—are unable to perceive? And is the price they pay for the privilege worth it? Young Abelardo arrives at the hospital to see me after these devastating visions (he calls them glimpses), and how can the price he pays be calculated: loss of balance, trembling, bags under his eyes, sickly yellow skin, stuttering, sweaty palms and glassy, unfocused eyes. Dealing with an illness as devastating as melancholy, and given the serious situation of our city, any responsible physician—and I count myself among them—should not disregard any working hypothesis.' What do you think about that?"

"It seems rather unprofessional for a physician to make a diagnosis of a nervous illness based on a passage in the Bible."

"He was a very special physician—the only one I ever consulted because of liking him. You know how skittish I am about physicians. Luckily, at my age, the next time I need to go to a doctor will undoubtedly be for an autopsy."

"I would rather skip the pathologist and be seen by a hairdresser just in case someone looks in my coffin. I wouldn't want anyone to say about me what that doctor says about you: bags under the eyes, yellow skin, glassy and unfocused eyes. Ugh!"

VIII

Oh, God, why art thou acting as if thou slept,
Seemingly unaware of the tribulations which
Cause us Mexicans to weep? Awake!
Allow not our enemy to say, "Where is
Your God, who seems not to run to help you
In this conflict?" Arise! And wielding thy
Mighty sword, take vengeance, vengeance, as
The blood of this innocent people flows!

CARLOS MARÍA DE BUSTAMANTE

WHAT A SHAME, Dr. Urruchúa, that you, for whom the possibility of preventing pain during operations became a bona fide obsession, who sometimes used hypnotism or bleeding even though you recognized that they weren't enough to produce complete numbness or suppress involuntary muscle movement, never found out that scarcely a year after your death, in 1848, a physician in Edinburgh, James Simpson, discovered chloroform as a general anesthetic. In deference to your memory, I was present at one of the first operations performed with chloroform in the Hospital of San Pedro and San Pablo, and you can't imagine what a wonderful experience it is to open a container, soak a handkerchief in that blessed liquid with its sweet and penetrating smell, place it carefully over a patient's nose and mouth, and then watch the lips change miraculously from an anguished grimace to a perfectly relaxed peacefulness.

Surgery on a patient profoundly asleep—the miracle for which you so steadfastly hoped and prayed!

Neither were you able to learn, which was another shame, that at essentially the same time as you, the Austrian physician Ignaz Semmelweis started to require his students in Vienna to wash their hands in a solution of calcium chloride before attending a birth. That same idea—isn't it strange the way human ideas develop and come to fruition—was at the root of Louis Pasteur's findings in 1865, when he published his theory that germs cause sickness, the scientific foundation of antisepsis and asepsis.

You ought to see—right there in the same hospital where you worked so many years—the steaming basins in which scalpels, needles, thread and scissors are disinfected before operations.

Physicians no longer assist with a birth without washing their hands, *plus*—incredible as this seems—disinfecting their instruments!

I vividly recall you telling me that you were convinced that "some harmful agent" must pass from the dead to the living via physicians who treated both. That agent—decomposed organic material—undoubtedly caused the blood poisoning which took the lives of an astounding one of every three women who gave birth.

Don't think that every invention dazzles me! I have lived long enough to see some things and be amazed, but also to put progress in perspective. Some inventions like the incandescent electric light bulb, which has lightened our nights (even though it has driven spirits away), or photography—you ought to see the modern cameras with tripods and bellows, which puff out a little cloud of white smoke when you take a picture—seem unquestionably useful. I think that others will actually impoverish us, or complicate our lives even more. One example is moving photography, apparently called cinematography—which I fear could soon do away with theater. Another invention that people are starting to talk about is the gasoline-powered automobile, which would take from us the pleasant slow trot of our irreplaceable horse-drawn carriages.

There are other inventions, like the telephone, to which I simply can't accustom myself—it's just a personal quirk. I think I mentioned something about this to you some time ago. I have always felt such surprise and happiness, as you well remember, from the astonishing fact that we can go into a café, order a glass of absinthe, and moments later the glass is on the table. At times I have felt like kneeling down at that moment to thank the Lord for such a gift. Think about it, doctor: a bit of air is expelled from our mouths, accompanied by movements of the tongue and jaw, and the miraculous result of such a simple act is that a glass of absinthe appears, something vital to me in the afternoon. Well, the invention of the telephone extends the effects of expelling air and working the jaw to ... an infinite distance! Our voices form a sort of invisible spider web throughout the city, echoing over and over. I tell you I just can't get used to it! It exceeds my capacity for astonishment.

Where is our world heading? It's a good question for a physician like you, Dr. Urruchúa—wherever you may be—who would have appreciated chloroform as anesthesia, but would still today have used a verse from the Bible to diagnose a nervous disorder rather than using some comfortable treatment from traditional medicine. Since this chronicle belongs to all of us who had something to do with that black year, I am including here some of your notes.

IX

It wasn't just the arms and the training that distinguished them from our armies; above all else it was their superior diet and their drinking whiskey every morning.

MANUEL BALBONTÍN

UNTIL A SHORT TIME *ago I believed that my sheer exhaustion from spending all day working in the hospital would keep me from useless thoughts and reflections, but ever since Abelardo planted the topics of melancholy and nervous disorders into my head, I have taken every opportunity to accompany colleagues to the San Hipólito insane asylum to observe firsthand the admittedly extreme manifestation of the other world.*

It was like staring into an aquarium to find that the fish were looking back at me, a little cross-eyed, sleepily producing errant bubbles.

Or, the opposite, being the fish looking through the glass at the doctor whose clinical eye is magnified through the glass.

Deep down, *what is the difference?*

Now that I have studied them, I believe what dooms some unbalanced people is the way in which their outward behavior is perceived as unbearable by society. Tics, manias, physical degradation and oral or motor problems make it very easy to label individuals and separate them from the mainstream.

But when we look a little more closely at them—for example, by listening to some of their arguments—we discover they aren't as crazy as the doctor thought. Or, even worse, we find that the doctor is not as sane as we would like to think.

For example, there is a woman who perceives that things suddenly shine with an intense brilliance which paralyzes her, leaving her eyes as big as saucers and hands twisted into knots. I saw her during one of her husband's occasional visits. He naively tried to cheer her up by talking about their home and small children. She suddenly screamed and protested bitterly: how could he waste her time talking about annoying, dirty children when the important thing right then was the indescribable beauty of the glimmering designs the evening light formed on his shirt each time he moved his arms? What a vision, I thought. But the poor woman didn't spend long in her paradise. Her incursions into that world of beauty became shorter and shorter until they finally disappeared and all that was left was horror, fright, paralyzed eyes and a frozen, twisted mouth.

As I wander through the rooms and see the faces and gestures of the people, a slight shudder comes over me, and I see myself in the faces of those people, and there beside me flowers the rare and fleeting testimony of another reality: perhaps a series of a distant glimpses into that reality, a door left slightly ajar through which rays of living and burning light enter our existence: a wink of friendship, a smile which is more of a horrid grimace, a trembling, beckoning finger that says, "Come, Dr. Urruchúa, help me understand the world and my mental state, and let's be friends, since we are so alike," a gesture which moves me with painful compassion, then terrifies me, a tic which seems suspiciously like one a favorite cousin of mine has.

I remember a patient with an inoperable tumor in his stomach told me, "Blessed is physical pain, doctor, because it makes us forget our truly insufferable pains—those of the soul."

A front of contrasting winds stirs and a gust blowing the other way brings me back to my supposedly real reality, the reality outside of the asylum, the day-to-day variety, of sane physicians and men who—now here is madness!—are at war with the most powerful country in the world.

My final conclusion—I have no other choice but to conclude—is that the only positive quality of our president ... is that he doesn't drool.

The Mexican constitution has never been in effect. The government is despotic, and I am certain that it will continue so for many years to come. The elected officials are not honest and Mexicans in general are not very smart.

SAM HOUSTON TO PRESIDENT ANDREW JACKSON,
FEBRUARY 1833

AFTER READING PARTS of my chronicle with a slightly more tolerant attitude, my wife asked me this question: "Do you think those notes from that doctor friend of yours (whose surname I can never remember) about insanity can possibly be of general interest? After all, the city was on the verge of being invaded by the United States."

"To me they seem absolutely indispensable to understand what happened afterwards. He was absolutely correct when he stated that Santa Anna's only saving grace was that he didn't drool. That statement could help us to reinterpret our country's recent history. Besides, those notes reflect Dr. Urruchúa's humanity and why he abandoned life after treating pains which destroyed all of us."

"I think you are including it for merely sentimental reasons."

"That's also true. Sometimes as I write, I get the feeling that we are together again. Maybe even closer than in those days."

"Will you feel closer to Isabel when you write about her?" she asked with a mischievous spark in her beautiful eyes.

"I would love to find out. Especially because the most important part of our relationship started precisely when I stopped seeing her."

"You've always managed to complicate your life. And as you do so, you complicate the lives of other people as well."

Halfway through 1847 I stopped seeing my fiancée, Miss Isabel Olaguíbel, when I discovered that her father was in favor of the American invasion. They lived in the city, but on weekends would go to their mansion in Tlalpan, with its ceramic tile from Spain, its fireplace with bronze and lapis lazuli decorations, its wrought-iron balconies and a marble stairway flanked by two dazzling white porcelain figures—long-maned lions that seemed to jealously guard the entrance to the house.

Sunday meals with her family were insufferable, but I truly loved Señorita Isabel Olaguíbel with her languid, shaded eyes in which deep black pupils seemed to shimmer in perpetual arousal, her movements and gestures as precious as an embroidered heart.

Her father, Don Vicente Olaguíbel y Torre, tried to force me into becoming a connoisseur of cockfights—his own children had bags of excuses not to go with him—but what he nearly accomplished was to plunge me into bankruptcy.

On Sundays we would go to the town square, in the shadow of the whitened chapel called El Calvario, where they would set up the pit for cockfights. The truth is that I did enjoy going—it distracted me from my nightly anguish and I liked the environment. There were very few places like that one where the rich and the poor could naturally rub shoulders.

Once a fight was set, a man wearing a straw hat and an unbuttoned shirt would bark at the top of his lungs:

"Here comes the fight! Here are the roosters! The first match will be fought with open blades. Gentlemen, place your bets!"

Bookies would come out of the woodwork, shouting and adjusting odds and taking bets, announcing the names of the roosters and their handlers.

"Ten *pesos* on Saldaña ... Six *pesos* on Ledesma ... The betting for this match will close soon!"

And that is where my problems would begin. Although I was a penny pincher, just to irritate my potential father-in-law I would always bet against his rooster, no matter what, and of course I would always lose. With his markedly receding hairline, a round belly that preceded him so far it seemed separate from the rest of his body, a curved nose proclaiming the triumph of decrepitude and his oily skin, Don Vicente would slap me on the back and say, needling me:

"You're going to lose, my young friend."

He would explain to me in an unbearably pedantic tone that the most famous, well-bred roosters were from San Antonio el Pelón, near Cadereyta, and the ones from Tlacotalpan in Veracruz. But—and don't ever forget this—roosters from Tepeaca and Xochimilco had a terrible reputation.

I would then place my money on a rooster from Tepeaca or Xochimilco, which would cause Don Vicente to take a deep breath, take off his wide-brimmed hat and wipe the sweat from his head with a scarf. Then he wouldn't say a word to me for a long stretch.

At the command of a judge, bettors would clear out of the actual pit, leaving just the handlers and the starters.

The handlers were covered with feathers. They held the roosters close to each other, whipping them into a frenzy by making them look into each other's eyes, inciting them to try to strike out even before the fight began, which naturally reminded me of the constant confrontations between our combative politicians. Then, with a gentle push, they sent the roosters into the fight, like letting go of a rocket at take off. The handlers would stay squatting, a stony intensity on their faces.

Within the whirlwind of beaks, feathers and blood, at some point one of the roosters would suddenly pull up lame, incapable of lifting its claws again. That was the rooster I had picked, of course.

I would lose with a bittersweet taste in my mouth.

Arguments and the sound of money mixed with music festooned the winner. Handlers and starters would dart from place to place spouting details of the combat and the announcer would finally call out:

"Come collect your winnings! The doors are once again open!"

Meanwhile back at home, at exactly two o'clock in the afternoon, Isabel's mother—lovely, maternal, wearing a graceful smile which made her look younger, and gesturing with hands as sleek as birds—would announce dinner was ready. The Talavera place settings shared honors with the tablecloth embroidered in Aguascalientes; the glass pitchers contained drinks of various colors, and elaborately folded napkins elegantly rested beside the plates.

She would show off, one by one, the dishes on the menu: bread soup with slices of boiled egg, garbanzo beans, parsley, peppers and cheese; chicken breasts, with red *mole* on one side and green *mole* on the other; in the center of the table a tray of beans, radishes, green onions and strips of pork cracklings. Dessert included coconut cookies, caramel sauce and jelly-filled *roscos*.

As we would start to sit down, Don Vicente would enter the room with the heavy sound of his shiny *federica* boots, beaming and full of energy. Standing there he seemed even fatter than he actually was, his enormous gut swaying rhythmically from side to side.

The first thing he would do was announce what had happened that morning at the cockfights.

"Young Abelardo once again lost this morning, I'm sorry to say," he would state, and then instead of speaking to me he would turn to his daughter, who, as usual, would look down at her soup. "Why don't you convince him to allow me to instruct him, Isabel? If there's anything I know in life, it's cockfights, as you're well aware."

A silence would follow, creating an icy atmosphere all around. Isabel would answer, full of nervous anxiety, but packing an explosive punch:

"Stop asking him to go with you, please. He doesn't enjoy it. Haven't you seen that? Abelardo, isn't it true you don't enjoy going with my father to the cockfights?"

"If I didn't enjoy them, I wouldn't go, Isabel. On the contrary, I'm coming to enjoy them more and more and starting to understand them better," I would argue, a spoonful of thick bread soup with boiled egg sticking in my throat.

"It certainly doesn't seem that you understand them at all," Don Vicente would answer drily, not looking at me as he added bits of cheese to his soup. "It actually seems like you enjoy losing your money. Even Rafa Madariaga observed that last Sunday: 'It seems like your future son-in-law enjoys losing his money.' That pains me because it might be thought I am making you lose because of bad advice."

He would then ignore me and start to criticize or scold one of his children, Isabel's younger siblings, for some reason or another whether they deserved it or not. He was a little more considerate with his wife and daughter as long as they didn't talk back to him and maintained absolute silence.

He would lead the conversation as if conducting an orchestra, and I—suffering from the nervous tension and a host of concerns overwhelming me at the time—tried to eat with my eyes glued on my food or some imaginary object on the ceiling, or on the iridescent prisms of the candles, or out the window on the distant trees or the group of servants saddling the horses.

After a third glass of wine Don Vicente would become even more sententious, invoking family tradition and the moral precepts he had inherited. He would emphasize his statements by leaning back in his chair, then solemnly inserting his hands in his vest pockets, which ended up making his belly look even rounder.

"Don't ever forget that if we Olaguíbels are anything, we owe it to honorable hard work. We are not aristocrats, but a modest, liberal family."

He would make reference to his obsession with time and punctuality. Isabel would look at the ceiling with an annoyance which, luckily, her father never seemed to notice. He would pull from his vest pocket a bulky gold time piece, and with the clean, rounded nail on the tip of his index finger move the minute hand ever so slightly to ensure that it accurately reflected the time (always, every Sunday at that time, his watch was either ahead or behind, which gave him the valuable opportunity to set it to the proper time in our presence).

"You were all born into a cacophonous, chaotic time. What a pity. I was born at a time when family life was ruled by a clock. Just listen to those chimes," he would say, and we all listened most attentively to the grave, clear chimes of the grandfather clock in the parlor. "They used to awaken us early in the morning with their imperious call—at exactly two they brought us to the dinner table and at ten they would give their absolute directive to go to bed."

Other weeks it was:

"My father lost a fortune in mining. Mining, as is well known, was greatly reduced after the wars of independence, and with disastrous results. But his shrinking fortune only increased my father's pride, and eventually he was reborn from the ashes, like the phoenix."

He liked to trot out the image of the phoenix as often as possible. Undoubtedly he read somewhere or someone told him about the symbolism of the phoenix, and citing it made him feel learned.

Looking at his children, he would then propose a rather awkward toast:

"To my father ... your grandfather."

Then he would lift his cup and we all had to toast his father, the grandfather of his children.

But one Sunday Don Vicente, in his preferred pose of leaning back in his chair, made a statement which pushed me over the edge:

"As a moderate liberal, I am convinced that the American invasion will be a golden opportunity to put an end to the despotism of military dictators like Santa Anna, and that once the Yankees win the war and occupy the entire country they will impose federalism and a liberal form of government."

My stomach contracted and a wave of bitterness rose in my throat. I couldn't swallow the bite of *enchilada* with green *mole* in my mouth. Trembling, I moved my glass of *jamaica* water and saw that a drop of the red liquid had fallen onto the pristine white tablecloth, a tiny drop of the past—it had to be the past, and soon enough I would be in my own house remembering the shameful scene as yet another of my nightmares—which one of the servants would coldly wipe away with a moist towel from the kitchen as the table was cleared.

"Mercy! I've spilled *jamaica* water on the tablecloth!"

"It's just a drop, Abelardo, think nothing of it. That will wash up splendidly," Isabel's mother said kindly.

But to the astonishment of the family, which on this occasion included an uncle who had just arrived from Querétaro, I threw my napkin onto the table with verve, stood up, and bowed in a ridiculous, stiff way that was completely unwarranted. In a jerky stammer, I explained that it would be impossible for me, absolutely impossible, to stay and eat with them after the outrage I had just committed. "Please understand me when I say that a stained tablecloth is a stained tablecloth, something for which a person can't just apologize lightly, especially at the table of a family as decent as yours. I need to leave immediately so that you may finish your excellent meal at your pleasure. No, please don't get up. You've already been too kind to me. Tomorrow I'll send a formal, written apology to Isabel to beg forgiveness for what has happened here." And I headed for the door, bowing the whole way, each bow stiffer than the previous one, with a forced smile on my face which could only have looked insincere, my teeth gritted as they were.

As I returned home I felt horrible for having hurt my dear Isabel that way—after all, she was the only person in that family who meant anything to me—but I felt a measure of consolation at the thought that I had spared myself the sleep-inducing conversation after dinner, and even more importantly the mazurkas and nocturnes played in the parlor on the piano with its inlaid woods of various colors. At the end of each number, Isabel would look at me questioningly and it was my solemn duty to nod in approval, letting her know that indeed she did possess some modest talent for playing the piano.

The next day it was Señorita Isabel herself who sent me a letter in a sealed, heavily perfumed pink envelope, but I hardened my heart and didn't even open it.

I felt the same type of indignation and disbelief which came from the comment of my future father-in-law, when some of my friends from the Progreso Café—friends who stopped attending our meetings, naturally—took up arms against the federal government in February because Vice President Gómez Farías required Mexican clergy to pay a fifteen million *peso* bond. How could they even think of opposing the federal government with the Yankees practically breathing down our necks? Such a phenomenon could only take place in a time such as ours, when chaos and general uncertainty reigned. The same people who fought for independence from the Spanish yoke stopped feeling any patriotic zeal, and little by little started to replace it with harsh criticism and desperation in light of the stupidity of our insufferable politicians. Unfortunately for everybody, the one did not warrant the other. In fact, the absurd confrontation made it impossible for the auxiliary government of Veracruz to function, and I felt compelled to write an article in *El eco del otro mundo* which created several more enemies for me:

What blindness among Mexicans! How prone we are to canni-
balism! The inhabitants of a country occupied in the north and
on the verge of being invaded from the west devote themselves
to their favorite pastime: stabbing each other in the back.
Because precisely when the invader—the Lapdog of the Anti-
christ who has come to earth to find converts—is more visible
than ever and fanning infernal flames all around us, instead of
setting aside their grievances and ideological differences to go
out and engage their true enemy, the enemy who will swallow
all of us, some of our most honorable Mexicans try to start a
wicked and shameful civil war. Given these actions, complain-
ing about bad luck seems utterly out of the question.

The people stirring up the masses said that the name by which they were known, the *polkos*, came from their unbridled passion for dancing the polka, which was all the rage. Others said that it came from their taste for *pulque*. The truth is that they were given that name because they were considered, and rightly so, the vile instruments of President Polk, undoubtedly often without even realizing it. Whatever the case, their relationship with the clergy seemed to have been the cause of their absurd incomprehensible actions.

Religious scapulars, medallions, ribbons and relics by the
dozens hung round the necks of the objectors, especially the

luxury-loving comfortable youth who made up the majority of our wealthiest and most elegant social class.

I later learned of a letter from Moses Beach, an undercover agent of the United States government who had infiltrated Mexico during the war, to Secretary of State James Buchanan, which put everything into focus:

Precisely when the troops of General Scott landed on the shores of Veracruz, the most crucial maneuver of the war took place—an uprising against the government in Mexico City—which tipped the advantage toward the United States. Barricaded in convents where their loving mothers took them food and bedding, the polkos have withstood the pounding of the army for nearly ten days, thanks to the support they enjoy from the leaders of religious orders. When I learned that the Church needed fifty thousand dollars to keep the uprising going one more week, I used funds made available to me from the State Department, and I made an open-ended loan to Bishop Fernández Madrid. I consider this expenditure more than justified, since General Scott had scarcely disembarked with the artillery at Veracruz and needed some time to overcome the defenses of the port.

When Dr. Urruchúa read my article in *El eco del otro mundo*, he immediately clicked his tongue and spoke to me in his most stern, scolding voice:

"Fine. But you are far too emotional with obvious points, and I also think you are starting to hallucinate in some of your writing. What good can come from saying 'the Lapdog of the Antichrist who has come to earth to find converts'?"

"I'm opposed to the dirty dealings of the Catholic Church, but I'm a sincere Christian."

"Well, I think it is the most unfortunate phrase I've ever read. You have to understand that the Devil is nothing more or less than the human choice to become distant from God. Don't be giving him a body and autonomy. Why don't you try to think about something else, anything else? Why don't you try to spend your valuable time in something other than an anguished, breathless anticipation of invasion?"

But how can anyone think of anything else, I wondered, when everyone who laid eyes on me, my dreams, the conversations I overheard, everything I read in the news and even the glittering stars reminded me of the same thing?

That's why I preferred to focus my attention on the signs—most of them recent, but others from before—announcing that which was imminent, that which I anxiously awaited. Any attempt to flee it just made things worse for me. Some of the previous signs seemed particularly significant. For example, this article published over fifteen years earlier, in 1830, by Manuel Mier y Terán in *La voz de la patria, The Voice of the Fatherland,* announcing the forthcoming loss of Texas:

Texans are in collusion with the greediest, most covetous country on Earth. It was that way yesterday, and it is that way today. The ambitious Americans have taken control of everything within their grasp. In less than half a century they have cunningly taken ownership of the rich, extensive territories which were formerly ruled under the Spanish and the French scepters, and of even larger and more bountiful areas that belonged to Indian tribes, countless Indian tribes they have subjected by force, which is exactly what they would like to do with us Mexicans.

Which is true—how are we any different from the Apaches who lived on the vast lands which they owned until the Yankees mercilessly exterminated them? What better mirror could there be to reflect our situation, I wondered, as I ran my index finger along my throat, imagining the decapitation I supposed would not be long in coming.

Mier y Terán also described the careful steps the Americans had taken in preparation for the *coup de grâce* to be applied to its chosen victim:

They begin by sending explorers and businessmen, supposedly to "aid" economic progress. Nevertheless, the greedy eyes of some of those American explorers and businessmen immediately are transfixed by the richness of the soil. They measure it, calculate it and then they invent an imaginary price for it. They hypocritically pretend to respect the rights and sovereignty of the country in question. Soon enough they provoke some political conflict. Or several political conflicts. They weaken the authority of the legitimate owner of the land. Then they take it over. That is exactly the precarious position in which Texas finds itself today. Are we Mexicans simply going to stand by with our arms folded in the face of this situation?

Three years after that passage was written, Vicente Filisola, general commander of the region, issued an official report on his initial activities in Texas. He summarized the attempted uprisings on the part of the colonizers and made the following deduction:

There can be no doubt that their sights are set not only on forming a separate territory or state, but, inconceivable as it sounds, seeking independence from the Mexican federation.

Filisola cited the following actions as evidence of his findings: refusing to pay taxes, denying Mexican troops access to the border, disobeying state and federal laws, destroying public buildings and organizing an independent militia with exclusively American officers. In addition, more and more adventurers anxious for conquest flowed into the territory from New York.

"Don't you find it astonishing that Mier y Terán's vision about the expansionist policy of the United States from more than fifteen years ago is still so applicable today, in 1847?" I asked Dr. Urruchúa during one of our nighttime walks, but he didn't seem to hear me—his gaze was focused on an unspecified point on the horizon, like someone watching a ship depart. I had to follow up: "More than fifteen years ago Mier y Terán saw the intentions of the Yankees regarding our country and perhaps the entire world! Furthermore, after he presided over the commission to set the definitive border between Mexico and the United States, he agonized over our gradual loss of territory, and simply committed suicide in 1832."

"He did what?" Dr. Urruchúa asked with eyes that were back to reality.

"You heard correctly. When he saw that United States expansionism would end up swallowing us, he didn't wait around and committed suicide."

"What do you think about his suicide?"

"I understand it."

Dr. Urruchúa immediately changed the subject and suggested that I read some books along the lines of Thomas à Kempis' writings. Then he asked me why I had stopped seeing my fiancée, so beautiful, from such a good family and with whom I shared a love of theater and opera, as I had mentioned to him.

What really bothered me, though, was that a little while later he questioned the reliability of the chronicle I was writing because of my altered emotional state:

"If you aren't in a state of balance, I fear that your chronicle, into which you have put so much time and effort, will be far less than objective because it will be terribly contaminated by your nervous alterations."

"What about that 'state of balance,' doctor? Does it exist?"

"I can tell you this, my dear friend, you won't find it by licking your wounds. Come out of yourself and join the real world. Perhaps you will need to give up your visions and pay attention to people made of flesh and blood rather than the ghostly variety, and maybe listen to them and love them. Don't forget what Blake said: 'Gratitude is heaven itself.'"

"The first thing I should do is thank heaven for finding someone like you, doctor, and I mean that in all sincerity."

The doctor's eyes became visibly smaller behind his glasses when they became misty.

"Yes, sometimes ... I've been the same way at times, Abelardo, my friend ... I've felt to thank heaven for the mere presence of someone, for a gesture, for silence. Or just to know that you can simply talk ... and say something that you wouldn't say to anyone else, something suddenly so easy to express."

I couldn't think about anything but his words the rest of the day. Because it was true: how could I possibly achieve any sort of objectivity in my chronicle if my point of view was seriously altered? Understanding one's surroundings has to involve understanding one's own self, I decided. Or did things work from the outside in? Or should they develop simultaneously?

That night in my room, a subtle intimate feeling came over me. I served myself a little wine and lit my marble pipe (to which I would add, on special occasions such as that one, a touch of vanilla). The first mouthful of smoke I exhaled spread out like the foliage of a small tree, which always helped me concentrate.

Things change when we watch them intently. Observers affect what they observe. When a fool and a wise man look at the same tree, it is like two different trees, as Dr. Urruchúa informs me Pascal used to say.

How much can I influence this American invasion if I observe it intently, very intently, naïve as I am? What is it that truly causes something to happen? What is the unseen side of an event, the mystery which brought it here? (It would be very different to say "which brought it about.")

What, or who, brought the Yankees here to the gates of Mexico City?

Might we say that everything began on May 13, 1846, when the Congress of the United States approved a decree issued by President Polk?

Or was it April 25 of that same year, when Mexican cavalry ambushed and defeated a column of American explorers in Carricitos, Texas?

Or did it begin in 1842, when Commodore Jones tried to occupy Monterrey, California, believing that the war had begun? Might it be that the simple mistake of Commodore Jones unleashed all subsequent events?

Oh, such a role clueless people have played in human history!

Light flickered on the sheet of paper, then flew like a bird to my glass of wine.

I lowered my eyes, looked at the rounded tips of my shoes, then said to myself once more that I needed to try to understand the situation, it was my obligation, and possibly the only way I could regain my health and stop licking my wounds.

My shadow turned into two shadows, subtly, on the floor.

Where to begin? How should I go about it?

I rested the tip of my pen on my tongue for a moment. I turned toward the window, where the face of night pressed upon the glass. Threads of frost were starting to form next to the window frames. In the distance I saw the vague, expressionless sky.

Should I concentrate on my city in its current form? (They say there are two hundred thousand of us and our subsistence depends on the annual consumption of seventeen thousand head of cattle, two hundred eighty thousand sheep, sixty thousand pigs, one million two hundred sixty thousand chickens, two hundred fifty thousand turkeys, one hundred eighteen thousand bushels of corn, three hundred thousand casks of *pulque* and forty-two thousand barrels of whiskey. There are four hundred ten lawyers, one hundred forty physicians, eight hundred forty-seven water vendors, ninety-four lottery ticket vendors, four thousand six hundred laborers, four thousand two hundred fifty maids, eleven dentists and thirty-four pharmacists. The average life expectancy of our population is twenty-seven.)

Or should I go back a few years in the history of the United States? (It must be remembered that, in effect, the methods used by the governments of Washington, Jefferson, Adams, Madison and Monroe were alike in uprooting and exterminating indigenous tribes from the land, expanding the borders of the country by using whatever methods necessary.)

Should I research other perspectives expressed by Mexican writers? (Friar Servando Teresa de Mier wrote in 1821: "To pacify the United States, Spain ceded Florida to it last year. The United States now occupies it, placing the Americans in the heart of Mexico. They had already taken possession of the Louisiana Territory, which was given by Charles IV to Napoleon without specific borders, and which Napoleon sold to the Anglo Americans. Thus the United States threatens to absorb us into its population, which is growing in a remarkable way. Each transfer of land is an affront to us as Mexicans, and not just because of the rights of our mothers, who were Indians, but also because of the agreements made by our fathers, the conquistadors, who gained it at great personal risk.")

How revealing it is that Friar Servando would have said that "the United States threatens to absorb us into its population, which is growing in a remarkable way," especially taking into account that in 1847, theirs was an astoundingly rich country with eighteen million inhabitants, while ours was terribly poor, with scarcely seven million. What else should we have expected? Of those seven million, roughly half made more than a *real* per day. Of the three hundred sixty-five days of the year, one hundred fifty of them were holidays. After taxes and obligatory Church contributions, only twenty-five percent of our income made it into the national economy. The country's production was unable to supply more than the needs of one-fifth of the population. In Mexico City daily salaries fluctuated between twenty and thirty *centavos*. Taxable holdings were worth about six million *pesos*. Eighty percent of the money in circulation was copper. Mines, which previously had been a source of income, were paralyzed. After 1835 chaplaincies had largely stopped lending money to farmers. The country's roads were infested with robbers, and fear and a lack of security had taken over. What kind of a future could we hope for?

Or should I also look to foreign points of view? (I don't believe in Rousseau's myth of the "noble savage," to which Columbus contributed so much by affirming in his letters to the Catholic monarchs that he had found here the best land and best people in the world. Neither do I share Voltaire's perspective—although I admire him in so many ways—when he failed to recognize the "degraded men" of this New World as his fellow beings.)

Or would dream analysis help me? (How can anyone understand in a deep way, for example, the Napoleonic wars, without being familiar with the dreams of Napoleon himself?)

And what about trying to get some help from magic, from palm reading, or perhaps from séances?

I was trying to sort all this out while surrounded by an astonishing myriad of simultaneities and coincidences, intertwinings and new starts.

Despite its constant restructurings and combinations, our mosaic world—or might we refer to it as a cosmic kaleido-scope—always manages to bring together essential pieces.

These thoughts helped me take courage: why should I not suppose that, at some point, my mental cobwebs would fall into line, strand by strand, with life?

What unexpected turn of fate could spring to life from my mental wanderings which would transcend the reality—and particularly the reality which was about to unfold—of my poor, ill-fated city?

The destinies of two peoples, of millions of souls were coming together, and would soon transform into one large group in the conflict; the frightening mixture of individual solitudes would be transformed into one enormous body. And what would happen to that enormous body—Americans and Mexicans mixed together—in the future, in fifty, one hundred or two hundred years? How would that body adapt, transform, or maybe even break apart?

At times, when I managed to gain a little distance from myself, from my obsessions and anguish, I felt the need to review the facts with the attitude of a sentry perched on a watchtower scanning the horizon. That attitude did wonders to put my anguish into perspective. I felt the need to consider each event with the greatest possible latitude, not just as a single event, but from every imaginable angle, starting with a verbal formulation, in which I had an almost magical confidence. Things simply seemed more real when I would put them into written words. I felt that by writing down events I was conserving them, like family portraits hanging on the wall.

Perhaps it is true that the history of the world shines in any bronze uniform button of any soldier, whether Mexican or American, who was undoubtedly engaged in combat as I was writing those lines. When we focus completely on that button (third from the top), we see every confrontation of man against man which the world has ever known, and perhaps more importantly, their determination or lack of determination, which in this case is the same thing.

Could I possibly manage, perhaps just for a moment, to enter that new dimension from which it would be possible to see, all at once, everything that the eyes of the inhabitants of Mexico City were seeing? It was two hundred thousand pairs of eyes, each as stunned and confused as my own.

The reality—our frightening urban reality at that time—would stop unfolding. It would petrify into a vision where the "I" would disappear annihilated. But that annihilation was a triumphal blaze, I told myself, I repeated to myself, I wrote down.

I had not yet discovered the poetic writings and divine inspiration of Santa Teresa of Ávila, which helped those poor notes take shape and my life take an unexpected turn when a woman I madly loved gave me that book.

PART TWO

I

Homeland, homeland of tears, my homeland.

GUILLERMO PRIETO

O NE MORNING IN 1847 I heard the unmistakable sound of a carriage parking at the gates of my home. My maid hurriedly responded to the knock at my door. It seemed strange because of the hour of the day—I had just awakened and was still in my robe—and it was even stranger that the visitor was the mother of Señorita Isabel Olaguíbel, whose name was also Isabel. She was wearing a dark veil, which complemented the somber feeling she conveyed. Nevertheless, her perfume was sweet and insistent, like a morning aroma. I offered her a cup of hot chocolate, which she accepted, and then with a shaky voice she told me how her daughter had been.

"Ever since you stopped visiting she hasn't stepped out of her room, and she barely eats. I understand your concern and chagrin over the vulgarity of spilling *jamaica* water on the tablecloth, knowing as you do how fastidious my husband is, but let me assure you that you were immediately forgiven, and as far as we are concerned, the entire event has been erased from our memories as if nothing ever happened. It certainly shouldn't have led you to leave our house so upset and embarrassed."

The situation was actually more serious than what Doña Isabel had originally described to me. Some time after refusing to eat, Señorita Isabel had begun to experience fevers and strange aches all over, and several physicians paid her visits. She was given arnica treatments, they spread a fine cloth over her skin, they applied cantharidal plasters for her fever, but nothing seemed to help. She even developed such hypersensitivity that physicians and pharmacists who visited had to keep their distance from her because of the medicinal odors that stuck to them. Once the professionals left the house, they had to sprinkle cologne in the room to mask the smell. Only then, it seemed, could Isabel really breathe once again.

"And it has all been in vain. Now she doesn't even want to see the doctor, every day she eats less and less, and she cries for hours at a time. One of our servants told her about some folk-healers from Peralvillo who work miracles, and she seems willing to go see them ... as long as you go with her."

"Me?"

"You. She says over and over that she won't go if you don't go along. Actually, if I may ..."

"Please, ma'am, say whatever you would like. You can't imagine how deeply your daughter's situation pains me. It seems my absurd reaction has played a prominent and unforgivable role in her state."

"Please say no more about forgiveness. Spilling on the tablecloth was so insignificant. That's what put my daughter in her current state—because you insisted that your action was somehow unforgivable."

"Well then, please forgive me for having said it," I replied, smiling.

"As of this moment you are forgiven for anything you may say or do. Agreed?"

"As a friend of mine says, repentance transforms the past, so you can now speak as if anything that happened that Sunday, no matter how painful, has been wiped away as if it had never happened."

"I didn't want to say this to you so directly, but what my daughter needs, in addition to medical help for her strange illness, is to see you. Yes, you. Don't make that face. I wouldn't be here if not for ... sometimes, in our family we feel so desperate and powerless ... In my case ..."

She inhaled as deeply as she seemed capable, became very pale, tilted her head back so far it looked as if it were detached from her body, and finally closed her eyes.

I called for camphor and my maid helped me lay her down on the sofa. I undid the top button of her black dress.

When I had her smell the camphor, she opened her eyes back up, but with a look I had never seen in her. My maid left us alone in the room.

At that moment I committed the second mistake in my incipient relationship with the Olaguíbel family. The first was to believe that I liked Señorita Isabel. The second was to discover that whom I really liked was Doña Isabel. Her eyes had the splendor of lightning, and they made me blush when she fixed them on me as she came out of her strange swoon.

She was about forty-five. But that meant nothing to me, because what I will never forget—what still affects me so many years later—as I remember her lying on the sofa in my parlor, was her air of a young woman from some prior century who had been asleep and awakened for me, just for me, with the top button of her dress open. She seemed to be awakening and returning to her true age, breaking free—as if shedding a skin—from the silent work of the recent long, unsubstantial years of her life.

While she was still waking up, I took her hand and discovered that encircling her neck, coursing through her veins, emanating from within, was a kind of shadow which hinted at a desire, perhaps a very old one, perhaps about to wilt and, worst of all, one that she may never have revealed to the world.

"Abelardo," she said after she was fully awake.

She said my name in a tone I had never heard before, laden with meaning far beyond the mere pronunciation of a name, my name.

I hadn't fully realized that I was holding her hand with both of mine.

If Doña Isabel's hand had been a bird, it would have suffocated.

Before getting up to depart, she made a comment which I felt had more to do with the amorous feeling we had just (had we really just?) discovered between us than to the momentary lapse she'd suffered.

"My word—I'm so very sorry. When it's not one thing it's another. Why is this happening to me? Why does my fragile heart betray me and falter precisely when I need it to be strong and true?"

I was going to ask her for details about that fragile heart betraying her, but I couldn't muster the courage.

As she left my home, the way she said goodbye seemed to indicate to me that there were more bursts of youthfulness left in her like the one she had secretly revealed moments earlier. I saw it in her half-closed eyes as she took leave. There was a crazed, aggressive light in them, but she would assuredly repent of it immediately.

She made one last remark, which seemed to indicate implicit regret on her part.

"Please help my daughter, Abelardo. Please. Nothing could possibly worry me and cause me such pain as the situation of my poor girl. I am certain that you will know, at the right time, how to help her, how only you can help her," she said, seeming to place emphasis on those last two words.

"I'll be with her tomorrow afternoon, Doña Isabel."

II

We don't want to see our sacred cathedrals converted into temples of those Protestant sects which cause such a scandal with their religious services; and instead of our tri-colored national flag, we don't want to see the stars and stripes we so despise flying over our buildings.

LUCAS ALAMÁN

"WHAT IF THERE EXISTS *a secret order to things, Dr. Urruchúa?" Abelardo asked me recently. "Where would this absurd war fit in? We can find a secret order to things in the most routine of events, in the simplest things. At least we sense it. Give it a try!"*

I did try and, lo and behold, I am starting to see things differently. The sound of a door slamming at the hospital superimposes itself over the face of a patient on whom I have just operated, and it also invokes a memory which seems to be wholly unrelated—of a very sunny street where I played as a child. Why these three things all at once? Their possible connections—sound, vision and memory joined in a fleeting and unrepeatable moment—seem like a complete entity in essence and meaning, something that with complete assurance awakens and widely develops once we are open and sensitive to it.

That is why, when those three events introduced themselves to me, I knew that the relationship was not a coincidence, especially given the identity of the patient.

His name was Wolfgang Fichet and he gave the impression of being prematurely aged and frail. He had a sparse grey beard. Nevertheless, his eyes were intensely blue. His wide forehead and the depressions at his temples betrayed someone who lives in a dream world. He wore a derby and carried a mysterious brown leather briefcase.

A doctor friend of mine had told him of my interest in the subject of melancholy, which is why he came to visit me. He wanted to open a practice in Mexico based on Mesmer's work. Had I heard of Mesmer? Did that seem possible in Mexico? He said he was planning to give it a try in Curaçao, where he was heading in a few days. I asked him why he had come to Mexico. He looked around, the wisps of grey hair on his chin trembled a bit, and then he answered in a soft voice. The wife of none other than Santa Anna had paid for his trip from Paris because she wanted him to examine her husband, who apparently had been suffering serious emotional problems. He said he had been unable to carry out the assignment—Santa Anna had flatly refused to allow it—but Fichet had offered the First Lady to return to Mexico for another attempt once the war with the United States ended. I asked him whether as long as he was here he could see a friend of mine who also suffered a serious nervous disorder, but he adamantly refused, making a gesture which left no room for doubt. He said his trip had been generously financed by Doña Dolores for him to pay a professional visit to her husband, and he had promised to treat no one else under any circumstances. He stated that his presence in our country was supposed to remain a secret. I asked if he could at least leave some information on Mesmer's method of treating patients, which was called "animal magnetism." He let me look over some of the papers in his briefcase right then and there. His clinic was located, with great symbolic importance, on the Place Vendôme in Paris, where Mesmer had imparted his first sessions. The original establishment was still the same: large open spaces, soft light, frosted mirrors in the corners, balcony doors open so that the breeze would make the velvet curtains sound like birds, giving the impression that the house was about to take flight. A very theatrical setting. Mesmer's disciple did the same thing that his master once did: he would appear suddenly in a lilac-colored silk tunic, reminiscent of the one Zoroaster wore, brandishing a long magnetic cane which he would wave near his chosen patients. He would pause before one, ask in a low voice the nature of his or her malady, and then listen intently. "Master, I cry at night, very softly, and I haven't been able to tell anyone about it." He would then bring the cane very close to a particular part of the patient's body at the same time he looked at him or her with unsettling concentration, a measure of concentration which by itself, he was certain, would begin the healing process. Very little time would lapse before patients started shaking, sweating, moaning, convulsing and at times even hopping, dancing and singing wildly, thus activating the famous redemptive "crisis." According to Mesmer, every nervous infirmity is like a fever: it needs to reach a point of culmination—it must be pushed to the point of culmination— as a first step toward finding the path to reestablishing mental and physical harmony.

I wondered what would happen if I tried to convince Abelardo to go to Europe, to spend time with his parents, and to try an "animal magnetism" treatment. I didn't think it would do him any harm. He would get to see Paris, he would yell, he would sing, and perhaps he would even dance—something that would help him come out of himself. He seems more pale and desperate every day here. Sometimes the mere mention of a piece of news—pretty much any piece of news—about the possible North American invasion of the city changes his mood from lightheartedness to apoplectic shock, and turns him a pale shade of yellow.

Doctor Fichet also told me about a system to put patients to sleep before surgery and keep them from feeling pain: hypnotism. Didn't I already know about that, he asked, with an astonished curve in his eyebrows. Mesmer's most faithful disciple, Count Maxime Puységur, had discovered it.

He hugged his briefcase to his chest. His tone of voice had steadily risen and his words became more and more heated and convincing.

Out of sheer love for art and science, surrounded by his vast possessions at Buzacy, Count Puységur became determined to practice magnetic treatments in accordance with the prescriptions of his master. His patients weren't hysterical nobility of the feminine persuasion, but cavalry soldiers, peasants and *people from surrounding towns. On one occasion, using the tip of his magnetic wand, he magnetized a young peasant by waving it over and over again across his forehead, but rather than causing him the anticipated convulsions, or at least some form of spasms, the young man fell into a strange state of lethargy, becoming completely motionless and impassive. When the Count ordered him to walk toward a nearby tree, he walked that direction with his eyes closed as if sleepwalking! He ordered him to lie down on the ground, and the young man did just that, then to get up, and he obeyed. The Count's surprise intensified when, without waking, the patient responded with absolute coherence to his questions. He performed a brief demonstration of the phenomenon with the young man in a half-empty Parisian theater. Other peasants offered to participate in the entertaining experiment. The Count learned to choose the candidates most open to suggestion. He discovered what seems obvious to followers of Mesmer today: upon waving the magnet, or some other object, in front of the subjects and asking them to concentrate intently, a strange sleep ensues. The Count even managed to give some post-hypnotic orders which the subjects would precisely carry out when they awoke. Later on other physicians perfected the system to anesthetize patients before surgery.*

I couldn't allow Fichet to go without giving me a demonstration of this strange and apparently revolutionary procedure of anesthesia. I promised absolute discretion, then took him to a room in the hospital where we had a patient with a tumor the size of a grapefruit in his cheek. The poor man had such a small chance of surviving the operation we were planning that there was little to lose in experimenting with him. I invited several colleagues I completely trusted to come with us into the room, and on one side of the patient's bed I arranged my surgical instruments for the operation.

Fichet's long fingers started to run up and down the patient's body as if they were playing an invisible piano, from the crown of his head across his face and chest down to his upper abdomen. The muscles in the patient's deformed face, undoubtedly swollen due to an extraordinary abscess in his gums, relaxed in a very noticeable way. His eyes soon became a pair of white marbles, then placidly closed. A nurse seated to his side wiped sweat from Fichet's forehead. Sixty, eighty, one hundred, one hundred twenty additional passes, each time expanding the length of the imaginary keyboard.

The patient's body tensed up each time the magnetic fluid touched it.

I felt my heart tighten and an enormous anxiety came over me.

Twisting up his mouth, Fichet explained, "Sometimes it takes more than an hour to get patients completely asleep, and you can never guarantee that they are one hundred percent out. Several patients have awakened right in the middle of surgery, which is truly horrible."

Disappointed, I figured he was saying that his system wasn't going to work in an emergency hospital like ours. Sometimes we had to resort to operating on patients in the very entrance of the hospital, on the first slab of available concrete we could find.

The patient was slowly sinking into his pillow, as if into foam. He also began to snore quietly, with small whistling sounds and a regular breath.

After about an hour Fichet was exhausted. He cracked his knuckles and wiped his face with a towel the nurse handed him. He went over to the window for some air and took a couple of puffs on a cigarette which he lit with trembling fingers. Then he sat next to the bed, took one of the sick man's hands, and checked his pulse.

"See that? Just a little while ago it was nearly a hundred. Now it's seventy."

He lifted the man's arm, and the hand dangled lifelessly. He asked the nurse to do the same to the other arm, which had the same result. When he let go, the patient's hand fell precipitously, as if a cord which had been holding it up had been cut.

"Everything's ready. You can start to operate."

I started to explore the tumor. Its roots were in the man's jawbone, but it had spread out and almost filled his nose. It had also reached the socket of his right eye and was starting to obstruct his throat. I asked the nurse to have the probe ready, just in case, to go into the internal ear through his nasal passages, and if necessary into the occipital cranial cavities. I then described to Fichet and my colleagues, step by step, what I was doing.

"I begin by tightening the skin," and I pulled the skin tight and cut into the man's cheek with a scalpel. "I make a small incision here and cut the underlying connective tissue. I open his cheek all the way to his nose. From time to time I pause to tie off blood vessels ... Are you following me? By the way, what would we do if he woke up?"

"What do you give your patients to put them to sleep?" asked Fichet.

"Rum."

"Well, if he wakes up, give him a generous shot of rum. Do we have any other option?"

Fichet seemed even more nervous than me, and only out of the corner of his eye would he look at the swollen face that had turned into a bloody pudding of skin, bones, teeth and hair all mixed together. The gauze was greedily absorbing blood. Every so often the nurse would raise the man's head to let him cough and spit into a bowl the blood that had accumulated in his trachea.

At a certain point I announced loudly, "Let's finish up!"

I introduced my fingers into the patient's throat and pulled out the root of the tumor, which looked like a small green toad ready to jump. At that moment the patient came to, his eyes wildly out of orbit, lifted his head slightly, and then nearly bit my fingers off. I'll never forget how immensely black his eyes were, jumpy like rubber balls, suddenly open. Luckily, he immediately passed out.

III

I arrive here as the savior of a people subjugated by corrupt political parties and an ambitious and murderous military.

MANIFESTO FROM GENERAL WINIFRED SCOTT
UPON TAKING THE CITY OF JALAPA

WHENEVER I FELT DEPRESSED—which was more and more frequent—certain newspaper articles seemed to urge me to leave this insufferable city. The opportunity was certainly there. Why shouldn't I leave? Without any great difficulty I could join my parents in Europe, which they repeatedly asked me to do in their letters. With so many doubts about the chronicle I was trying to write—Dr. Urruchúa said it was too hermetic when he read part of it—I was lost within the dark absurdity surrounding me. I was wholly lacking the will or the ability to take up arms. With my nerves more frayed every day and a feeling of horror at the impending American presence, why was I staying?

My dear Dr. Urruchúa, you knew why I was staying, didn't you? Even though I let you down at the moment of truth, although I wasn't with you—and with those who were with you—at the battles of Padierna, Churubusco, Molino del Rey, and Chapultepec; despite all that, you knew I wasn't going to leave the city, no matter how many times they told you my house had been abandoned and I had vanished into thin air. Only you knew why, and for that reason when you and I had the same dream on the same night—my dreams have always been powerful, and it is quite possible that I transmitted my dream to you, and moreover it was a nightmare that had to do with the future of our city—you fixed your eyes on me and simply asked: have you considered leaving us now that the ghost is almost here? I answered no, that I wasn't going to leave you or my friends in any way, shape or form. Nevertheless, I need to confess that in the depths of my heart I was looking for an excuse to leave, and my supposed commitment to stay with you and everyone else was ambivalent, to say the least.

"Because if you have to leave, for example, to Paris, there are physicians specializing in nervous maladies whom I myself would like to meet."

"Don't even bring that up, Doctor."

"Don't dismiss the idea so quickly, Abelardo my friend. They manage miraculous healings using a method called 'animal magnetism.' All you would have to do is let them wave the magnetized tip of a cane near you and then allow your fears, your fury, and also your innermost desires to be exorcised. Some people dance, others sing, and yet others scream ..."

"Please, doctor, don't even suggest it. Can you imagine me dancing, singing and screaming in the state of depression I'm in?"

"Maybe that is exactly what you need."

When you helped me at those difficult moments, it struck me that to point out your own weaknesses, you would refer to a third person to keep from hurting my feelings.

"Not long ago ... someone was talking about himself with true sincerity," you told me. "Someone who was very desperate and who sees life simply as a precarious postponement. Postponement of what? He doesn't even know himself. I tried to give the impression to that person that I am entirely healthy and full of vigor, and I suppose that helps him trust me. But I wouldn't want that person to find out what I am about to tell you, because adding one weakness to another doesn't help anyone, and may even generate a negative force, and that just wouldn't do." I thought that at any moment his plaintive voice might crack. "You know, I am very much like that person. I believe that I have arrived at a similar point in which tangible items start to lose their meaning, to fade. My hands feel like they are covered with the residue of dead moths. Do you understand? Not at all."

He continued: "At some point the moment arrives when a person has to come to grips with himself, has to bump his head against a mirror. You never know when that moment will come, but you have a feeling, an intuition. The worst part is you can't talk about what can't really be expressed. It's like trying to explain the color blue or purple, or what you perceive to be blue or purple. What would be the point?"

Was that the night when almost without realizing it we happened onto the Plaza de Santo Domingo and sat down on a bench at the edge of the square? Or had we just left the hospital, where I had come to get you as I had done so many times before, and we walked along Espíritu Santo Street toward the Progreso Café, followed closely by my carriage in case it rained? But it had rained earlier in the day and the evening sky was as clear as could be, and we heard music coming from some place, probably from one of the cafés with its doors propped open in that area. Or maybe it was from a theater, because I seem to remember that it was a string quartet, and it was not the kind of number they play at that hour in the city's crowded cafés.

You didn't say anything else. The fervor with which you had just spoken made absolutely clear what had till then been latent. I lowered my head, as if to indicate that I hadn't understood anything, as if I hadn't understood that I hadn't understood anything.

At times like those, one extra word can be fatal, can topple everything that has been built with something like a snail hissing in the flames.

Overhead, a new musical note, tense and sustained, was taking on meaning, and then another note joined it, not to further the melody but to sacrifice itself in a chord which became increasingly beautiful, which gave purpose to our walk. As we crossed the street you started to stumble, and when I reached out for a moment to steady you I recognized the energy in your muscles and a strength in your bones which I hadn't realized they possessed. The sky was transparent glass, behind which was more glass, behind which was another layer of glass. The planets floated there as if on a peaceful sea.

"No, doctor, I won't be leaving," I finally confirmed.

Ironic how long everyone thought that I had really left.

I 𝒱

Mexico will be smaller—half its size—it is true, but if it salvages its status as a nation and its independence and sets out to work hard, with dedication and integrity, it will still have more than enough resources, natural and human, to become one of the leading and most important nations in the world.

EDITORIAL FROM EL ECO DEL COMERCIO, MAY 9, 1848

I CAN'T TELL ANYONE *to stay. How could I? I simply suggest, just as I did with Abelardo, that if people are able, they depart from the city as soon as possible. Why would anyone want to stay? I have a very religious niece, Leonor, who is determined to stay in her home, despite having two small children. I read a passage of the Bible to her in order to raise, very subtly I believe, her sensitivities about what could happen to us, or what was about to happen to us.*

At a family gathering, I practically forced her to invite me for a hot chocolate at her home. It had to be at her home, and preferably without her husband or children. Her eyes full of surprise, she asked what I was going to tell her or ask her and I said the truth: I simply wanted to read her a prophetic passage from the Bible.

"Tell me which one and I'll read it. Juan and I always read from the Bible together. You don't have to come over."

"I need to read it to you myself," I insisted.

I care deeply for her because she is the only daughter of my sister, may she rest in peace, and her children are so small, so full of family traits, and so unbearably mischievous, that the mere thought of what could happen to them if they stay here when the city is invaded melts my heart.

Leonor has beautiful chestnut eyes with golden flecks, and a very delicate mouth and chin, but putting on weight doesn't become her and she inherited my sister's ample hips, which swing as she walks. That afternoon she wore a green cambric dress with a blue belt and had a silk ribbon in her hair which fell to the middle of her back. Every time I saw her—and I saw her very little because I absolutely could not tolerate her husband—she asked me why I didn't have a wife like her, or like my sister, or like my mother, or at least like one of my aunts. Why had life taken me to a dead end in which I had nothing more to my life than my routine work in the hospital and a loneliness which I tried to ignore? Confronting that loneliness would be like looking at myself in the mirror when I got home from work in the evening: I wouldn't see my face but rather a black void, a funnel making repugnant gurgling noises.

Leonor took me to a small room next to the entry, which they called the chocolatero, *the chocolate room. She enjoyed showing off her new house. The table in the middle of the room was covered with Chinese tablecloths. Butterflies were beautifully mounted and hung on the walls. On the mantel of the fireplace was a porcelain clock from Saxony from which little musicians would emerge on the hour, playing tiny violins and flutes and accompanied by diminutive ladies with broad-skirted dresses— it was a treasure which delighted the children. Juan's family crest was prominently displayed on the walls (which intensified the negative feelings I had for him). Despite the political situation of the city—of which she understood absolutely nothing—Juan's fabric business was doing wonderfully, and he had opened a new outlet on Misericordia Street.*

"People keep buying fabric, which means that the country can't be in such terrible shape," she said as she brought in a basket filled to the brim with crescent rolls surrounded by artfully folded starched napkins.

After we partook of two cups of thick hot chocolate and several sweet rolls with cream—which felt like a brick in my stomach—I told her very succinctly my thoughts about the war we were in with the United States, that the possibility of the city being invaded by the Americans was very high, and therefore I thought she should flee with her family as soon as possible because—and my voice broke—the city was going to be filled with corpses.

"Ay, uncle, you see death everywhere because so many people die in the hospital."

I decided to go directly to the Bible, which she considers our best guide to life. I read the passage and asked her to read it to Juan that night. I think I accomplished my goal, because she seemed quite frightened and even pale.

"'When ye shall see Jerusalem encompassed by armies, then know that the desolation thereof is nigh.' I'm going to repeat that: 'When ye shall see Jerusalem encompassed by armies! When ye therefore shall see the abomination of desolation, spoken of by Daniel the prophet, stand in the holy place. Then let them which be in Judea flee into the mountains and let them which be in the cities flee them immediately, and let them that be in the field not turn back to any city. And let him who is on the housetop not come down to take any thing out of his house and him who is in the field not look back. And woe unto them that are with child, and to them that give suck in those days! But pray ye that your flight be not in the winter, neither on the Sabbath day, for then shall be great tribulation such as was not since the beginning of the world.'"

V

In this war, the flag of honor and justice will belong to
Mexico, and the American flag, I am ashamed to say, will
stand for dishonor and slavery.

JOHN QUINCY ADAMS

I HAVE OFTEN EXPERIENCED cycles during which what
is truly significant revolves around a central void, like a
newspaper I had yet to read or a page I had yet to write. During
those turbulent years everything became so saturated that the
only reasonable thing to do was to recognize without quibbling
the ties between things, and to take into account, certainly, the
meteor showers I would undoubtedly experience the moment
I stepped into the street. In that frame of mind I jumped—and
that jump is what intrigues me now—from reading the Gospels
to a note in *El Monitor* which referred to a priest, exiled from
Spain, who had declared that he was rabidly anti-American and
had organized a guerilla campaign against Scott and his men!

I rubbed my eyes and took a little walk, then read the article
again. I confirmed that such a person did indeed exist.

The main part of the article was a communiqué sent by
General Rebolledo from Veracruz to the Minister of War:

*It is my honor to communicate to you the damage inflicted on
our enemies at the hands of the guerrilla forces of Celedonio
Domeco de Jarauta, the Spanish priest living in exile here, so
that you can pass this information on to the Supreme Government:*

75 men killed.
86 horses and mules disabled or killed.
In addition, the following supplies were appropriated:
28 barrels of wine and liquor.
23 bundles of miscellaneous supplies.
14 crates of munitions.

It gives me great satisfaction to report this message to you, adding that the guerrilla forces in this area have been enjoying a notable rise in numbers. Calculations suggest that the number of guerrillas operating between Perote and Veracruz is greater than 300 men, which makes communication for the enemy more difficult, as guerrillas have made a concerted effort to interfere with it for several days.

I beseech you to make the foregoing known unto the President of the Republic, along with my greatest consideration and sincere appreciation.

Who could this Spanish priest be? Exiled among us, his Christian faith undoubtedly prompted him to launch guerrilla warfare against the Americans.

That—not the hypocritical Church cozy with the *polkos*, with American emissaries, or with our corrupt politicians—is the Church which inspired me to increased my faith in Christ, in justice and in liberty.

I remembered enthusiastically the names of some of our national heroes who fought for our country's independence, starting with Hidalgo, the priest of Dolores; Morelos y Pavón, priest of Carácuaro; Mariano Matamoros, priest of Jantetelco; Sixto Berdusco, priest of Tusantla; Eugenio Bravo, priest of Tamazula; Marcos Castellanos, priest of Palma; José Manuel Correa, priest of Nopala; Ignacio Couto, priest of San Martín Texmelucan; Miguel Gómez, priest of Petatlán; Joaquín Gutiérrez, priest of Huayacocotla; José Manuel Herrera, priest of Huamuxtitlán; Antonio Macías, priest of La Piedad; José María Mercado, priest of Ahualulco; Moctezuma Pérez, priest of Zongolica, and many others.

I have compiled a list of twenty-six such parish priests, along with twenty-eight other priests.

The ranks of the insurgents included men from various religious orders, among them an Augustinian, two Carmelites, four Dominicans, eleven Franciscans, one from the order of Hipólito and six from the order of Juanino.

What admirable people! They fought not only against a concrete enemy, but more importantly against the dark shadow of the reactionary ecclesiastical institution which tried to bind them down. This is exactly what happened during the Inquisition.

A profound curiosity was kindled within me to meet this Father Jarauta, a Jesuit priest, especially as I reflected on the words written not long before by Carlos María de Bustamante:

It is noteworthy that the guerrilla forces are the ones that have waged the only true, tenacious resistance to the American enemy, attacking and weakening its forces and disrupting its convoys; but let us not become delusional—the success of these guerrillas cannot become the norm among fighting forces in Mexico because our soldiers lack the necessary spirit, and young dandies in the capital cities could never be organized because they have become corrupted with vice. Guerrilla warfare requires men who don't have a drop of doubt in their thought processes or who have an unshakable religious faith, much like the men who fought in the Crusades, or knights in medieval times, or men who can place their bodies in front of a wild bull.

I interrupted my work—the quantity of information I was gathering had started to overwhelm and confuse me even more—and that same afternoon I went to visit Señorita Isabel at her home in the center of Mexico City, as I had promised her mother.

As I rapped the door's golden knocker, shaped like the jaw of a lion, my heart was beating as if about to burst from my chest. How would I manage to avoid, in that house, remembering her mother's brilliant eyes?

A quite serious and polite servant wearing white gloves opened the door and told me that he had instructions to take me directly to young Isabel's bedroom.

"To her bedroom?"

"Yes sir, to her bedroom. That is what I was told to do."

We walked across a courtyard shaded by four orange trees. Flowerpots and birdcages adorned the hallway.

I felt so nervous that I couldn't take my hand from my head, running it through my hair to my neck again and again.

We passed through a large room with brocade curtains and wood and wicker furnishings. As the stairway turned toward the bedrooms there was a large painting of the Crucifixion.

"This way, sir," the servant said in a very quiet, ceremonious voice, as if he were also incredulous to be taking me to her bedroom.

Isabel was lying on a honey-colored silk *chaise longue*, her head perfectly upright, her hair in ringlets, resting in a cloud of soft cushions and indifferently holding an open book in her hands, her legs covered by a fringed blanket with a floral pattern. The only feature of her face, consumed by reclusion and suffering, which maintained its beauty was her pair of enormous dark eyes, their brilliance intensified by fever. Somehow hers was a tormented and mysterious beauty.

"Abelardo," she said as soon as she saw me, beckoning me with a languid white hand.

Her neck was barely visible, covered by blue lace, and suddenly she seemed to be wearing far too much makeup, almost to the point of caricature, like her face was covered by a powder mask, an impression perhaps affected by the closed velvet curtains and the flickering candlelight. It seemed absurd for me to be there, alone with her in her bedroom. I sensed her mother's hand in every detail, from the room's décor to the heavy powder on Isabel's cheeks. My beloved Señora Doña Isabel. I could imagine her positioning her daughter on the *chaise longue*, combing her hair, applying the makeup, and placing a book in her hands with a false sense of disdain.

Out of the corner of my eye I looked at the bed with its canopy and white quilt. On her dressing table were flasks of many colors and a porcelain jar with forget-me-nots painted on it. Her chest-of-drawers was enormous and her armoire, in the corner of the room, featured four doors with carved moons. Next to the window was an eight-sided clock with Roman numerals.

"My dear Isabel, how could I have ..." I said, taking a seat facing her, and then I gave her hand a prolonged kiss.

She answered every question with a smile and then rang a small bell. We were brought tea and a tray of wrapped candies, and then left alone. She looked deeply into my eyes, which created a spark in hers, and stated, without a hint of doubt in her voice:

"I love you."

"I love you, too, Isabel."

But she continued as if she hadn't heard, and in fact intensified her voice.

"... and I am willing to show you my love wherever and whenever you desire."

She must have seen that her words affected me, because she reverted to a mere hint of a smile and closed her eyes ever so slightly. Then she pursed her lips and blinked over and over. I asked how she was feeling and she answered with alarming sincerity.

The problem was her father, whom I could not tolerate. He loved me, but I hated him. After that Sunday when I bolted from the table—and everyone realized the true source of my anger: her father's pro-Yankee ideas—Isabel went mad and told him what she had never dared say to him before: that he was a bad father, hateful, arbitrary, a traitor, and worst of all, she talked openly about the lover he had in a house in Mixcoac, a well-known secret to everyone in the family. Her father slapped her, her mother fainted, and her siblings and the uncle who'd just arrived from Querétaro took the two women to their respective bedrooms.

"I suppose that if your father finds me here, the least he'll do is kill me," I said, looking at the door.

"Stop worrying. He's out of town. My mother took care of everything."

"What about her? Where is she?"

"She's not here either. She wanted us to be completely alone in the house. The servants have been given very strict orders not to bother us unless we call them."

I took a deep breath without even looking at her, and then asked what happened after I had left. I remembered what Dr. Urruchúa told me: "You are a mere boy, Aberlardo, and the only thing you can't bear is for someone to point out your childishness."

Isabel seemed to talk to me with more and more sincerity, which was a little troubling given our circumstances.

For days she had refused any sort of food. She lost so much weight she almost disappeared, becoming even more transparent than how I saw her now. The best, most expensive physicians in the city came to see her, but she rejected them all. Each time she looked in the mirror of her armoire, her eyes glassed over with an evil happiness. Her father would feel so guilty if something terrible happened to her.

How frustrating it was when she learned that he, who didn't care to enter much into the world of women, barely asked about her condition and spent very little time at home. Her anger led her to intensify her efforts. Her mother, who couldn't stop crying, gave up, surrendered, and proposed that the two of them go to the mansion in Tlalpan. People would probably just think that it was a precaution linked to the imminent Yankee invasion. Her poor mother would personally prepare and serve her daughter her meals. At first Isabel rejected the offer, stubborn in her desire to waste away, but she finally yielded, as kindness triumphed over her calculated, self-destructive vengeance. The problem was that her emotional state had become seriously affected and she couldn't shake a fever, even though its intensity had decreased, thank the Lord. One of the servants told her about a miraculous healer who lived on the outskirts of the city, near Peralvillo, and her mother had the (brilliant) idea of asking me, begging me to accompany her. After all, who else could accompany her, because the area had a reputation for being dangerous and they couldn't confide in her gossipy siblings, let alone the most trusted of the servants. She was determined to regain her health and stop causing her mother problems, such as new confrontations with her father.

I ate another coconut cookie—it was my third—and with a grimace that never quite became a smile, I told her that I would accompany her wherever and whenever she wanted.

"My mother decided to go get you despite the fact that I told her about the letter I mailed to you which you never answered. I immediately understood why, and there is absolutely no need for you to apologize. She said she was sure she could convince you because she knew how much you love me."

"Your mother is a woman of finely tuned intuition, and she knows when two people are in love, I have no doubt about that."

"Nevertheless, before I consented to allow my mother to get you, something very special crossed my path."

It couldn't have been another man, I reasoned, since she hadn't left her room. What then? I couldn't have been more surprised when she told me:

"I have decided to become a nun."

"You, a nun?"

"Look what I'm reading," she said, handing me a book.

It was an old leather-bound autobiography by Santa Teresa de Ávila. I leafed through the first few pages and found an underlined sentence which I will never forget: "Answered petitions cause more pain than those which go unanswered."

When taken in concert with the following passage in Saint Mark, it was frightening: "Therefore, I say unto you that whatsoever thing ye ask in prayer, having faith that ye will receive it ... it shall be granted unto you."

I had never read Santa Teresa, but that sentence alone was enough to forge one of those sudden mimetic, mysterious and progressive connections between an author and her possible reader.

Had Isabel's mother carefully prepared the theatrical production I was witnessing—Santa Teresa's book, the underlined section and her daughter's desire to become a nun? At each turn I admired her calculating intelligence more, and my need to see her increased as well. What would have happened if, when she awoke from her fainting spell at my house, her moment of youthfulness had not been as fleeting as I supposed?

I processed each and every word Isabel spoke as if it were in a secret coded language that had to be deciphered.

Which was preferable? To die consumed with hatred for her father or full of the highest and purest love of God?

At some point, Isabel felt the Virgin Mary's presence, she

prayed fervently, and felt an invisible hand comforting her head. Unfortunately, shortly thereafter a nervous attack overcame her, her fever rose, the mystical images became distant, she felt the agony of being alone, the lack of communication in her family, the abandonment of a world deaf and dumb to her, and then she went to Father Luis, a priest the family had known for many years who had administered her First Communion. Because she believed herself at the edge of death, she made a complete confession, which she'd never supposed she would ever do with anyone. Father Luis suggested the convent and she replied with an enthusiastic "yes."

"But ..."

"But what?" I asked in desperation. I was drinking her words like the most intoxicating of wines. I assumed that the other Isabel was dictating these words to her daughter. Why not? She was undoubtedly hiding in the folds of the velvet curtains, telling her daughter what to say, as if prompting an actor.

"But I overheard a conversation Father Luis had with my mother."

"Oh."

"I was feeling much better and had gone down to the kitchen for a glass of water when I heard the voice of Father Luis in the dining room."

"Can you remember the exact details of what he said and how your mother responded?"

"I remember it perfectly."

"Tell me everything."

"Father Luis said, 'My dear Doña Isabel, your daughter Isabelita, under the influence of Santa Teresa, has decided to become a nun.' I heard my mother let loose a horrified scream. Father Luis continued, 'Santa Teresa was none other than the most accomplished woman of her era—a poet, a founder of convents, a true intellectual.' My mother retorted, 'Those stories do nothing for me, Father. Most nuns never become more than poor, vulgar, hypocritical, withered women. The life of a nun, full of drudgery and hypocrisy, may well be the worst possible life in the eyes of God.' Father Luis responded, 'Calm down, Doña Isabel. Why can't you imagine that Isabelita, given her talent and dedication, is closer to the high spiritual plane inhabited by Santa Teresa? What abundant worlds and universe full of resplendent suns resulted from her life in the cloister and her abnegation!' And my mother, in a half-mocking tone: 'What would you recommend be done with my poor daughter to lead her down that exceptional path?' And Father Luis, now in rare form: 'It is absolutely necessary, for the time being, that Isabelita attend more of the Church's religious celebrations. She needs to hear more sermons, attend more masses and novenas, become an active member and participant in a religious order, visit the sanatoriums in the city, and voluntarily take care of the sick.' My mother: 'What if she refuses, knowing her the way I do?' Father Luis: 'At first it is true that such activities can seem cumbersome, mundane and away from the path that would lead toward a life of contemplation and rapture. But little by little, learning to enjoy such humble menial tasks, and with the help of frequent holy prayer, she will come to recognize the right path.' When my mother said nothing in response (she was undoubtedly stunned), Father Luis became more brazen: 'My dear friend, you will see how the Catholic Church has a very shrewd way of putting us onto the path leading toward God. You'll see how Isabelita comes to recognize the wisdom of our holy predecessors and all the religious rites they established. The ceremonies and pomp and circumstance may seem insignificant and even frivolous to her right now, but when she turns around to leave, she won't be able to, because the holy cells of the cloister will have closed behind her. At that point she will come to appreciate the things she did not value previously, and she will see the world she left behind as absurd, including her resentment toward her father, her frustrations with her fiancé and the competition she feels with her siblings. She will return, with more fervor, to the work of Santa Teresa, reading it much more calmly and with increased concentration, so she will not end up in despair. Because at first it can be very discouraging to compare one's own life to that of Santa Teresa. It could cause real grief to find out that what you thought were banal, unimportant events were grave sins to her. And the opposite is also true, that we often think some things are more significant than they actually are. It can be a painful test to consider oneself a saint before actually becoming one, and this is something I can tell you from my own experience. That is why reading Santa Teresa over and over is important, but without any particular goal or ambition. That alone will bring about a miracle, I am certain ...'"

"What did your mother say to all that?"

"She didn't say another word. I simply heard her bid Father Luis goodbye at the door, then she came upstairs to tell me to keep reading Santa Teresa's book, but without any particular goal or ambition, and to please finish it soon so that she could read it."

"Did you finish it?"

"Yes, and I'm starting to read it again."

"And did your mother read it?"

"Of course. She marked certain passages, and then she counseled me to read it again."

As soon as I left Isabel's house I hurried to find a copy of Santa Teresa's book. I never would have imagined that the autobiography of a saint would replace my obsessive reading of newspapers, which had gone on for months. (Later on I came to learn, *In Puebla people are clamoring for arms to defend their city, but the state government has none to give them. Santa Anna can't provide them either, instead having chosen to abandon the city—once again we see him abandon a city which is about to be attacked. He says that he must go protect the nation's capital. Encountering hostility there he decides to present his resignation as President and Commander of the Armed Forces. This resignation, as was the case on so many occasions, implied that it was merely a temporary situation, a laughable bit of pantomime.*)

I read Santa Teresa's book voraciously, until light from the candles dimmed and I discovered that it was once again daytime.

I read it as if Doña Isabel were reading it with me, imagining that all three of us—she, Santa Teresa and I—were experiencing the same rapture. Here is a revealing passage:

Here, where the soul currently resides, there is no way to resist or to take preventative measures. A light as if from the heavens comes along with an energy so strong that you feel yourself being lifted up like a cloud or an eagle. You allow yourself to be carried upward without knowing where you are going. Even though we delight in it, our weakness and human nature lead us to lament that which we leave behind. For that reason we need a courageous soul, not so much for what has been stated, but in order to risk everything, no matter what, to place ourselves into God's hands, to go wherever He guides us, because once you turn your entire soul over to Him you must go wherever He desires.

I read with such enthusiasm that my heart started to beat like a bass drum. Did a light from Heaven precede Santa Teresa's levitations? Fortunately, since I felt completely and totally removed from any state of holiness, I didn't feel myself in danger of levitating. That would have been all I needed. Not even Dr. Urruchúa would have believed it, and he may even have taken it as a joke. Or maybe he would simply have sent me directly to the insane asylum, assuring me that there I would suffer less than I am suffering right now.

I also underlined the following lines:

At times I wanted to resist and would do so with all my might, as if fighting a formidable enemy, and I would always end up exhausted. Other times it was impossible because He would lift my body and soul from the ground to where He was. This happened very few times, because my resistance was weak. One time He went to where we, a group of nuns, were kneeling in the choir to take communion. It saddened me, because it seemed extraordinary, something we could talk about for a long time, but I told the nuns not to breathe word of it to anyone. Eventually I became very accustomed to what the Lord would do. Once I was participating in a holy festival and I lay down on the floor.

People could see there how my body was elevating. I begged the Lord to spare me further mercies of the sort which were so public because I was tired of everyone talking about me. But that was how it was—even when I wanted to resist, incomparable forces would lift my feet. And I would feel terrible because of my desire to resist. After all, you don't get very far resisting something the Lord wants, since nothing compares to His power.

I opened the window to contemplate the new day. The sun seemed about to dispense with the immense morning shadows. Someone said that if no one pays attention, there is the risk that the sun won't come up. And if the sun really doesn't come up one day, will it be due to rebellion? So every day someone has to be awake to encourage the sun to come out—even if just for the last time, for today, come out! They say that one time the sun became sick in Egypt, it went blind and they had to send a god to heal it.

Moments later it had already taken on the form of a showy orange.

At those times, early in the morning, it was easy to think of the people who were starting to inhabit the streets as tiny figures in a scale model, moving about a city which was the size of a small stage in a children's theatre, entering and exiting houses and establishments which were actually nothing more than façades, illuminated by candles from behind the stage.

Wasn't this the city, Mexico City, where at one point the inhabitants wanted to build a fortress for God, an island of charity and honest labor?

Oh, the unending night of my homeland—in danger, blind, boiling over!

Furthermore, in a moment of fleeting vanity, that morning when I finished reading Santa Teresa's book, in contrast with the tragedy headed our direction I imagined myself completely enlightened, all-seeing, called to receive revelation, and I had the dark assurance that there existed a place from which all things could be seen, as if from the center of a wheel. Why not?

Was there some hidden spot in this ill-fated city possessing that mysterious energy which raised Santa Teresa from the ground?

And if our entire city were to levitate, would the Yankees dare invade it?

It seemed to me that the sun had interrupted its illusory orbital movement, and was simply decorating the tops of the poplars behind the house.

Never have I felt the way I did that morning, my heart beating with such vehemence, interrupted at times by disconcerting pauses which made it seem like it was about to stop beating altogether.

I calculated that if the validity of a testimony like Santa Teresa's were called into question regarding that *other* world and the mysterious power which energized it—and which caused her to levitate!—human testimony in general would have to be declared invalid as well. What would become, then, of history, of the history which we were living that very day in 1847? Would anyone in the future believe us? And would our point of view, and the point of view of each chronicle written, have a subsequent effect on what would happen there? Things change when they are watched closely. Two plus two equals four, plus the one doing the math.

Because if we are able to catch a mere glimpse of that *other* world which Santa Teresa mentions, and we believe in it, what a transformation we would see in humanity, which is stuck in the rut of accepting only that which it can see or touch. All you have to do is see how people give themselves over to pleasure, ambition and war. They would act differently, and would certainly temper themselves, if they didn't treat pleasure, ambition and war as a support against Nothingness. Actually, if men were certain, absolutely certain of their continued existence, they wouldn't be able to think about anything else. Pleasure and war might survive under such circumstances, but they would have far less luster and color, since their intensity is proportionate to the attention and energy we invest in them. They would fade like the light of a candle when the sun comes up. War and pleasure would be eclipsed by happiness.

Did she, my beloved Doña Isabel, know what would happen to me upon reading that book, which she managed to get to me after so many twists and turns?

And in addition to physical attraction—which I was led to believe she also felt toward me—my relationship with Doña Isabel came from *somewhere else*, perhaps even in a prior life which we shared. A pair of dreams confirmed that to me.

XI

When I take walks through the streets every morning, I always ask myself the same question: How is it possible for this city to still be standing?

CARLOS MARÍA DE BUSTAMANTE

*S*HOULD I ABANDON *those controversial meetings in the Progreso Café, which in my opinion assuredly give the impression of feigned indifference, or worse yet, of frivolity?*

They often ask me, "Dr. Urruchúa, why don't you, once and for all, say what you think about the situation in which we find ourselves? Why so reserved lately?"

I'm afraid that if I were to give my opinion, I would shortly wind up in a confrontation with some of those friends. For example, with Gamboa. What can an aristocrat such as he understand? He lives as if the French Revolution had never taken place, and thinks that the word idealism is "vague."

I cannot, nor should I, give them my opinion, because my reasoning may seem too simple and direct to them. I could talk this through with Abelardo, with whom I seem to communicate very well, but the poor man is too overwhelmed with his dreams and visions and, from what I have read, his supposed chronicle, which is highly hermetic, to spend time listening to me.

Here is my opinion: war with the United States is purely hypothetical—there is no war as such. For there to be war two parties have to want to fight. In this case only one side has any interest, notwithstanding the indignation of the people and some generals and a few exceptional soldiers. Stated another way, when the Yankees learn how slight the opposition is that they face, they will simply destroy the cities through which they sweep and take as spoils whatever they please. Unless it occurs to them to take control of the entire country, at which point we would hand it over to them.

107

Mexican history can be portrayed as a gradual widening of the circle of the wealthy. It started with the conquistadors and widened to the clergy, to be joined by landowners and eventually us, the descendants of Europeans. It seems impossible to have wealth reach the impoverished masses of the general population. Powerful interests labor in opposition to such a process. Each time the circle has widened it has been accomplished by drowning the country in rivers of blood, thereby making it easy prey to foreign predators and throwing it into chaos. It becomes fertile soil for the appearance of counterfeit saviors and venal leaders, who make it possible for "decent" folk to make a fortune and hang on to it through repressive violence or a corrupt legal system.

What, then, is Mexico for Mexicans in this day and age, but a labyrinth, a vague ghost, a faceless monster?

The United States has quickly discovered, in something akin to discovering veins of gold in a rock, that our politicians merely pretend to fight against them, when in reality they are fighting each other. And as they fight each other, they are hoping to gain the sympathy and favor of the invaders. Talk about a charade. The victim, as always happens, has been the common people—among which I include the soldiers, most drafted against their will—who end up paying for that lack of patriotism with their blood. I can't conceive of a sadder tragedy. These poor souls give their lives—as we saw in Veracruz and Puebla—for a simple lie called Mexico, which does not exist except in bombastic speeches, official seals, and land plundered by both citizens and foreigners.

That is the painful and chaotic state of our political reality today, as I see it. It reminds me of when my mother asked me to unravel a ball of yarn. Everything went perfectly well at first, as the yarn unwound cleanly without any snags. It fascinated me that the flabby mass of yarn could be made up of such a simple long strand, which went through my fingers without difficulty. Oh, but what evil (with a lower case "e") waited, hidden but ready to break up harmony and order. My fingers—acting as an extension of my entire body—encountered a sudden interrup-

tion in something that resisted and strained. The yarn which before had flowed toward me had become tangled, the process stymied by a knot!

My mother looked at me with a little grin which is echoed on my face each time I encounter a problem in my profession or I try to understand the situation through which my country is passing, then said:

"Let's see if you can straighten that out."

VII

As far as I am concerned, your Excellency, I assure you
that I would prefer to die a thousand deaths than see my
country humiliated by a hypocritical and greedy people,
as is yours, which, while trumpeting liberty, enslaves people who have the misfortune of being located nearby.

JUAN NEPOMUCENO ALMONTE, 1844

WE WALKED ALONG, avoiding puddles, through miserable neighborhoods whose adobe huts seemed to wear
dirty faces. There were street vendors, pigsties, animals grov-
eling in the mud and dogs with matted fur scratching at their
mange and fleas. Some of the women, on their knees grinding
corn, paused when they saw us walk by. Their taut arms almost
seemed to become one with the grinding stone, their withered
breasts hanging within their blouses, their pupils glazed and
remote.

The tenuous, depressing light filtered through the air onto
the ground. Whistling gusts of wind, which tested the leafless
branches, raised the hair on my neck. Was I nervous? Was it
fear of walking beside Isabel, with her pristine white dress
and parasol, knowing that she could faint or collapse at any
moment?

Outside one of the huts was a set of four shelves loosely
held together doing its best to showcase some merchandise.
There were packets of herbs and containers of dark liquids
which people would buy as they left the house after a consulta-
tion there.

After being outdoors, the murky darkness inside the hut,
illuminated only by a tallow candle, seemed doubly impene-
trable. I had to wait a few seconds before I could make out any
of the shadows. There were chipped earthen pots, sections of

tree trunks serving as chairs, ragged bedrolls, crosses made of wood and palm leaves, and a niche housing a candle which threw light on the golden image of the Virgin leaning over the Christ Child. A small brazier smoldered meekly in the corner.

The weak light of the tallow candle trembled, transforming things with its macabre glow, creating mad shadows.

Fortina, the *curandera*, or folk healer, was a woman of indistinguishable age, quite thin, with sallow leathery skin which retreated into the crevices of the bones in her cheeks and arms. She wore her hair in braids. Seated on a bedroll she would receive people, while another woman, a little younger and not as thin, would go about the room, giving the impression that she was navigating more by touch than by sight. From the sound of coins it seemed as though she was counting money, then she would package new bundles of herbs and blow on the brazier to coax an occasional flame.

With a greedy, well-aimed eye, Fortina seemed to evaluate Isabel, followed by an almost imperceptible hint of consent.

"Have a seat, little one. Tell me what ails you. Your face indicates your problems are more emotional than physical."

She shouldn't have said that. Isabel burst into tears. Fortina helped her lie down on a mat next to some herbs and started to speak quietly to her. Isabel answered with a grief-stricken face. She hiccupped and whimpered, and slow tears wet her cheeks. I kept standing and could barely hear their conversation.

A short while later Isabel, who had regained control of herself, started to get up, beginning by pushing up from her right elbow on the mat; she then made a pass with the back of her free hand across her face, as if to remove the remains of her crying, the cobwebs she had to clear away from her life.

"See that?" Fortina asked, once again using her normal voice and smiling at her with large yellow teeth and eyes that were in continual motion, as if trying to discern things hidden to everyone else.

"Yes," Isabel answered as she paid for and took the package of herbs they offered her.

Once outside again, it seemed imprudent for me to make

any comments, and Isabel simply told me that Fortina had asked about the place where memory causes such pain and the other where dreams do. She also prescribed a tea to be taken very hot each time she woke up in the middle of the night.

I wondered whether I should consult with Fortina about that place where dreams cause pain. Unfortunately, events were rolling forward, the Yankees were at the gates of the city, and I never had opportunity to do so. That very morning I had read a news article that terrified me:

The Americans now have the new Colt firearm as well as the most modern, overwhelming and brutal Rinngold and Howitzer cannons. Our army, by contrast, is limited to the cannons it inherited from the time of Spanish control and the old harquebuses purchased from England at the time of the Napoleonic wars.

Were we really expecting to confront the most powerful and bloodthirsty army in the world?

Isabel didn't seem at all worried about the invasion we were going to suffer. Something happened during her visit with Fortina which changed her. An unidentified strength, a happiness, breathed life into her from that point on. Without becoming overblown in effusive clamoring or histrionic gestures, it was there, present and certain, visible and tangible.

We still managed to go with her parents one night to the theater. Don Vicente demonstrated a disarmingly pleasant manner toward me when we met and Doña Isabel smiled at me over and over, but without making direct eye contact.

We went to the Teatro Principal to see a performance—as a matter of fact a rather poor performance, as the actors flubbed almost every line, possibly because they were also nervous given the shadow looming over the city—of *A Star Behind a Cloud*, a comedy in three acts by Juan Miguel de Losada.

I ended up sitting in the balcony box between Isabel and Doña Isabel, although I felt that it would have been more appropriate for Don Vicente to be next to me. Perhaps he opted to sit behind his wife to avoid a new confrontation with me. Or was it she who once again choreographed everything? What I do know is that from the moment the lights went out and the velvet curtain went up, a gust of warm air enveloped us—the mere idea of breathing the same air she did made my heart beat more rapidly—and I distinctly felt her arm on occasion coming close to mine. It was something almost imperceptible which no one else would have noticed. The four of us remained very formally in our seats, our hands properly positioned on our laps. At times we leaned forward slightly and put our hands on the balcony rail. At one point Isabel took out her green taffeta fan.

The murmurs, the applause and the air trembled, surprisingly stopped, and spun around all together. The same gust of air which prompted Doña Isabel and me to heave frequent sighs seemed to hover near our seats like an itch and was moved by the fans, or would pass by our faces like a caress.

There was a scene in the play during which I felt her arm particularly close to mine, precisely when the main character said:

> *Oh, if my wife only knew*
> *Of the love which consumes me,*
> *All the while thinking I am happy,*
> *How she would pity me.*
> *Only pain and tears*
> *Await this soul,*
> *Crushed into pieces*
> *By such a hopeless love.*

She sighed, which was a precise—and precious—admission that what the character said rang true. She was hiding something in her diaphragm, in her lungs, in her throat. The emotion of being near each other forced us to hold onto the air we were sharing, as if it were going back and forth from one mouth to the other.

In no other circumstance, ever, have I experienced such an amorous emotion. Although I boast of enjoying certain intuitions and near visions, I can scarcely relive that night in the

Teatro Principal. Try as I might to remember details, few come to memory, and it does little good to obsess over it. It is as useless as trying to remember details from a dream when all that remain are a few threads when we open our eyes.

I do remember that during the blackouts of the play I would close my eyes for a moment and take leave of myself, floating in an absolute availability, waiting for something propitious to occur. Only love allows us to yield ourselves, to break free from that moving framework of contacts which make up our lives, to make ourselves available like a card in a deck waiting compliantly to be shuffled and dealt.

During one of those blackouts I leaned my shoulder toward her, and from the brief contact I had with her arm a wave of warmth swept over my entire body, brought color to my cheeks and made my temples throb.

It was a moment that our poor inadequate timepieces could never measure, but during that brief moment I could feel Doña Isabel disintegrate voluptuously at my contact.

It seemed a flame had been lit at that spot where I touched her.

At that moment, a character in the play seemed to share with me (with us?) the emotion of the moment:

Those who love and then become separated leave their souls in that which they love.

And it seems to them that what they leave there will be their immortal soul.

Where did we leave our souls, beloved?

In my carriage on the way home, I was struck by the abundance of the wretched, Indians and common folk on Mercaderes Street. At first I thought they were participating in a festival, but I soon discovered that they were holding a street protest, shouting insults against the Yankees who would soon be arriving, but also against the Mexican government and especially Santa Anna. Some of them held torches. The wind battled the flames and lifted dense spirals of smoke skyward. We scarcely managed to get past them—my driver directed his whistling whip as much at people who came too near as at the horses—and a rock broke one of the carriage's windows. The scene seemed to foreshadow what would shortly take place.

I thought it opportune the next day to deliver to Isabel a book of poems by Juan Miguel de Losada, author of the play we had just seen. Since Doña Isabel and I were secretly exchanging books—sadly enough through her daughter—I assumed that she would find it and read it, especially a particular poem, so I creased ever so delicately the upper corner of that page:

Before the altars of your being, I sacrifice
My existence for your anxious love.
I worship you! You already lived in the
Chapels of my soul before I met you,
At night you would always appear
In the shadows of my solitary room.
In silver hues the moon painted
Your likeness everywhere I looked,
And the hours passed one by one
Never altering the illusion.

Just a few days later, during a visit to her house, Isabel, who felt completely better, and I would even say reborn, asked me in her clearest voice:

"Do you really think there is a strong chance that we'll die here when the Yankees come?"

"I absolutely do."

"Before that happens I want to spend time with you. Invite me one of these days to your home."

I remembered what her mother had asked me to do: "Help my daughter, please. Nothing could worry me more and cause me so much pain as the situation in which the poor girl finds herself. I believe that you will know, in the heat of the moment, how you alone can help her." And she emphasized the dangerous final words, "help her."

VIII

And what about God? What role has He been assigned
in this war?

LA COLUMNA, EDITORIAL FROM APRIL 8, 1847

G ENERAL SCOTT SUFFERED *some of his most anxious
moments subsequent to spending ten weeks in Puebla. The
guerrilla warfare, organized by a priest by the name of Father
Jarauta, had seriously affected his supply lines, dysentery had
gained a toehold with his troops, and many of them lost their
enthusiasm for moving forward. But General Scott will not be
stopped, and his campaign strategy continues with astonishing
precision. Since leaving the road from Ayotla to Peñón to head
toward Chalco, Xochimilco and Tlalpan, nothing has halted his
march, meaning that the head of the army of the United States
now has a free path to the capital, which will shortly be his.*

It pains me to confess this—especially to you, Dr. Urruchúa—
but once the Yankees arrived in the Valley of Mexico, and during the bloody battles of Padierna, Churubusco, Molino del
Rey and Chapultepec, I was in my home safely hunkered down,
blissfully happy, making mad love to Isabel. I was free from
my demons, liberated from my ills and wounds, aloof from the
city in which I was living and even from the world. I seemed
to experience a level of energy which I had never imagined
I could possess. I slept better than ever, and without taking
doses of lime and passionflower. I didn't read any newspapers and had no idea what was happening on the streets (my
domestic help had been given strict orders to open the door to
no one, no matter what, to give the impression that the house
had been abandoned). I had a richly varied food supply in the
cellar which would have allowed us to stay there several weeks
without any sacrifice at all.

Afterwards, I found out that while some of my friends fled the city or openly proclaimed themselves in favor of the American invasion, others courageously took up arms to defend the city, and some of them even died. Dr. Urruchúa came down with a stomach disorder from which he never recovered, and was on the verge of a nervous breakdown after not sleeping for several days because he was treating the wounded and helping to bury (or burn) the dead.

Therefore, confessions such as the one I am making right now—which my wife has been so insistent that I divulge—attest to the fact that in every religious faith the vast majority of people have an anguishing need to *give an accounting*. To whom? To a friend who died, like Dr. Urruchúa? I am certain that he has given me his forgiveness. To a handful of possible readers? I doubt I'll have many. To the soldier I stabbed? We were at war and I didn't see any other option. To my family? My wife clicked her tongue at me disapprovingly when I told her that she should also forgive me. To my posterity? Anything is possible. But might it not be related, in an involuntary way, to anticipating that meeting with Him who gave us our souls and who could take them back whenever He pleases? Anything that could temper that meeting cannot be considered trivial, especially if, as I have always thought, it is through writing that the meeting becomes possible.

The fact is that from the very first time I was with Isabel, a very rainy afternoon as I recall, I decided that I would not leave my house again. Especially when she said:

"My mother knows I'm with you and she certainly must know that chances are great I'll stay here several days."

"What about your father?"

She smiled with a smile that seemed to go deeper than her lips and teeth.

"My father is probably happy that I've disappeared. Besides, my mother has undoubtedly made up some tall tale which has made him even happier. I know him well."

That first afternoon we spent together turned out surprising for both of us. It was obviously surprising to Isabel because it was the first time she had made love, and it was for me because I had no idea of her sensuality. Might it have been a trait she shared with her mother, perhaps something she had inherited from her? At first I thought the attraction I felt for her derived precisely from her languid, dark eyes, which communicated a constant stimulation, with intensely black pupils that reminded me of her mother. Soon her ardor, combined with her natural sweetness, captured me, and she took on a highest value all her own. My relationship with her mother had to do with *before*, while hers had to do with a passionate present.

Her cheeks had recovered their pinkish color and I immediately thought that all of her pores were opening, and in a state of anxious waiting. She was wearing a diaphanous white muslin dress with a blue sash dotted with gold flowers, and she had kidskin gloves as well as a small purse made of velvet and glass beads. Several days later, while her dress was being washed, she had to wear one of my mother's robes, which was somewhat disconcerting to me and provoked a new conjunction of faces—that of her mother, of mine, of herself—but there was no way she could have kept wearing her own clothes for so many days straight.

She never stopped talking, batting her eyes and waving her hands, as if she were keeping time to a secret melody. We were in the courtyard, drinking tea on a marble table next to a large wooden cross under some poplar trees. She mentioned how well she was feeling—the tea Fortina had recommended was miraculous—and she allowed me to kiss her on the lips, which were slightly open. Her hands started to sweat when I held them too long. Later it started to rain and I invited her to the living room to have a piece of candy and a cup of wine from Burgundy, which lifted her spirits even more. I showed her my library. We sat in the black leather chairs and I read her the first fragments of the chronicle I was trying to write about the grave events assailing our city. She wanted to read some of the most recent pages I had written, in which I described what had happened in the Teatro Principal when I was seated next to her mother. I did not allow it, of course. I stood up to take the incriminating sheets (which I never should have shown her) back to the desk and their place at the bottom of a drawer. She caught me and blocked my path with an attitude of confrontation.

"You have something there you don't want to show me. Let me see it."

"Soon enough, when I have made corrections. The way it is written right now I wouldn't show it to anybody."

"I don't believe you. Tell me the truth," she said while her eyes studied the depths of mine.

"Absolutely not."

I shouldn't have said it in such a definitive way, because she pounced on me like a whirlwind and, giggling, tried to get the damning papers from me. I put them behind my back, so Isabel reached around me with both hands to try to reach them. I managed to break free from her arms and raised the papers high into the air. She then tried to reach them, standing on the tips of her toes, leaning on my chest. What did I do then? I managed to put the papers behind her back, leaving her defenseless as a prisoner of my embrace, which allowed me to kiss her at length and move her toward the sofa—discreetly leaving the sheets on the desk.

We went up to the bedroom—she never stopped batting her eyes and opening and closing her hands, as if she were squeezing lemons with them—and then she spent an eternity in the bathroom.

I had foreseen the possibility of these events, which is why that very morning I had been quite sure to have cleaned and shined the Spanish tiles installed all around the bathroom. They made it glow, the tiles a stunning white with images of green stalks from which tiny roses bloomed. I also had the creamy enameled wrought-iron tub cleaned. I bought new towels, a toothbrush with a silver handle, carbonate for dental hygiene, perfume, lotions, combs and hair brushes, handkerchiefs, and found a leather case which had belonged to my mother, with tweezers and nail files in a variety of styles and sizes.

To my surprise, she came out exactly as she had gone in,

except more nervous. I had to shut off the light for her to get undressed.

In the bathroom with my ear to the door, I heard various articles of clothing fall to the floor. Some of the heavy ones landed loudly, while others were mere suggestions, alighting like birds, until the dry thud of her boots let me know that I could come out, wearing a robe, of course.

The darkness was broken only by a wedge of indirect light from the courtyard, and I could see the line of her body under the sheets, her phosphorescent eyes looking at me from the darkness.

Because I still couldn't believe all this was happening, I knelt down next to the bed without saying a word. I kissed her hair, her forehead, the bridge of her nose, her cheeks and her chin. Was this really Isabel, the only girlfriend I had ever had, the mere girl who had just recovered from a serious nervous breakdown, who had thought about becoming a nun, and whom I had considered as precious as an embroidered heart? Those fragile flowers of her hands were trembling as she clasped the sheets. She responded to my kisses with a smile. Her eyes, a pair of full moons, were in ecstasy.

I asked the most absurd and awkward question possible in that special instant: "Why are you doing this?"

After a profound sigh, or perhaps it was more like a sob, she responded in a very guttural voice:

"Because if I don't, I'll die. That's why."

I slowly lowered the sheet, fighting back the desire to do so in one fell swoop, in order to discover her naked body, whose mystery had been blockaded until then

"Who else has seen your body like this? Your mother, but many years ago. Anyone else?"

"One day I discovered a cousin looking at me through the keyhole of the bathroom."

"That's different. A physician could have also seen you, but that's different. What you are doing now, by letting me see you the way I am, is giving yourself over to me entirely."

"I'm quite nervous."

"You'll be fine. As the poet said, the only virginity that matters is this one, the one that precedes the first profound view of our body, and is lost beneath that view."

"And how do you feel? Tell me how you feel. That will help me feel less nervous."

"Me?" It was the worst question she could have asked because it stripped me of my false security. "I don't know, I feel like a bird hovering over a small island where I have been wanting to land for a long time."

"Maybe it would be better if you didn't land, if you just stayed there in the air for another day."

I should have anticipated that frustrating answer. I pretended that I didn't hear her and lowered the sheet a little more.

"Let me see you. Give yourself to me. Your body is happy, even if your conscience of a properly raised, decent girl still gets in the way. Think how frustrating it was that your skin, all of your skin, had never experienced true light—that of someone else's gaze. This is the light of a real day, the most faithful mirror, the only beach with sunlight."

I think that was the moment when she jumped onto me and told me to hug her, just hug her. I felt her shrink and withdraw into my arms, as if putting up a barrier, refusing to give in. Perhaps she was crying without showing it openly, hiding her tears.

We stayed that way for a long time. I felt her press against me over and over again, like a series of waves. We stopped shivering (which we'd been doing for no reason, since those days were warm).

I awoke when the morning sunshine was spreading bluely upon the windows. I confirmed that she was still sleeping soundly, with the expression of a newborn baby that good people wear when they rest soundly.

I opened the window. A lovely, penetrating aroma drifted in. I stood there, looking at her as if in a trance until I saw her wake up and stretch beneath the sheets. Her misgivings had faded from her eyes and a wild glimmer sparked like lightning.

I myself prepared her a bath of water treated with medicinal herbs that helped the body to recover and facilitated expectoration after a tiring night, as an herb vendor from the Portal de las Flores had explained. I rubbed her back with the soft natural bristles of a brush.

The aroma of rose-scented soap combined with the warmth of the air, and Isabel lathered herself with both hands, slowly applying the suds to her body as if she were discovering it for the first time, as if love had given her a new one. The greenish color of the tiles gleamed liquidly through the steamy mist.

This bath interregnum, a break from her arid traditional existence, helped Isabel break free from time and the rancid tradition of the Olaguíbel family, which, knowing her father as I did, could not have been easy. The moment she started to stand up—a goddess emerging from the water—I handed her a white towel that she wrapped herself in. She had re-entered her tedious realm of being a clothed woman, of her name and surnames. Each article of clothing—and regretfully almost every day she had to put on the same thing—seemed to tie her down to the history of the city in which she was living, and to the history of her presumptuous family, returning each and every year of her life to her along with a mountain of useless, painful memories. You could see her future in her face as visibly as the powder mask I had found her wearing the afternoon I had gone to visit when she was suffering from such a strange and mysterious ailment.

Our time together was marked by an almost ceremonial set of activities that we repeated every day. (Toward the end there were days when we did not have hot water, and Isabel would come out of the water shivering, but I would rub her with turpentine and mustard and she would warm up immediately.) I loved to see her sleep peacefully, to guess her dreams behind her closed eyelids, to see her get out of bed early in the morning and then see the sheet which had covered her fall gracefully to the floor. We would bathe, eat together, have a drink, walk through the garden, play cards, and before we knew it the day would slip away like flowing water. We would extinguish the light on the nightstand and slip into bed, enjoying the feel of the sheets and the mattress which was just the right firmness. Every night we found one another in bed, as surprised as the first night.

Sometimes she would put the light on the floor because she said she liked the look of the glow around the bed.

She took absolute possession of the house and the domestic help. She was fascinated by the box of keys and bells at the entrance of the kitchen, and she experimented with each one, trying each key in all the cupboard locks and trying the sound of each bell. She did a thorough inventory of the pantry and the cellar, then calculated in detail how long the food, wine, cooking fuel, ice and milk would last. She immediately ordered the servants to put on caps and better aprons, and at first they looked at her a bit resentfully, scowls on their faces. But when they saw that she had my unconditional support, they yielded to her authority. The same thing happened with my driver, who at that time ended up working as a gardener.

I could spend hours in the shade of our poplar trees in the courtyard, watching the clouds, my mind void of thoughts, wholly given over to the world of the body, my senses attuned to any demand of pleasure.

There were no more flames in the air, just clouds, which at times moved so slowly that it took all day to see the shapes of a lion head and a mountain range dissipate. I spent hour after hour immobile, knowing how useless it would be to walk around, because I was inexorably in the middle, at the absolute center, of what I was contemplating.

Usually obsessive when it comes to time, I laughed when I discovered that my watch had stopped because I had forgotten to wind it.

We stopped thinking about hours of the day and started paying attention to the placement of the sun in the sky to guide us when to eat and sleep. I observed the slow movements of the rocking chair and the glare of the sun. Trees swayed around us. Sparrows announced dusk's arrival.

I've never again experienced such days. The earth's bounty

was matched by that of the sky, and my soul seemed to merge with each of them in turn. I breathed deep sighs of contentment, and finally dared to gaze serenely at things.

Now that I have returned to my house in Tacubaya, I move from empty room to empty room invoking ghosts and memories. I once again see Isabel in the creamy enameled wrought-iron bathtub—which has been replaced by an awful chipped pewter tub—and I feel my heart so full of tears (possibly due to seeing so many near visions, a lack of sleep and the nervous tension I am once again experiencing), that the smallest noise sounds like wailing. "Do not under any circumstance allow your altered emotional state to take you to the point of tears, my friend. That would be a dangerous warning sign," Dr. Urruchúa used to tell me. But under these circumstances, at my age, how can it be avoided, and why would I want to avoid it?

Shadows shift and the drawing room unexpectedly fills with the sound of a chord from the piano which was there. The chord rings out again, as if a hand had fallen upon invisible keys. The vibrations dissolve into the silence.

I've seen the figure of Isabel from that first night reappear in my old bedroom. Her face was still only partially visible and a yellow halo surrounded her silhouette. I thought I could sense the trembling of her skin in its recently reborn state. I thought back to what I had wondered all those years ago: "What experience has your body had with the world?" Also repeated were the sensations, groaning, silence, smells and horrors of war outside the home (which we didn't see, but imagined). Everything came back, took possession of my imagination, took on form and color. Was it really me back then?

Inevitably my enthusiasm was tempered by grave anxiety, by the slipperiness of the images. I saw that the sphere—the aura enveloping Isabel—wasn't stationary, but spinning around her, like a planet rotating on its axis.

"It's leaving!" I exclaimed, terrified. It was similar to my worst crises of melancholy when I would lose the memory of a dream which I knew had been important.

I discovered that, like the moon entering its final phase, the aura which enveloped the ghost of Isabel was slowly vanishing, ever so slowly, taking away my delectable vision, until all that remained was a dusty bedroom in need of paint.

All the shadows retreated, overcome by the granulated light breaking through the dirty windows and, grumbling as they went, dissipated into the rest of the house.

Once again I was alone, lost in the empty house. My only companion was the guilt I felt knowing that while I had been there, my city had been subjected to the most savage battles.

IX

In Mexico all that is authentic and noble is weak and ephemeral. The only strong and lasting thing here is the power of lies.

FRANCISCO ZARCO

M Y DEAR ABELARDO, *how I have missed and needed you during these tragic days. I sent people to look for you, but they told me your house was abandoned and you had undoubtedly fled the city in such a hurry that you did not even have time to say goodbye to your friends. Given the chaos in which we live at the moment, your departure is justifiable. Everything is justifiable.*

We have certainly lived through remarkable times in this city, marked by the burning metal of pain and tragedy. When will they end? Sometimes I feel like I can't go on, that I'm going to burst or faint or fall asleep standing up or start yelling and run around outside like a lunatic. I wonder whether, even being a doctor, I'll stop distinguishing between human body parts, or whether I'll lose the capacity to amputate an extremity or use a scalpel to start an incision. But I continue on because all that has to happen is someone with a wound shows up and the cobwebs of exhaustion and desperation flee. Who was it that said there are places in our heart which don't exist until grief and pain appear? I spend night and day in the Hospital of San Pedro and San Pablo and also manage to visit our tiny battle-front hospitals, at least the ones that have been thrown together on the run, working with the paltry resources we have available, which seem fewer and fewer every day. We apply bandages using dirty fabric used who knows how many times before (we have to salvage even the bandages from the dead, because no matter how stained they may be, we don't have the luxury of discarding them). I'm surrounded at every hour of the day by my patients and their refuse, making a great effort, to this very day, to become accustomed to their sputum, mucus and pus, their belching, the thick breath when their mouths open, their vomiting and regurgitation marked by lumps and foam which sometimes splatter on whomever is nearby, and the nauseating odor of their urine and excrement. I am trying to become accustomed to amputating an endless number of arms, legs and fingers, to removing bullets from the most unexpected places (I just extracted one from a man's palate), speed-stitching wounds caused by sharp instruments used as weapons, cutting off gangrenous skin, cutting a burned eye out of its socket, pulling loose teeth, removing parts of blackened fingernails. I try to turn a deaf ear to the sounds of my saw, to the moans and groans of wounded men biting on a piece of wood or a handkerchief and squirming like worms. I try not to pay attention to the closed eyes of the men whose faces are full of an unending expression of anguish, rebellion and disbelief. "How much longer, doctor? How much longer? What's the point of all of this?" "I'm about to finish, son. I'm almost done, I swear." And the procedure continues, the saw going back and forth to sever a gangrenous extremity, bone-dust flying. And our only anesthesia is a good swallow of rum. (Nothing worries me so much as the possibility of running out of rum. Truth be told, we physicians make use of it from time to time as well.) All this is done with the help of colleagues as sleep-deprived and worn out as I am.

Sometimes I pray, "Help me, Lord." I usually pray for myself rather than for the wounded, because despite my long experience, while I operate I am worried to death—and lately I have been operating day and night—and my supplication is like a fist that pounds unceasingly on a door, the fist of a person who desperately wants to enter a house which he knows ahead of time is closed to him, without any possibility of anyone (Anyone?) opening the door.

The lucky ones faint, which almost always happens when the scalpel makes its initial incision. Who can stand to watch or suffer that kind of spectacle? With my nose buried in the *entrails of a patient as I operate, my entire body tenses up in a sensation which includes disgust, compassion, defiance, rage and tenderness. I can't get over the surprise, perhaps a bit naïve, when I save someone's life and then he smiles and thanks me.*

"Thank you, Doctor. God bless you. How can I ever repay you?"

On the other hand, in some cases just a few days later the very same soldier returns wounded even more seriously than before, and the question arises:

"What's the point of all of this, doctor?"

Sometimes when a badly wounded soldier arrives and is bleeding to death on our makeshift operating table, I make a completely idiotic remark to my assistant:

"Look at how much blood there is in a human body, even a small one!"

All the values and ideals the assistant has formed with such effort about his altruistic profession and esteemed teachers must crumble at that moment.

All of us—the wounded, nurses, physicians—have nerves as taut as the strings on a guitar. One of those assistants, whose name I cannot remember, had been without sleep for several nights and was helping me with a delicate operation. He observed how, with a single incision, I cut through cartilage and separated the soft tissues of the thorax. He suddenly threw the bandages into the air, started to sweat and tremble, and collapsed at my side, going into a series of convulsions. He got better several days later, but we discovered that when he would see blood, even one drop of blood, he would start to convulse and lose consciousness.

Nevertheless, despite my increasing desperation over each new operation, I am convinced that when all is said and done pain is relative. Could it be that I am merely trying to cheer myself up? Perhaps, but I have the impression—I wish I could prove this scientifically—that pain, when it passes a certain threshold, provides its own anesthetic. Before we get hurt, the sting of pain seems very sharp, at times inconceivably sharp.

But is it really? I think that when it hits, it injects at the same time its own narcotic, and somehow we manage to bear up, or we immediately faint. I've seen this during long years of work. I have always told my patients to stop worrying about future pains. We never have to worry about future pains: anticipating them is worse than their eventual reality, because nature is not yet ready to handle them.

I like to remember, over and over, a patient with an inoperable stomach tumor who told me, "Blessed is physical pain, doctor, which distances us from pains of the soul, because those are truly unbearable."

Or even better, the comment from a woman who was suffering a serious nervous malady: "I am acquainted with another type of crying, doctor. I don't know whether it is more or less painful, but it is different. It is a crying which is almost imperceptible, often muffled by a pillow or hidden behind a dark veil, and which anticipates no relief or end. It is a dry kind of stifled, tearless, and almost always nocturnal crying, resigned to never being noticed, to never receiving any help or aid, because it would never even know how to ask for them."

As she said this, I glimpsed in the infinite sadness of her eyes a hint of that secret crying of which she spoke.

Right now the city is sleeping, and I wonder with a bitter taste in my mouth what will happen within a few hours. As I write in the light of a sputtering candle, caressed and comforted for a few minutes by the silence of the night, I think about how much I would have enjoyed saying goodbye to him, warning him against the danger of feeling guilt: the black beast of life, as Burton called it, so influential in his nervous disorder, convincing him that he would not be judged by anyone—here, now, nobody cares what their neighbor does or does not do—and perhaps before saying goodbye, drinking some absinthe together and talking about any sort of topic, or perhaps we could have finished that conversation we had until early in the morning on one of the benches in the Plaza de Santo Domingo about the philosophical theory of "three lives" which he'd read about somewhere: this temporary transitory life; the transcendental life, consisting of memories based on prestige and glory; and finally the supposedly future, unending life in which believers place their trust. Abelardo thought this concept should perhaps be expanded to "four lives" (which satisfies our obsession for finding new forms of life), which would be in essence this fleeting life, the life of glory, the future life, and, pay close attention here, a second future life.

"Listen to my reasoning, doctor," Abelardo explained very slowly, his eyes trembling in their sockets, as if looking for something in the distance, in the newborn day, a proof of what he was saying. "Believers in a future life imagine that it will be so different from this life that, since this one is essentially provisional, the future life will be essentially definitive. What if, as we begin the next life, we are informed that it will be just as provisional as this one, that just as in this life we will need to work toward the next one, in the next one we will have to work for the following one, and in that one for the next, and so on without end?

"The ship of philosophy could never be dismantled in any port. Each port sends it off to sea once again on a new, never-ending voyage. Similarly, it is quite possible that death is not the definitive shipwreck we envision it to be, and perhaps the next life will not be a permanent port either."

My thoughts are once again like moths flying dangerously close to flames which can burn their wings. I have to ask myself what would happen if Abelardo and I had gone to Paris with the excuse of getting treatment in the "animal magnetism" clinic, and we had discovered that city together, just as we have discovered our own city during our nighttime walks?

My candlelight is now so dim that I can scarcely see my own writing, even when I write in large, clear script and refrain from adding the flourishes I typically use.

Why am I not in the least overcome by sleep when last night I scarcely slept three hours, and why if I were to lie down right now would I only sleep at the most four hours? Might it be that Abelardo left me his melancholy disorder when he departed?

I had the fortune of being one of the boys at Chapultepec Castle. Amidst them in the clamor of combat, surrounded by dense smoke and explosive powder, I learned to love my country with unbridled passion.

JOSÉ TOMÁS DE CUÉLLAR

PRECISELY WHEN MY LIFE finally looked to me like a peaceful, silent river, marked by inane but harmonious daily routine, with a current that had carried me to that September afternoon which seemed like a waveless sea, a sea in which I could leisurely drift along floating on my back, caring about nothing and feeling no guilt about what might be happening outside my house in the city; precisely on that rich afternoon as I was smoking my marble pipe on a sofa in the living room, lost in the circles of smoke drifting upward, I heard Isabel scream in my study, although it may have been more of a shriek.

I left my pipe in the ashtray and ran to find out what was happening.

Behind the curtains the afternoon was in agony. An intense, fleeting blue in the corner of the balcony window announced the beginning of night.

Isabel was seated at my desk, the pages of the chronicle I was trying to write spread out before her in the fragile light of an oil lamp. She raised her face very slowly, reminiscent of someone being rescued after nearly drowning. It was a face devastated by such tremendous anguish that I felt ashamed to look at it.

Or was it rage?

I struggled to find a way to cast a veil over that unbearable scene. But what name can be given to misery when the person we love most is suffering from something we have inflicted?

With a guttural, almost incomprehensible voice, she read:

"'What I do know is that from the moment the lights went out and the velvet curtain went up, a gust of warm air enveloped us—the mere idea of breathing the same air she did made my heart beat more rapidly—and I distinctly felt her arm on occasion coming close to mine.'"

"Isabel, let me explain."

But my words only exacerbated the turmoil in her eyes, which glanced at me briefly before turning back to my writings, with a grimace that showed her deception and made her stop to take a deep breath before continuing.

"'She sighed, which was a precise—and precious—admission that what the character said rang true. She was hiding something in her diaphragm, in her lungs, in her throat. The emotion of being near each other forced us to hold onto the air we were sharing, as if it were going back and forth from one mouth to the other.

"'In no other circumstance, ever, have I experienced such amorous emotion.'"

"Please, Isabel, that's enough. What you are reading is a sort of novelized chronicle and I had to invent that absurd situation to infuse interest into the plot. Your name and your mother's name were the first ones that came into my mind because I was so close to you. Do you understand?"

But she didn't listen to me and kept on reading; during moments when her voice would become clear, she read my words with an intensity I never would have imagined them to possess.

"'During one of those blackouts I leaned my shoulder toward her, and from the brief contact I had with her arm a wave of warmth swept over my entire body, brought color to my cheeks and made my temples throb. It was a moment which our poor inadequate watches could never measure, but during that brief instant I could feel Doña Isabel disintegrate voluptuously at my contact. It seemed a flame had been lit at that spot where I touched her.'"

"Isabel, what you are reading is pure literature, and not particularly good. It has nothing to do with reality."

She breathed deeply and then read one last paragraph, unfortunately the most incriminating.

"'I thought it opportune the next day to deliver to Isabel a book of poems by Juan Miguel de Losada, author of the play we had just seen. Since Doña Isabel and I were secretly exchanging books—sadly enough through her daughter—I supposed that she would find it and read it, especially a particular poem, so I creased ever so delicately the upper corner of that page.'"

When she was about to read Juan Miguel de Losada's poem—and what a poem it is—I went over and grabbed the papers from her. She attacked me like a tornado and amid cries and shouts, erupting and foaming at the mouth, she slapped me, leaving a deep scratch on my cheek. Her eyes were two small crazed birds in their orbits.

"I never want to see you again!"

"Isabel, listen to me for a moment," I begged, speaking very slowly to try to seem under control.

"Never, never, never, never!" she insisted, as if hammering a nail.

She took a few steps away, glared at me with fire in her eyes, and haltingly said:

"I want to go home."

I breathed in as much air as a runner about to start a race and then impulsively, but in a highly lucid state—like lightning in the darkness, like falling stars in the middle of the desert—I took out of the center drawer of my desk an old dagger with a marble handle that I'd inherited from my grandfather and pressed it forcefully against my own chest, right at my heart.

"Isabel, if you leave, my only option will be suicide. I can't live without you. It would be completely impossible for me to live without you," I said with a voice that seemed to flow inward. I had indeed decided to follow through with my threat, and that decision created a strange bittersweet taste in my mouth. "With you I have discovered a world which I simply could never leave."

I sensed a flicker of compassion behind the mists which veiled her eyes, despite her harsh response:

"Do whatever you want."

"I swear I will."

She blinked her eyes, became perceptibly pale and, with a voice tinged with anguish, asked a question which hurt me more than the tip of that dagger at my heart:

"Do you love my mother?"

The question negated any possibility of committing suicide there in front of her, because if I didn't answer it would be admitting guilt, and plunging the blade into my chest at that moment would be the equivalent of *making love to her mother*, in my estimation. For that reason I couldn't lie to her. There was just no point in lying to her.

"Yes ... I love her." I felt my voice lose its strength until it was barely audible. "But I also love you. They are two completely different types of love, and they have nothing to do with each other."

Color once again filled her cheeks and her nose started to twitch in indignation; she lowered her head for just a moment and then left in a huff.

At that moment, the only thing I could do was exactly that: anything. I could stab myself or not stab myself. I could think of myself as either courageous or cowardly. I could run after Isabel or remain quiet. I could watch myself act from within or from outside myself. I could center my thoughts on God or think about nothing at all. I could imagine myself as a character in a tragedy or a comedy. I chose the latter, and since I felt completely ridiculous standing there, alone in my study, I had no choice but to lower the dagger and put it back in the center drawer of my desk. That experience had its advantages. I learned to anticipate what was going to happen to me as if it were not actually going to happen to me. As if it were to happen to someone else, to an *other* who was also living at that moment in the same house and had been jilted by the woman he loved. Even today, so many years later, I can fancy the same thing if I put my mind to it. I close my eyes, and even if just for a moment, I see myself as if from the ceiling. Or from even higher—much higher. It's remarkable the distance from which a person can contemplate oneself. As well, this experience helped teach me how to control my anguish. I found it best, at that distance from myself, to give in completely to anguish, not putting up any resistance and maintaining a constant awareness of being in anguish; in fact, if I can recognize it every morning and be deserving of it, if I cherish it and become worthy of it, I then manage to free myself, to a certain extent, from its most damaging consequences.

A moment later my driver announced that Señorita Isabel had ordered him to drive her home immediately. I nodded my consent, aware that silence and immobility could also be a form of self-destruction. Why didn't I run after her? Why didn't I force her to stay in my house until I could convince her of my love? Would that have even made a difference, since I had just confessed that I also loved her mother? Could she ever accept that? I remembered the night when Isabel asked to read the final pages of my chronicle. Why did I simply place them in the drawer of my desk instead of putting them somewhere more secure? In fact, why didn't I destroy them, since I knew I wasn't going to finish the account? I should have foreseen her looking for them in that spot, the only logical place to look.

I realized that if I stayed in the house I'd flirt again with the idea of stabbing myself, so as soon as my driver returned, I went out to see what was happening in the city.

✳ I

Chapultepec, my forest, my place of enchantment, nest of
my childhood; seeing you in ruins is like seeing the man-
gled body of my own father.

GUILLERMO PRIETO

MY EYES WERE STUNNED—confusion and panic appeared on every street corner.

"Here they come!"

"Here they are! They're already here!"

"They've taken Chapultepec Castle, and tomorrow they'll
march into the center of the city!"

"They're such blond giants!"

"They'll crush us!"

"They've come to kill us because we're Mexicans! Just
because we're Mexicans!"

"Just like they killed off the Apaches!"

"They'll squash us like flies!"

My friends at the Progreso Café—I had guessed that if some
of them were still in the city they would feel the need to get out
of their houses and meet with their friends—gave me a summary of the latest events in the city.

Once his reinforcements arrived, Scott left Puebla and
started the ascent toward Mexico City during the first week of
August. They said that he was surprised to find no resistance
in the mountain passes, which would have been so strategi-
cally opportune for Mexican attacks. Nevertheless, Santa Anna
had already begun the farce which would culminate—he had
undoubtedly anticipated this would show up as a scene in a
play—in one of the most painful and bloody tragedies in our
history. Santa Anna, his five thousand men and thirty pieces
of heavy artillery waited for the enemy's arrival at the Peñón
Grande hill. The obvious problem was that, with the help of

his spies, Scott found a route which allowed him to go around towards the south. On August 17 he entered through Tlalpan and destroyed the Mexican defensive strategy.

Three days later a Yankee column attacked and occupied the hamlet of Padierna, in San Ángel. Santa Anna and his troops, those five thousand men who were the "flower of the Mexican army," showed up that same rainy morning in a nearby hamlet, unsure whether or not to attack. They engaged in a strategy of dubious worth: to remain still, always remain still, as in a game of statues.

From an adjacent hilltop, with the help of a spyglass His Serene Highness saw how the courageous general Gabriel Valencia personally confronted the ferocious invading army, sword in hand, leading his men armed with bayonets. As the afternoon came to an end, General Valencia was regaining control of Padierna. Santa Anna closed his spyglass and withdrew.

At two o'clock in the morning, when General Valencia, brimming with enthusiasm, was dictating his part in the war, two of Santa Anna's officers presented themselves, saying that their mission was to help the various Mexican forces "come to an agreement regarding future operations." They indicated that Santa Anna's orders were for Valencia to retreat from Padierna as soon as possible.

"Why?" Valencia asked, his eyes in amazement. "If General Santa Anna will lend us his support and attack their rearward this very morning, we will have pinned the Yankees into a position from which escape is next to impossible."

"The Honorable President simply gave his orders for you to retreat immediately from this place. Period."

"But why? We just managed to recover this spot, and at the cost of how many lives!"

"The Honorable President did not give his reasons."

"Then tell your Honorable President that I'm not going to move from here, and that tomorrow I will defend this spot with even greater enthusiasm, and tell him to go fuck his mother."

The messengers returned to deliver the message from Valencia to His Serene Highness—which undoubtedly included the message about his mother—and soon they were back in Padierna.

"The Honorable President wishes to repeat the order for you to retreat, and he sends no explanation. He stated that if you choose to disobey, he will simply issue orders to have you executed tomorrow without any delay."

Valencia stared down the threat of execution. All his officials approved of his valor and disobedience. They would keep on fighting, with increased enthusiasm, and they would seek to triumph despite the contrary instructions and the high rank of the President of the Republic.

At daybreak Valencia confirmed that Santa Anna and his troops had departed from the nearby hill.

The Yankee artillery pounded Padierna with all its strength and razed it to the ground, despite the valor of the Mexican soldiers. They say that defeated and under threat of execution, General Valencia had to flee in disguise to Toluca. Everything, including the disguise Valencia wore, was tragically theatrical.

The next stage was located in Churubusco, a strategic point in the defense of the city, with its old convent surrounded by adobe and straw huts, lush vegetation and rows of ripening corn ending at the foot of the old walls. Churubusco was on the route between Tlalpan and Coyoacán, and was a swampy area with abundant flowers. Two generals were present: Manuel Rincón and former president of the Republic Pedro María Anaya. There were two regiments of *polkos* determined to vindicate themselves after their shameful actions of the previous February. National Guardsmen, who witnessed the cowardly retreat of the "flower of the Mexican army" from the battlefield, made ready to defend their posts with pathetic flint rifles held together by string and baling wire—practically props. As a matter of fact, in their ranks was one of our finest comedic playwrights, Manuel Eduardo de Gorostiza.

The forces were comprised of thirteen hundred raw recruits, most of whom had never participated in an armed conflict, surrounded by an army four times their size and more than four times their superior in terms of training and artillery.

Santa Anna gives the order for them to fight in a loud voice with grandiloquent gestures. Then he retires with his army to the National Palace. The strategic inefficiency of Santa Anna includes turning around and around in circles to the point of getting sick, hiding behind curtains, or entering and exiting the stage over and over through various trapdoors, but with no particular purpose. His assistance in Churubusco consists entirely of providing, at the last moment, seven cannons and one carriage with several boxes of ammunition.

"We are in a convent. We are defending not just our country but Jesus Christ and His church. Death to the demons of Protestantism!" shout the *polkos*. (It is worth remembering that just last February they took up arms against the federal government because Vice President Gómez Farías imposed a loan of fifteen million *pesos* on the Mexican clergy.) The cry is seconded by the members of the St. Patrick Irish Battalion, which, once the conflict had begun, cast their lot with Mexico and Mexicans, whose misfortune is similar, in political and religious terms, to Ireland and its relationship with England.

The Twiggs division attacks. Others provide reinforcements. The Yankees surround the convent on all sides. Heads emerge over and over from the embattlements like targets at a fair, some of them wearing hats, some donning kerchiefs, and some wearing nothing; some are young and others old, and some are ghostlike in clouds of smoke which diffuse their silhouettes.

Their ammunition runs out and so they turn to the supplies sent to them by Santa Anna, but they find it is all nineteen-weight ammunition, a caliber far bigger than the fifteen-weight bullets which they need. The cartridges do not begin to fit in their arms.

"That son of a bitch Santa Anna knew it! He wants the Yankees to crush us like rodents!" shout the *polkos*.

The explanation Don Marcos Negrete gave me seemed the most logical one:

"Since the defense of the Churubusco convent was going to be executed for the most part by civil forces, most of them well-known for their virtues and considerable fortunes, Santa

Anna decided to place them in a trap and then wipe out all trace of their heroic stand."

But the *polkos* don't surrender:

"Open the other boxes! Let's use the practice ammunition as salvos, even though there are no bullets! We can at least use rocks in the cannons!"

After several hours of heroic combat, the convent suddenly returns to its heavy silence, just as when the monks used to return to their cells after afternoon prayers. High up one of the walls a white flag appears, since nothing can be done. The Mexican soldiers abandon their strongholds, come down from the walls, and stand in formation in the center of the courtyard, all at attention. Twiggs arrives and recognizes the courage of the vanquished. He directs a question to General Anaya:

"Where are the munitions?"

General Anaya looks at him with penetrating eyes and responds in an unwavering voice:

"If we had munitions, you would not be here."

He should have clarified:

"What Santa Anna left us is nineteen-weight bullets, useless for our guns."

A summary military trial was immediately exercised against the Irish and several members of the Saint Patrick Battalion were hanged. Others were whipped or branded with the letter "D" to identify them with the infamy of being deserters.

At Molino del Rey it was the same story—a farce marked with real blood. Scott's spies informed him that next to Chapultepec Park there was a foundry in which the city's bells were being transformed into cannon barrels, and that there was a large storage of gunpowder in a place called Casa Mata. Attack that house, destroy every instrument of battle which could not be transported and return as quickly as possible to the headquarters were Scott's succinct instructions. Eight hundred invaders attacked the locale in the early hours of the morning of September 8, captured three cannons and began their retreat.

But Colonel Manuel Echegaray and his five hundred men of the Third Light Battalion left their positions to pursue the

Yankees. He recovered the cannons. He came within shooting distance of enemy lines and asked desperately for support to attack. The cavalry of General Juan Álvarez, stationed in the Los Morales *hacienda*, was sent by Santa Anna to engage in combat "at the opportune moment." But the libretto stated otherwise, and the order was never given nor did the cavalry move, "they were not supposed to move," struck by the same illness of pretense as the president. Things being so, Colonel Echegaray agreed to return to Molino del Rey with the recovered cannons, which caused no small stir of jubilation among the troops. When tragedy is being staged, any accomplishment, however modest, should be interpreted as encouraging and cause new, although ultimately painful, hope.

The next day, the Americans reorganize into three columns. One attacks Echegaray and is rebuffed. The second attacks Casa Mata and is also turned back. The mission of the third is to stop the cavalry which Santa Anna sent to Los Morales *hacienda*. However, since Santa Anna had cast mere extras in this cavalry, they do not move, remaining "dishonorably immobile," and as a result the American column splits up to provide reinforcements for the other two columns. In new attacks, the Yankees achieve victory.

"Don Marcos, how could the librettist have allowed this to happen?" I asked. "Because you and I know that Something or Someone not us is writing this drama in which you and I and everyone meeting here, along with everyone fighting on the outskirts of the city, is merely a character with an assigned role, but notably absent is the hand of the author of the play. Who could have possibly conceived of this horrid play of which we manage to catch mere superficial glimpses? Each scene is woven into a bigger whole, and the fabric consists of every battle, every fallen hero and survivor, each triumph or defeat, each figure which appears on the stage before or after us."

"I understand. Santa Anna is simply a terrible tragicomic actor. But who in hell cast him in our play in a role that affects so many innocent people?"

"Who?"

And the biggest tragedy, Chapultepec, was still fully to develop, so my friends had not yet heard of it.

My wife asks, "What was it that José Zorilla wrote about Chapultepec Castle?"

I find the citation and read it to her:

Whoever has not seen Mexico City from Chapultepec Castle has not seen the Earth from the privileged balcony of Paradise.

"That must have been so tragic for those young cadets whose lives ended there, don't you think? The instant prior to the battle when they contemplated, even if just for a moment, life from the most beautiful spot in our valley. Write that down."

"I'll write that you told me to write it."

"Fine, but say it. Imagine what it must have been like for those youth to die there, at that precise spot."

"It seems worse to have died for a country in which honor had been abolished and cowardice enthroned."

Besieged by an enormous enemy (in every sense) which they could not overcome, abandoned to their fate (Santa Anna, naturally, was in the National Palace: he already knew the denouement of the play), those young cadets, who were between thirteen and twenty years old, resisted the invading force despite the authorization they had been given to retreat if they should so desire, if they should so choose, if their instinct for survival so dictated. One of them, Felipe Santiago Xicoténcatl, died as the code of honor dictated—wrapped in a Mexican flag—from fourteen separate bullet wounds.

Early in the morning of September 13, Scott gave the order to take the strategic point General Nicolás Bravo was defending. Amidst the ruins of the castle—they had been bombing it for twelve straight hours—and the pounded hilltop, there were only two options: to flee shamefully as many other soldiers had done the night before, or die. The first option had been illustrated over and over by General Santa Anna himself; the second option was the option of a dutiful, patriotic soldier. In that absurd war against the United States, many Mexicans faithfully fulfilled their commitment, but the combatants of Chapultepec deserve special commendation because they knew that they were the last combatants of the army who would be able to do so, who still had that obligation, because the invader was at the very gates of the besieged city. In addition, in a very practical way, abandoning Chapultepec meant leaving one of the main sources of the city's water in the hands of the enemy. Scott could merely have blocked off the aqueduct to kill us for lack of water.

The motifs so familiar in the unrelenting tragedy of our history seem to have been perfected in Chapultepec: fear, desertion, improvisation, clumsiness, avarice brandished like a right, simulation, but above all else, in a superlative degree, heroism.

The Yankee sharpshooters advanced through the forest. A wave of birds flew off from the trees as if to announce what was happening. In addition to gunshots, cannon fire rang out, followed by flurries of rocks careening down the hill and sounding like an earthquake. Blue uniforms climbed the hill like lizards, appeared and disappeared behind *ahuehuete* trees nearly a thousand years old, and simultaneously brought the forest to life and a contrasting death. Many of them stayed on the flanks, but other soldiers in blue advanced, advanced relentlessly, like actors on the set of a harrowing nightmare, but a nightmare which does not wake the person sleeping.

One column moving upward toward the castle was turned back by Felipe Santiago Xicoténcatl and his faithful companions of the San Blas Battalion. But only temporarily. The fire from our arms slowly became lighter and lighter and the dense clouds of smoke started to lift. Quitman's troops surged forcefully with their bayonets flailing, as if emerging from the earth itself, and took the castle. Among its final defenders were the students of the Military Academy who fired their final cartridges, engaged in hand-to-hand combat and heroically gave themselves over to death. "To that death which is not death, because its cause is higher than life itself," as Victor Hugo wrote.

What I feared most was becoming reality. My secret plan—
to die while embracing Isabel, holed up in my house, with
my eyes closed tight so as not to see the Yankees when they
invaded—had failed because of my clumsiness, a simple act of
carelessness which unleashed fate.

Having gathered information on the events of the preced-
ing weeks, I tried to continue my chronicle, but it turned into
such a mass of unconnected and unfinished ideas and events—
there were far too many unanswered questions because of my
flight to that *other* world—that I decided to destroy it. Pages
and pages were blackened and consumed in just a few seconds
by the providential effects of the chimney's flames to which
they were condemned that very night.

But then I slept several hours and kept writing. What else
could I possibly do to avoid a complete breakdown, with a dagger pointing at my heart, my nervous disorder out of control,
reverting to a fetal position and possessed by the devil? But no
one could have vouched for my condition, since even insane
asylums had been converted into temporary hospitals for the
troops.

Early that morning I was still writing when my driver came
into the study and announced what I had so feared, what
my hallucinations and the lights had announced to me for
months.

"Sir, it appears the Yankees are here."

I put down my pen and prepared to leave.

My driver asked with a most austere gesture, "Don't you
want to take some kind of weapon, sir?"

"A weapon? Me?"

"I believe it would be most prudent, sir, if you will pardon
the suggestion."

I thought it over a moment and then took from the center
drawer of the desk the marble-handled knife which, hours earlier, I had pressed against my own chest.

PART
THREE

I

The sound of the final cannon shot was like a signal to
General Scott from Santa Anna to enter the city.

CARLOS MARÍA DE BUSTAMANTE

✠ HAT MORNING OF September 14, 1847, even the sun
seemed to have interrupted its illusory orbital movement and for a good stretch crowned the thick treetops in
the Alameda. The ruddy sphere, suspiciously weightless, cast
the city in a discordant yellowish tone. At that moment, when
things looked like they were inside a trembling gelatin, we saw
the first Yankees parade past us.

It was worse than the worst of my hallucinations.

Among the haughty generals donning their parade uniforms with white plumes and gold stripes, riding their gleaming horses, their unfurled flags showing off pieces of the
sky—an emblem of their insatiable ambition—to the sound
of drums and bugles, and with pennants waving and fire-
arms sparkling, they tried to hide what could not be hidden:
the disastrous appearance of the mass of troops, the aura of
infamy in which it marched, and the human degradation which
bordered on bestial.

They were enormous, freckled, absolutely unrefined and
seemed on the verge of exploding with their red complexions.
They marched with long, ostentatious goose steps, wearing
blue jackets with gold buttons, rather dirty and ragged. Their
neckerchiefs, their kepis with square visors, their backpacks
and thick cartridge belts were all splattered with mud. Many
of them were limping, had their arms in slings or their heads
bandaged, or displayed open wounds. Others were eating raw
squash, tomatoes, yams, crusts of bread, or drinking directly
from bottles. They constantly spit on the ground.

These were our new masters.

The sun glowed on their faces; they whispered to each other in the haughty tones of people who know themselves conquerors, and when they noticed us—insignificant, slack-jawed, clumsy—they smiled or laughed openly like an audience at a circus.

We ran behind them, following them to the Zócalo.

On the way, balcony doors opened to wave an American flag, to offer greetings, smiles, kisses, roses, dahlias, carnations or perfumed handkerchiefs.

A shiver of contempt ran through me, contempt for my city and everyone in it—why were we allowing this to happen? I felt particular contempt for those damned people who, now I really, vividly felt it, and not just as a literary metaphor, were rolling over and even welcoming the demons of the Antichrist.

It crushed my heart to see that delirious, aimless multitude follow their kidnappers down Plateros Street, moving like a huge, uncoordinated animal.

The crowd consisted mostly of the dregs of society, but here and there I could see a hat, a cane, or a dress which betrayed a "decent" individual.

From the Zócalo came the sound of a growing, fluctuating, murmuring crowd.

Most of the people congregated in the center of the square, but others spread out into every nook and cranny, wandered through the archways, climbed the ash trees, lingered on the sides of the streets, climbed onto the rooftops or bunched together in windows.

The voices turned into a jumble of predictions based on remembrances, and each new prediction seemed to increase the sensation of horror and justify the anger we were feeling. From time to time we could hear loud sighs, far more painful than any complaint.

The entire plaza vibrated and every sound echoed in magnified, sonorous tones.

We all had our eyes glued on the National Palace because we'd heard that General Scott had already taken possession of it, and that before long he would appear on the balcony to deliver us a message.

I reflected on how the foundations of that same palace had registered the voices of Montezuma, Cortés and the first viceroys. Not long ago it had heard other cries, with crowds like this one gathered in the plaza, such as, "Long live the army of the Three Guarantees!" "Long live independent Mexico!" "Long live the Plan of Iguala!" And then, seven months later, "Long live Agustín the First! Long live the Emperor and death to Congress!" The walls still echoed with more recent cries: "Long live General Santa Anna! Long live the father of the Republic!"

This is the plaza in which the great monument to our independence was to be erected.

Indignantly, we heard the grave lament of the Cathedral's main bell, swelling and then bursting like a golden bubble in the morning's vehement air.

Suddenly I could hardly breathe. An agony seemed to pervade everything. I thought that I was going to die, right there, surrounded by inquisitive, stunned, broken faces. But it wasn't me or my body that was going to fall completely apart, I realized. It was the world.

I blinked over and over, then opened my eyes as best I could. Vertigo took hold of me. Figures came near, disappeared, or became fuzzy. Things changed sizes.

But no, it wasn't just that my ability to perceive was wavering, the fact was that at that moment General Scott had appeared on the balcony of the National Palace. He was huge, arrogant, wearing a dark blue uniform with glistening stripes and medals, and he started to address us in a moving speech ... in English!

"Mexicans, dear Mexican people! Listen to me! We have come, we are here to save you from your politicians who can never come to a point with one another; we have come to save you from the corrupted Mexican army ...!"

The crowd's discontent was made known through a nearly deafening whistling. A poor woman near me worked her arms like a windmill as she shouted:

"We're gonna crack your head open, you filthy bag of bones! The least you can do is talk to us in Christian!"

Or:

"You foul Protestant! Go back to the hell you came from!"

Another voice was even more earthy:

"We'll see whether you keep speaking English when I personally break your balls!"

There were all sorts of shouts, but each had the same tenor and was tinged with the same anger:

"Go home, Yankee son of a bitch!"

"Go ahead and keep talking, idiot! What do we care since we can't understand a word you're saying!"

"Who do you think you are, asshole?"

"We're gonna kick your butt all the way home!"

One man in rags yelled something quite profound:

"Get out of here, damned Yankees! Here we are, dying of hunger, and you come to take away our last crusts of bread!"

Some started a chant:

"One, two, three ... Hey, Yankees! Go fuck your mothers!"

Cries against Santa Anna started to bubble up as well:

"Where's Santa Anna?"

"He left. They say he left the city!"

"The coward left us here alone!"

"Santa Anna should fuck his mother, too!"

"Hey, Santa Anna! Go fuck your mother!"

The gestures these people used to convey their sentiments were as expressive as the words they accompanied.

Santa Anna, who had indeed fled from the city at the head of an army of four thousand men on horseback and five thousand on foot, would later write in his memoirs, *My Military and Political History*:

The people of Mexico City failed to resist the imposing presence of the invaders, who proudly took possession of the city. The people gathered together, started to form into small groups, and slowly became angry at the notoriously arrogant nature of the Americans.

It was the people who took action against that arrogance without any help from Santa Anna and his army.

In a corner of the plaza, standing on a bench, a man put his thumb and index finger into his mouth and produced a whistle so shrill it forced all of us to turn toward him. It was Próspero Pérez, who had a reputation as an orator of the masses. With his eyes flashing and his long disheveled hair, he looked all around with disgust and finally asked, in a powerful voice:

"Are there no men here?"

Then he yelled it again. And then again and again:

"I'm asking are there no men here! By my way of thinking, men—real men, that is—wouldn't allow themselves to get screwed and just stand by and do nothing. You're getting screwed and then some. It's as if every single Yankee entering this city is throwing his crap at you. Their very presence does it. Can't you see? You should at least look up and see it. Damn, it's falling right on your heads and you don't even see it. The women did and that's why they are actually setting an example for us with their determined attitude and shouts. Listen to them! They're yelling 'Out with the Yankee shit!' And you so-called men, are you going to just sit there with your arms crossed as you get covered with crap from head to toe?"

Someone responded, "What are we supposed to do? What can we do to keep that shit from falling on us, Próspero?"

His response was blunt and put an exclamation point on his rant:

"Aren't the very rocks from the building rooftops here calling to us? Listen to them! They're saying, 'What are you waiting for if we are right here and ready? Use me! With my patriotic help, beat the hell out of the Yankee invaders!'"

His speech ended exactly when a Yankee soldier raised the American flag over the National Palace. Many of us practically stopped breathing. Enraged shouting mixed with muffled moans and sobs, although plenty of people chose to put their heads in the sand and not look at all.

However, the Yankee soldier failed to complete his task, because when the flag was at half-mast, a very accurate bullet coming from a nearby rooftop cut him down.

When they saw his body collapse like a marionette whose strings have been cut, and the American flag at about half mast, the multitude let out a prolonged howl and attacked the Yankee soldiers who were on both foot and horseback near the doors of the Palace.

There was no place to take cover, so even the densest and most fearful of us realized that it was impossible to retreat, that we were being swept by a wave of people, that we could go only one direction, even if we thought we were headed toward an abyss.

"Death to the Yankees!"

The crowd turned into a huge animal, clumsy but brutally impulsive, headless and disjointed.

Children got caught in the torrent of people, and those who lost their balance and fell couldn't get up and were trampled. They were the first to start crying.

Who would have supposed just a few minutes earlier, as we watched them parade down Plateros, that those huge, haughty Yankee soldiers, so blond, laughing at us like they were an audience at a circus, would end up running terrified in every direction, driven by the crowd? Their weapons couldn't protect them for long because the masses fell upon them in increasing waves.

"Death to the Yankees!"

There was total chaos and confusion. The columns and battalions seemed to have disintegrated. In their frantic retreat like frightened ants, Yankee soldiers threw down their weapons, hats, sword sheaths and ammunition belts.

Some Yankees were pulled from their horses and thrown to the ground, and then the people showed them no mercy. A riderless horse with three hoofs and a bloody stump seemed to be trying to bite its own tail in a crazed frenzy.

My entire being was filled with uncertainty. Fear overcame me and I started running to get out of the plaza, bent over, out of joint, my head in a fog, thinking as if in a trance that one of those bullets which I heard intermittently was destined for me, that I was running toward it and could do nothing about it. Or that one of those glimmering knives or bayonets was waiting to put an end to my shameful actions. Many times I tripped, slipped, was pushed, fell, got up and caught my balance. I felt keenly ridiculous to flee that way, so clumsy and unable to stay on my feet.

"Death to the Yankees!"

I was covered with dirt and sweating profusely. My teeth were chattering and my fists were clenched so tightly my fingers hurt.

One time when I fell I managed to see—inside a cloud of dust—a group of women scratching, biting, stripping and spitting on a Yankee soldier, who seemed in shock and writhed as if in convulsions.

Another soldier seemed already dead. A sticky white substance oozed between the curls of his blond hair, and his face—a brutal face which death had not yet altered—was covered in blood. A pair of poor, wretched people stared at him in fascination, as if he were still warm prey. They nudged him with their feet again and again, a bit fearful he might come back to life and arise.

One woman hung a Yankee soldier's bloody underwear on the end of a pole and, laughing and jumping around, brandished it like a triumphal banner.

Everything was happening as if in a dream. The struggles, the fighting between adversaries, the shouts, the gunshots and the scattered corpses were all real images, belonging to the world of real reality, so to speak, but they hovered in a kind of fog.

"Death to the Yankees!"

I was about to leave the plaza when the hand of a wounded Yankee soldier grabbed my ankle and I finished him off with my knife. I decided to leave it in his chest so that it wouldn't end up in mine, considering the way Isabel had abandoned me.

At that moment the entire city ignited in a sudden blaze, infected by a sun which precisely just then was opening a sumptuous peacock tail over the horizon, a horizon terribly distant to those of us in the capital.

The American army found in the common people of Mexico City its fiercest opponent since stepping on Mexican soil. It must be recognized that in addition to fighting the Yankees like demons, the common people and the more than one thousand prisoners Santa Anna ordered freed from the jails of Acordada and Santiago Tlatelolco, looted a fair number of offices and businesses.

As Melchor Ocampo wrote, it was impossible for Mexico to resist the Yankee army with its own army. Instead, defense by the common people was the most effective way:

Since it is not in the cards for us to imitate the barbarous but heroic and sublime courage with which the Russians razed their sacred capital in 1812, let us at least imitate the tactic shown us by our fathers and our people in the glorious struggle for Independence ... Peace for Mexico City would only be a seal of disgrace, the best possible condition for the new conqueror. In a word, it would be reverting to a state even worse than that of its own black slaves.

II

War, blood, extermination, revenge—not peace purchased
with an insult, flashing a smoking sword from the rubble
of omnipresent death. Not shameful, cowardly peace, but
blood, fire, extermination, revenge, and in the din of the
awful slaughter the sound of law being dictated to the
vanquished.

JOSÉ MARÍA ESTEVA

AFTER WALKING LIKE a zombie for hours through the
streets and alleyways near the Zócalo, to the outer limits
of the conflict, I finally found my carriage and returned home
immediately.

The rest of the day I stayed in front of my fireplace, drinking wine and smoking, with my cheek quite swollen thanks to
the blow the fallen Yankee had given me. My hands trembled,
shivers ran up and down my spine like snakes, and I had to
inch closer and closer to the fire to warm the ice I felt in my
gut. At some point I nodded off and had a dream which has
recurred from time to time throughout my entire life. I'm at
the edge of one of the city's canals and there is a large sun
perched in the sky. The entire canal is a sun, an immense, chaotic knife which lashes at my eyes, while above me a very blue
sky presses down forcefully against my neck and shoulders,
forcing me to look without ceasing at the water. Suddenly I see
in the distance a naked body oscillating gently to free itself
from the rushes in the canal, then it finally manages to make
its way to the bank where I find myself. The sun illuminates
its cadaverous face, so pale that it is nearly transparent. It has
wide-open blue eyes, the same eyes the Yankee soldier had
when I stabbed him with my dagger. The thing that torments
me about the dream is that, despite the cadaverous face, those

eyes are alive, very alive, and they always look at me imploringly, pleadingly. But I have never managed to figure out what they want.

In the evening I went out onto the roof to contemplate the city which was illuminated by intermittent lights—very similar to the lights I saw in my premonitions—little red stars which must have been gunshots or puffs of fire from cannons or houses that burned like straw.

There was a growing noise, something like a wave about to break upon the beach.

The sky was vividly clean, decorated with stars which contrasted with the tumult and agony—agony above all else—here below.

The entire city buzzed.

I imagined—oh, how naïve I was—that Santa Anna had returned with his army to defend us from the invaders. But no, it was nothing more than members of the National Guard and the common people of the city engaged in battle. The former had arms and ammunition and were located in strategic locations—waiting for opportunities to shoot American soldiers who were madly circulating around the city, some on foot and others on horseback, seeking to weed out the rebels.

The only weapons the common people had were fingernails, teeth, rocks—those rocks which, according to Próspero Pérez, were beckoning us to fight—sticks, machetes, sling shots, bottles, flower pots and even butter knives. Boiling water and oil thrown from windows was one of the most common practices and one which inflicted the most damage. People created barricades of stones, but also of dressers, tables, chairs, beds and crates.

I knew that night I wouldn't be able to shut my eyes, so I asked my driver to take me to the Hospital of San Pedro and San Pablo, which, on the outskirts of the city, would be more easily accessible.

III

I learned that in the main plaza there was a regiment of
enemy troops occupying the Palace and that on its roof
the American flag was waving, but truth be told, I did not
have the courage to go and see for myself.

CARLOS MARÍA DE BUSTAMANTE

DR. URRUCHÚA HAD LOST so much weight that his pants
were baggy and his shirt slid all over his body. His lack of
weight and color seemed to have accentuated the turbulence
in his eyes behind his foggy glasses. He embraced me warmly
without asking a lot of questions, as if we had seen each other
the day before. After walking down a dismal hallway, he showed
me the back wing of the hospital housing the injured who had
most recently arrived, of which there was a multitude.

The friends and relatives of the injured waited in a foyer
outside the patient rooms. Dr. Urruchúa could scarcely pass
through them: here and there they tugged on his white gown,
made demands, begged him to tend to their victims and
demanded that he brief them as they couldn't wait a moment
longer to know more. They sobbed and wrung their hands, or
doubled them into menacing fists.

The majority of the wounded were common people, many
of them women and children. There weren't enough stretch-
ers so they had to improvise with sticks and sheets. Some of
the patients were simply carried on people's backs. They put
them on the floor, lined up like packages, ten, fifteen and up to
twenty per room. The smell of urine and excrement was nauseating.

The wounded grunted, cried, cursed and emitted muffled
complaints as if in a monotonous choir of lamentations. Some
of them dragged themselves around, others pushed each other,

yet others ripped off their bandages. A few women wanted to go out and get some fresh air, while others just wanted to die. The most shrill cries came from the children, who otherwise slept curled up in little balls despite the gravity of their wounds.

The Yankee onslaughts had severed fingers and hands, had opened wounds, like one little girl who'd lost her leg in an explosion. As he helped her to breathe in some salts, Dr. Urruchúa asked me how she could still be alive.

He then asked some of his assistants to take the dead—which he identified with a simple glance—to the rear courtyards where, at his order, they would be burned. What else could we do with them, he asked me, his face dejected, consumed with sadness and a painful tenderness, unable to process the responsibility which had suddenly been thrust upon him. During the days when I did not see him, Dr. Urruchúa not only lost several kilos, but he aged several years as well. Stretch marks covered his face, grey peppered his hair and his body conveyed the distinct impression of fragility.

He gave the order and, yielding to the fire, the corpses piled atop each other started to blacken, then crackle, then bend as if coming back to life for a moment, their hair in flames.

It broke my heart to see that Dantesque spectacle; at the same time, just under the surface, a disturbing concern gnawed at me: how long could Dr. Urruchúa stay upright since, as he confessed to me, he had not eaten or slept for days?

At one point he pulled me aside to ask a favor. His opaque, tired eyes took on new life and started to gleam. He said that among the wounded was a very special person, a Spanish priest by the name of Celedonio Domeco Jarauta who had led the guerrilla warfare in Veracruz, and that very morning had shot, from a rooftop near the Palace, the Yankee soldier trying to raise the American flag over the National Palace. Had I heard about that? With pride I replied that I had seen it with my own eyes. He said that if the Yankees were to find him there in the hospital they would immediately recognize him—there were posters with the image of his face everywhere—take him prisoner and inflict on him unimaginable torture. Could I just imagine? I shuddered. Dr. Urruchúa must have seen it, because he quickly asked me point-blank whether I could take him to my home for a few days. After all, he pointed out, I was living alone, I was in a position to tend to his injuries and, perhaps, I could even allow him to receive some visits from a few of his guerrilla comrades who had come with him from Veracruz. Dr. Urruchúa pointed out that it was impossible for he himself to leave the hospital. He then raised his open hand to make a point. It emerged from the sleeve of his hospital gown along with his forearm, which looked like a pale snake. He said that he realized, naturally, should I accept I would be placing my own life in danger.

My heart skipped a beat. I would be placing my own life in danger, but I couldn't say no.

"I read something about him. He is a remarkable man. It will be a privilege to have him in my home, to help heal his wounds, and to receive his companions. My servants and driver are completely trustworthy, I can assure you of that."

IV

The affronts we have suffered at Mexico's hand since it achieved independence and the patient tolerance we have exercised have no parallel in the history of modern civilized nations.

JAMES K. POLK, DECEMBER 1846

FATHER JARAUTA'S HEAD was bandaged and during the trip to my house in Tacubaya he remained silent and kept his eyes closed. I arranged for him to stay in a hard old bed in the attic, surrounded by scuffed chests-of-drawers, chairs with one leg shorter than the others, tarnished and ghostly mirrors, enormous trunks and books with pages falling out. One of my servants swept and dusted as quickly as she could and helped me to change the bandage on Father Jarauta's head. We followed Dr. Urruchúa's directions as best we were able. The wound itself was large, but not deep, even though it had rendered him unconscious for several hours. We also gave him some arnica and administered smelling salts. My servant sent up a dish with honey, a little cheese and a bottle of wine. She then left the two of us alone.

Suddenly moonlight entered the room obliquely through a little window high in the attic roof. It absorbed the oil lamp's yellowish light and illuminated the dust suspended in the air.

He had the face of a man who had survived a terrible test, a fact crystal clear to me: his large watery, hazel eyes and thick eyebrows, his irises striated, marked with long dark spots that almost looked like tobacco stains. He had a hooked nose (*El Monitor* called it a "bird beak"). His cheeks were darkened by several days' growth of beard. His thick head of dark hair met his faded cassock at the neck, the cloth marked by blood and oil stains, and I saw that he was wearing beneath it unhemmed pants and shepherd's sandals that covered his filthy feet and their long toenails.

When we changed the bandage on his head, his entire body tensed up in what seemed to be a combination of pain, defiance, impotence, rage and nostalgia. But he didn't show any of that openly, and he made a forced effort to smile, turning up the corners of his mouth. He thanked us continually, his eyes blinking nervously, and he lowered his head ever so slightly.

He allowed me to help him remove his cassock—at times it seemed like I was pulling off his skin—then he ate and drank what we brought him and covered himself with a blanket.

He told me that the next day, very early, some of his companions would be coming to see him. He said that the doctor had given them detailed directions to my house, and they couldn't possibly get lost. (My stomach did an involuntary flip.)

He said that if it weren't for the head wound which made him lose consciousness for so long, that if he still had even an ounce of energy, he'd be fighting with his companions, that the Yankees were already familiar, very familiar, with how effective his brand of fighting was from the guerrilla warfare he and his followers had waged in Veracruz that kept the enemy permanently in check, hundreds of them killed, that lately the newspapers were understating numbers and even suppressing facts.

I put another pillow under his head and he cast me a red, watery look guarded by his heavy eyelids. Strands of light from the oil lamp intertwined in the thick hair on the back of his hand.

I asked him about the soldier who tried to raise the American flag that morning, the one he had shot with one expertly aimed bullet from a rooftop adjoining the Palace. He clicked his tongue and said, "That event was trivial and petty. As spectacular as it may have seemed to the people who witnessed it, we need to focus on bringing down the Yankees, if possible every Yankee who has stepped onto or will step onto Mexican soil. Not a single one should remain standing. Not a one!"

It was a premonitory sign that, like so many others, he had received from above.

He spoke in such a feverish tone—sometimes he had to take a breath between sentences, reinforcing his words with gestures or grimaces—that I was afraid he would leap out of bed and run to the city to join his companions. I'm convinced that he was on the verge of doing just that, so I patted him on the shoulder, insisted he get some rest, reminded him according to the doctor his injury had been really serious, and told him he should try to sleep. I was falling asleep myself. But then the wine must have given him a spark of energy, and his words were so compelling that we stayed up talking until dawn.

Just as the fight against Islam had occupied the thoughts of St. Ignatius during his youth, it had become the priest's obsession to help Mexicans fight against the Yankee infidel, something only a Jesuit would do. He urged me to remember the role of the Jesuits during the Counter Reformation, and that the event which created a sense of identity and rebellion throughout Spanish America was the decision of the monarchs to expel the Jesuits from Spain and her colonies. That alone had created a reaction which gave new impetus to the rebellion, as it had in every place from which they were expelled. That is why Michelet said that if they stopped a man in the street and asked what he associated with the Jesuits, the inevitable response was "revolution." Freedom was one of the key words in the teachings of their founder. They had brought modernity to the New World, and they sponsored the studies which opened our eyes. Instead of hunkering down in scholasticism, they wrested power from the adherents of the teachings of St. Thomas who had dominated political thought.

Mystically integrated into the militant discipline imposed by Loyola, they set out on their mission, leaving behind all prior social and family ties, which they considered mere weaknesses of the flesh. Any material possessions they may have had ended up with the poor, mirroring what St. Ignatius did in Montserrat: exchanging his elegant clothes for those of a beggar before he began his pilgrimage. Regarding rituals, they were frugal to a fault and did away with ostentatious and pompous ceremonies, dedicating very little time to fasts and vigils which would weaken their bodies. They didn't waste their efforts feigning fictitious piousness, but were totally dedicated to the development of the spirit and, most particularly, of the intellect. They established schools instead of convents. Their lives were not sustained by alms, but by their own labor. And most importantly, they had dispersed to every continent to spread the message of Jesus. On more than one occasion all of this had led to conflicts not only with political governments but with popes themselves, at whose pleasure they officially served. Although that permission did not bear conditions and was a fundamental part of their order, they felt loyalty to the office of the Pontiff and to him as a person. Hence, they did not strive to show faithfulness and obedience to any particular pope, but to the supreme figure of the ecclesiastical hierarchy, to whoever occupied the throne of St. Peter, the highest representative of Jesus Christ on Earth.

Father Jarauta's voice was forceful but halting, resulting in long periods of silence which seemed appropriate to the story-line. They created an intense counterpoint and also helped the story to gel, finally settling like ash in the dense attic air.

The attitude and testimony he was sharing, along with his brethren, flew in the face of the concept many other Catholics held, which reduced Christianity to a sentimental "devotion-ism" (routine confessions and communions, nightly rosaries, chest-thumping, novenas, processions), or "angelism," bland and sickly sweet, in which truly pious people should become detached from tragic and raw temporal realities, from social injustices, and even worse, from the clear and ever more over-whelming manifestations of Evil, like what we were living at that moment in Mexico City.

We must not allow it: the clear intent of the Yankees was to take control of Mexico, exterminate its inhabitants, then con-quer the rest of Latin America, imposing the same barbarous domination, with the flag of the stars and stripes as its only symbol. They would then jump to Europe, subdue it also, do away with its culture and traditions, to conclude its long and sinister march in ... the Vatican, which they would invade.

"The Lapdog of the Antichrist who has come to Earth to find converts," I said.

"Yes!" he exclaimed, without a shred of doubt.

He added that every Jesuit was to be a soldier of Christ in this struggle. Were we shocked by the violence which they displayed in special cases? Remember that passage in the autobiography of St. Ignatius when he had just begun his pilgrimage on a donkey and he came across a Moor on the road to Manresa. They started a pleasant conversation, but when St. Ignatius mentioned the virginity of Mary, the Moor, not believing, let out a mocking laugh, and sped away on his horse. St. Ignatius wavered for a moment in his courage, but then reacted. A soldier of Christ could not allow a loathsome Moor to mock, just like that, the virginity of Mary. He decided to catch the Moor and pummel him with his fists. But he knew that a fundamental part of his recent conversion was to temper his violent character, so he decided to place the matter in Christ's hands. At the next fork in the road he loosened the reins and had the donkey choose the path they would follow. If it ended up being the same path as the Moor's, he would extract vengeance; otherwise he would resign himself to let it go. Happily, the latter happened. What if the opposite had occurred? Would St. Ignatius have been less saintly if, as he fully intended to do, he had pummeled the Moor with his fists?

The same character trait, that intolerance which was never fully tempered, that very broad concept of freedom, even led St. Ignatius to flirt with the idea of suicide on one of his strict retreats to a monastery, enticed by the temptation of throwing himself into a well. Did I know what had stopped him? First, his relationship with Christ, with whom he spoke aloud and to whom he confessed his weaknesses as he could never have done with anyone else; and second, his vocation for what would become the central pillar of his doctrine: contemplation, especially of a starry sky. This is what he wrote: "Contemplation of the starry sky always returns strength to my soul." That is where he found strength in his moments of greatest weakness. As he said this, Father Jarauta leaned his head slightly back to look through the small window in the attic ceiling at a bit of the sky, where a handful of stars were flickering blue.

Far from being a saint, I felt more like a circus clown who looks with his white face toward the black opening in the tent, his only contact with a starry sky like the one we were seeing at that moment. But for a moment, perhaps without him even being aware, it alters his sad condition of being a clown.

Without taking his eyes from the little window, Father Jarauta asked, "Have you noticed how orphan stars, the ones that have no part in a constellation, seem sadder and give off less light? From the very beginning man must have felt that each constellation was like a clan or race. Haven't you ever noticed that on certain nights, nights like this one, a kind of war is being waged up there, an unbearable set of tensions, something terrible yet marvelously alive and palpitating?"

He finished with a reflection which staggered me when I related it to what was happening at that very instant in our city:

"The opposite of death is not transcendence, or even immortality. The opposite of death is fraternity. We need to think of the Crucifixion as a mere act of fraternity."

X

The great advantage of the United States is that everyone there speaks English. Here, within a radius of fifty
leagues, up to ten languages are spoken. That is why our
strength, a strength much greater than the strength of
arms, will come through the spread of Spanish.

IGNACIO MANUEL ALTAMIRANO

M Y SERVANT ALERTED US when the companions of
Father Jarauta arrived. They nearly toppled the house,
arriving as if in a stampede. Dawn was scarcely a greenish-
blue light. Father Jarauta nearly lost his balance standing up.
He asked me for some water to sprinkle on his face, carefully
avoiding his bandage. His cassock put a new shine into his
eyes. When he went down to the drawing room where his companions were waiting, the change was stunning: his look, his
hands, all of his skin seemed to be effervescent.

More than eighty people were in the group, including several women and priests, some wearing cassocks and others
dressed as civilians. There were farmers and beggars, but also
a few young people dressed very nicely, among them several
who said they were studying medicine. There were peons from
haciendas and workers from the outskirts of the city who work
one day with adobe and the next as water carriers or animal
herders. There were people who scrape out a living by gathering and selling small bundles of firewood and charcoal or by
killing rabbits. An old Spanish business owner, quite a talker,
surprised me when he invited us to his store to show us the
arsenal he kept there; he was a real jewel for this war. Some of
them, a very small percentage, carried rifles, knives and other
arms which they displayed with great ostentation. I saw anxiety,
terror and enthusiasm in their darkened, sleep-deprived faces.
They rubbed their eyes, made gestures, laughed hysterically or

171

comforted each other. Some of them never stopped talking, and they interrupted each other constantly.

They had spent the entire night killing Yankees—there was a large number of people scattered throughout the city attacking the Yankees with whatever means they could find, especially rocks and sticks—but they had also suffered numerous casualties. They mentioned the names of some of their fallen comrades, and Father Jarauta offered a prayer in their memory, followed by a moment of general silence.

The city council was desperately trying to re-establish order by publishing and posting notices demanding order on city streets, but no one paid them the least attention.

Someone who stealthily followed the Yankees from their Belén outpost reported that he could observe their progress by the cloud of dust they kicked up, and saw with his own eyes how they treated the people they came across with great cruelty, including women and children; he saw how they used the butts of their guns, axes and picks to knock down doors and then furiously attack the people's faces and bodies.

By contrast, in the San Antonio outpost near the place where a group of released prisoners from the Santiago Tlatelolco jail had taken refuge, someone else found American soldiers and horses scattered in the fields, their bodies viciously ravaged, with dismembered body parts lying amidst the rocks and potholes in the path. Some of the horses were wounded and in agony, shaking their long necks. A Yankee who was crawling through the mud, his bleeding hand clenched like a claw, pled for help. Purely out of compassion, he told us, our comrade simply finished him off.

People from the Callejón de López—a locale of ill repute which serves, rumor has it, as a refuge to the finest whores of the city—went out of their way to provoke the Americans, seeking to lure them into a difficult part of town. When they would succumb, even the children from the area would attack them, inflicting nasty bite wounds. In the western part of the city known as San Diego and around the section called La Acordada, a group of women who lived in an old building decided to throw vats of boiling oil from their windows at a passing company of Yankees. The soldiers hopped, hollered, twisted around and rolled on the ground like worms trying to take off the clothes burnt to their bodies.

Suddenly nervous laughter and mournful complaints ensued.

The fiercest battles were fought near churches and convents. Many "decent" folk also took to the streets and fought resolutely, while others expecting the worst improvised barricades inside their homes, and yet others blocked their doorways or abandoned their houses and the city altogether, taking nothing but the clothes they were wearing, such as what happened in Tacuba and Santa Clara, where Yankee forces suffered over two hundred casualties.

They say that when Scott was informed of the Yankee deaths in that area, he exclaimed, "I thought those people were with us!"

To which he received the response: "Not all of them!"

Yankee forces surrounded the convent of Santa Isabel to attack the rebels of Tacuba from the west, but their movements were discovered by a group of medical students. They spread the word and sharpshooters from the Juan Carbonero neighborhood arrived and almost entirely annihilated the invaders. Many of the patriots had turned the Minería Palace into their military base. Groups of students were seen there assembling ammunition while young ladies gave them bread and coffee.

But it was inevitable that the Yankee response became increasingly brutal. Impotent, disconcerted, they started to fire their cannons on the surrounding neighborhoods, regardless of the civilian population.

"They didn't leave a single house standing in Netzahualcóyotl."

One comment gave me chills:

"Yesterday afternoon the city government received a communication from General Scott warning that they would bomb the entire city if city officials did not do something to contain the rebels."

Father Jarauta asked, "Is that what he said? That they would bomb the entire city?" A flash of alarm crossed his eyes.

"Word for word. I have a very reliable source. And I have no doubt they are capable of carrying out their threat. Their casualties are now in the thousands and I bet their pride is severely injured."

"We need to pick up our pace then, finish them off. Nothing is more dangerous than a wounded animal," said Father Jarauta, adjusting over the bandage on his head a wide-brimmed Panama hat someone had given him, beneath which his nose and its shape of a predatory eagle's beak seemed especially prominent.

He seemed genuinely excited. Perhaps even more enthused than if he were officiating at a mass. He knew that what truly unites people, much more than religion or any other bond, is war.

Here was war.

Expending considerable effort, a fat old man dripping with sweat, his shirt-tail out, lifted a box from the floor to the table. He opened it. It was full of rifles. They flew out of the box. Father Jarauta set one aside and handed it to me. I took it in my trembling hand.

XI

Escandón owned carriages, cotton factories, a hacienda
and various silver mines—in addition to continuing his
activities as a moneylender—and at the close of the '40s
he became the most important financier in the country
due to his cozy relations with the North Americans.

BARBARA A. TENENBAUM

"YOU? YOU HAD a rifle in your hands? I can't conceive of
it, I just can't," said my wife, tossing the page back onto
the desk with an air far beyond scornful.

"Well, I not only held it in my hands, but I even used it from
a rooftop the next morning when the Yankees were entering
the city. One of Jarauta's companions taught me how to aim
with my eye closed, get a good look at the target, and finally
absorb the kick in my shoulder. That afternoon my driver
wanted to join the fight, so I gave the rifle to him."

"Did you hit anyone?"

"I didn't really want to find out, after the guilt I had for finishing off that wounded Yankee. I still haven't stopped dreaming about him."

She clucked her tongue, then shot off a friendly dismissal:

"You know, don't you, that those of us who know you well
see immediately that this is a highly novelized chronicle?"

"Don't you want to read more?"

"If Isabel shows up again let me know."

She turned back for a moment, still several steps from the
door, and with a sudden twinkle in her eye asked:

"Did you really love her the way you describe?"

"Absolutely."

"What about that feeling ... that you would be making love
to her mother if you buried the knife into your own chest?"

"I really felt that way."

Beneath her carefully guarded serenity, I thought I started to see another face emerge—tenser and with more color—like a wave from beneath sea.

"No wonder you didn't want to write about it."

"I warned you. Why were you so insistent that I include it?"

"I suppose I hadn't fully grasped how sick you really were at that point. Blake said it well—he who desires much but does not act engenders disaster."

She took several more steps toward the door but this time I stopped her.

"I knew that including Isabel would affect you."

She turned around and looked at me intently, taking her time to force a smile and then allowing it to disappear.

"That's what you think, is it?"

"I'm certain."

"The problem is that you think I'm the only one who will read your chronicle, so you take great delight in certain scenes, you exaggerate, and perhaps even make things up. I know you."

"You're right."

She drew a deep breath and then pressed her lips together, as if trying to hold back something she didn't want to escape. Then she said:

"I thought that after all these years, especially because I know you as well as I do, that I no longer felt any of what little jealousy I may have ever suffered. Maybe that isn't so. You know how much your little fantasies can sometimes affect me."

I never imagined she'd say that. Me, who knows everything about how she takes refuge in books, who knows what passages she reads in those books, who's aware of every bit of her physical being, who remembers each and every word she has ever used during our games of love starting from the very day we met, who can evoke, discover, and even guess what range of expressions, gestures, and looks she will use to communicate with me from the time we wake up together until the moment I hear her breathing deepen before falling asleep. I never imagined she would say that, and she knew she'd rattled me. Perhaps that's why, before she left, she smiled at me in a new way, like a new flower.

On the morning of September 15, we walked through various parts of the city through which the Yankees had recently passed. We witnessed demolished and collapsed adobe houses, foul smells at every corner, mountains of stones and charred lumber in the middle of which was often found a corpse, a severed arm or leg, or a moaning being pursued by a swarm of flies. Everything was a confused jumble. Even the people in agony seemed on the verge of turning to dust, soon to fall prey to the wind and be carried off like every other ruined substance.

During those days I saw so many dead that I almost got used to them, although later on they would come back to haunt me in my dreams, like the one I'd stabbed. Some were twisted like scrawled writing, their hands stiff or hugging themselves, as if trying to stay warm for no real reason; the eyes of some were long gone, blown out by the last thing they saw, and were turning cloudy and moss-covered; the mouths of others gaped open, as if trying to emit one last impossible scream they'd never get out.

The city government had notices all over the walls of the streets stating that resistance to the Americans, and not their invasion, constituted "a serious setback to peace and the common good." I saw people smearing mud and excrement on those notices, exclaiming:

"Death to the sons of bitches in city government!"

"Death to the Yankees!"

"Death to Santa Anna!"

At the urging of the old Spanish merchant, we went to his store on Santo Sacramento Street. Below ground level, at the far end of the cellar full of barrels and shelves lined with bottles, was a room which he opened with a rusty key after removing a double bolt from the door.

Father Jarauta's eyes would not have been more surprised if they had seen Ali Baba's cave. There were rifles, muskets and bayonets in cases up against the walls, bunches of machetes in their sheaths hanging from the rafters, supplies for horses, rope, bullet pouches, several boxes of ammunition, and a pair of powder barrels. Everything was in perfect order and ready to be used immediately. Why did the Spanish merchant have all this? Before answering, he covered his mouth to contain a nervous laugh which came out like a snort.

"I've had it ready for more than thirty years, since the War of Independence, when I was young, and like so many of my friends and relatives, I was fighting against you. But now that I am an old man we are fighting together against the Yankees."

He even told us about a cannon stored by a fellow countryman at his *hacienda*. Father Jarauta gave orders to several men to go retrieve it. I later found out that, sure enough, they found the cannon, covered by palm fronds, mounted and ready to be wheeled about for action. The problem was that after transporting it to the city with the help of several mules and positioning it in a strategic location, they couldn't get it to fire even once.

After we left the merchant's store, we separated into three or four groups. The last time I saw Father Jarauta he was about to mount a dapple grey palomino. The horse was still rather spooked after being taken from a wounded Yankee. I was struck by the way he spoke to the animal before mounting, as if he was letting it know about the battle they would face together, stroking its mane and haunches while looking tenderly—with a painful sort of tenderness—at the horse's flaming nostrils and foaming snout, its eyes wet with round drops that looked almost like human tears as they fell.

He then mounted and tightened the stirrup. That is the last image I have of Father Jarauta. He was a bit of a scarecrow with his filthy torn cassock, his hook nose, his wide-brimmed straw hat, carrying a Mexican flag on which he had inscribed his rallying cry: "Long live Mexico! Death to the Yankees!"

An unforgettable figure for me, for everyone who was privileged to be with him at those moments, and, I hope, for the history of our country.

That morning other religious leaders joined the fray, like Reverend Lector González, a swarthy well-built man on a shiny black horse, holding aloft a standard bearing the image of the Virgin of Guadalupe. He was seen fighting in Loreto and Peralvillo. Another rebel priest named Martínez fought with boundless courage and the sleeves of his habit rolled up. The Yankees hunted him down in the vicinity of the Ciudadela, but his final words ran like a burning trail of black powder through the common people:

"Long live Christ our King! Death to the Yankees!"

The saying caught on and many repeated the cry before dying:

"Long live Christ our King! Death to the Yankees!"

Several companions informed me that Father Jarauta was inflicting major damage on the enemy near Santa Catarina, and that large numbers of common folk were joining him.

At about noon a company of Mexican soldiers swept into the city—sent by Santa Anna!—which courageously engaged the American forces near the Mariscala bridge. Some of us went that direction, full of enthusiasm.

We set up on some nearby hills to watch. We saw large clouds of various colors—ocher, grey and orange—which the wind would shape and then rip apart, making it difficult for us to see much more than silhouettes. The truth is that we could hardly see what was happening, but what we could kept us on the edge of our seats. At times we could make out a bugle rallying the troops amid the incessant sounds of gunfire. We all pressed together, stretching our necks to see, our hats pulled down to our ears.

"I think we're beating the Yankees!" someone yelled, and the news spread.

We all started to chant, "Long live Mexico!"

Several people had brought spyglasses, so we passed them around. Up so close the scenes suddenly became intensely real. From the gun barrels came puffs of smoke that would extend and then suddenly reveal naked, astonished faces, light-skinned and dark-skinned both, hardened to the point of caricature.

There was plenty to witness in the intertwining of savage bodies and wild horses alone.

The possibility of victory is always encouraging. Several hours into the afternoon we saw more Mexican troops arriving—in a large group on horseback—at a gallop, passing very close to us. Dozens of horses came, enveloped in clouds of dust and accompanied by a shining sun overhead, but they seemed to travel with some of that sun in their midst as well. They were all crying out the same thing, which carried upward like crazed pigeons flying through the branches of the trees: "Death to the Yankees!"

It actually seemed that, at least in this battle, we were beating the invaders. We were finally offering in the city, in the very heart of the city, a worthy resistance, with a courageous, professional Mexican military!

For a few brief moments we saw how ridiculous our makeshift weapons had been—sticks, stones, kitchen knives, flowerpots, boiling oil thrown out of windows, and women's fingernails.

But soon enough—and even today, after so many years, I cannot believe it even though I saw it with my own eyes—as if in one of those abrupt endings of dreams in which we live out our fondest desires—our troops, our long-awaited Mexican cavalry, turned their horses around and began to retreat.

The man to my side asked me, or asked himself, "What? Did a bee sting them?"

An old man, very tall and thin with the skin on his neck so loose that it reminded me of a chicken, started to jump up and down like an excited child, and yelled, "Don't quit on us now, you morons! You practically had them sewn up like a blood sausage! Don't let them go now! Finish them off!"

A woman in a poncho, desperately pulling her hair with an intensity I had only seen previously at the theater, muttered over and over to herself, "Why does this have to happen to us Mexicans in everything we do? Why?"

The most surprised group of all was clearly the Yankees, who were paralyzed, their jaws dropped and sabers held in the air, so stunned they didn't even go after our men.

What the hell had happened?

The reason given later was very simple, and it ended in the humiliation of the captain of the cavalry: Santa Anna, safely inside the Peralvillo garrison, had sent them on a mission of exploration, a mission of exploration and nothing else, to find out the situation in Mexico City. When the soldiers received the shouted order from another officer, they did not question it for a moment—they retreated immediately, returning to the security of their garrison. As they had been properly taught, they did nothing more or less than obey orders, no matter their worth, period.

It is said that Santa Anna struck the captain across the face and demanded, "Don't you know the difference between exploring and attacking?" Then, with the entire regiment as witness, as if pulling the mask off a burglar, he ripped off the captain's stripes, medals and even jacket buttons.

That self-defeat was a crushing blow from which we, each and every one of us, could not recover. It forced us to recognize what had been constantly within our gaze but which we had not wanted to see: that the true enemy was in our own house. As another poor wretched man near me said after we witnessed that aborted battle:

"Our firewood seems too green to burn. I think we're screwed."

That realization, which has surfaced so many times in our history, should be recognized as the most courageous and mature acceptance of our situation: "We're screwed."

The American soldiers gathered up their wounded and quickly vanished.

We helped to gather some of the wounded Mexicans—there were plenty of dead on both sides left to rot in the sun, just as in many other parts of the city, which caused an unbearable stench—and took them to the closest makeshift hospital, where there wasn't room for even one more patient.

A very young soldier who was leaning on me during that stretch, his dislocated and bloody arm hanging like a rag at his side, asked me in a guttural voice with great effort, "What happened? Why did they leave? Why did they abandon us? Do you know?"

He may not have dared to ask the more serious questions: "Why did I sacrifice my youth? Is there an explanation for this futile suffering? Why do this for such a terrible mess of a country?"

During the afternoon it became clear that the battle's intensity had diminished and rumor had it the Yankees were starting to control a good portion of the city, although we could see in the sky brilliant lights and in some places intermittent fires, and still heard gunfire and a buzzing like the sound of bees.

Along with several companions I went down Verónica Street all the way to Tlaxpana and we went into the San Nicolás neighborhood to see whether we could help there. Our heads were hanging a bit—the aborted battle of Mariscala had devastated our morale—and we weren't sure what we should do, what we should say, what we should think, or even where we should go as we went through a cluster of adobe houses with cactus fences, many of them abandoned. A foul stream inched its way along the middle of a street.

"Fortunately, it looks like the Yankees haven't come this far. How lucky for the people here."

There were piles of excrement, clouds of smoke from burning refuse, men asleep sitting on the ground with their chins on their chests, women carrying a variety of things, children playing in the mud, famished dogs barking. We observed all this and took it as evidence that life in some parts of the city continued in its habitual routine.

A scrawny woman looked out of a half-opened door. She was barefoot and wore a shawl. Her dark skin was wrinkled and her eyes were glassy and so deeply set that they almost looked as if they had been screwed tightly into her cranium. Two malnourished children, wearing no clothes but with swollen bellies, clutched her skirt with little claw-like hands.

"These people really are lucky that the Yankees haven't come here," my companion kept insisting.

In the little church they were celebrating a mass for the wounded and fallen, and we went in for a moment to pray and listen to the sermon.

A short priest with no neck was proclaiming from the pulpit, in a voice as sonorous as a trumpet:

"Who gives strength to the Americans? Who gives them their physical prowess, their talent to manufacture better weapons, their ability to crush towns and people under their feet? Who gave strength to Hannibal, to Alexander and Napoleon? The devil? I don't think so. Wouldn't you agree with me that the source is God Himself, God whose goodness is unquestionable, the same God to whom we pray, the only God in whom we can believe? This is the God who came not to bring peace, but rather war. This is the same God who allowed the troops of the evil pharaoh to drown like cats and ordered Joshua to kill the inhabitants of Jericho. This is the same God who, we read in Isaiah, extended his hand over the land to shake it up and create conflicts between kingdoms which until that time had been in peace with each other. This is the same God who has brought us plagues and epidemics, the God of cholera in our city just fifteen years ago, and of smallpox just a few months ago. This is the God compared to whom our city government, General Santa Anna and the best of our soldiers are nothing."

His words caused me a sudden attack of anxiety, making me sweat profusely, and everything around me started to go fuzzy. I even started to fear, although this is absurd, that the Christ at the altar, who seemed inordinately high on the cross, might fall forward. I managed to control myself a little by breathing deeply.

The apocalyptic eloquence of the little priest echoed throughout the church's whitewashed walls, came to the foot of the altar and bounced off the dark altarpieces. For a time members of the disconcerted congregation—comprised almost entirely of the very poor and Indians—tried to hide their impatience by clearing their throats, shifted restlessly on the hard, poorly polished wooden benches and sought to quiet down noisy people. A shrill scream erupted from a small child in the arms of his mother, who left with him immediately. The little priest continued:

"That being so, what attitude should we have in face of the

inevitable invasion we are suffering at the hands of the United States army? What attitude should our government take? What should be the attitude of our Holy Church, the church of each and every one of us?"

He raised his open hands high above his head and suddenly changed his tone like a consummate actor.

"For a long time this city had the opportunity to have salvation, like every city in the world, like each inhabitant in particular. In His eternal mercy, God gave us the chance to choose, to make our own path. But this could not last forever. What have we done with this country since it was declared independent? Tell me: what have we done? Whom have we allowed to govern us? Tired of waiting for us to become more careful and responsible, and although I said 'tired,' I could well have said 'fed up' or 'exasperated' with each one of us, God has had to take matters into His own hands. He had to! He ran out of options! So He sent the Yankees to us as punishment. In summary: we Mexicans earned this invasion."

When he pronounced that final sentence, the diminutive priest dropped his shoulders and buried for a moment his chin into his chest.

"We had thought that it was enough to come to mass on Sundays to have God on our side and to give Him something from time to time. Things would work themselves out. But God is not lukewarm. He is anything but lukewarm. Those attitudes of whatever, of we'll see, of God willing, of tomorrow will come soon enough, of why should I get involved, those apathetic and irresponsible attitudes are entirely incompatible with His burning love or his vehement tenderness."

He raised his face as if it had been submerged in water to the point of drowning, and declared in his loudest voice:

"Make no mistake about it! God wants to see each and every one of us face to face. He wants to squeeze each of our hearts, so that at the key moment of our lives we can exclaim: "Lord, I beg of Thee to gaze ceaselessly upon me with Thy incandescent gaze. Burn me in Thy flames!"

He paused. He swallowed a big breath of air which, it almost seemed, would make him burst.

"Believe me, my brothers and sisters, when I say that this recognition and brightness illuminate us, clarify God's divine will and place us on the redemptory path of the cross. This very day, Wednesday, the fifteenth of September of the year 1847, by means of this torrent of blood and death and wounds and tears, let us accept that, as one of our most illustrious poets said, the emissaries who have arrived at our door are here because we called them. Yes, we called and invited our own invaders. Accept it. Let it become a part of you. Live it as an unavoidable truth, with all that it implies—shame, pain, but also the possibility of redemption. My brothers and sisters, may this American invasion not be just one more event in our history, but a means to our penitence and the possible salvation of our souls. And perhaps of the soul of our entire city. Do you understand me?"

The members of the congregation answered with a long and ringing yes. My companions knelt down behind a bench, placed their heads in their hands as if they were starting a profound search of their consciences, and soon fell asleep. By contrast, I was in such a state of distress and so in need of comfort that when the little priest lifted the consecrated host above his head, I thought I could sense an invisible presence as I never had before. Right there in that little church. It was an invisible presence, but it was more real, much more real than those transitive actors—the Mexican and American soldiers—and that transitory theater: Mexico City.

VII

I had an entire ocean of suffering in my soul.
All I had to do was open my eyes to once again feel the
pain of the city.

GUILLERMO PRIETO

I STARTED TO OPERATE *on the wounded early in the morning, I didn't stop all day, and I still found time that night—practically walking in my sleep, my head pounding, so tired that I thought my heart would burst—to visit the makeshift military clinic we had set up near Arcos de Belén.*

Outside a group of physicians, medical students and nurses huddled around a fire over which two earthen pots hung from a pair of sticks, thick smoke rising from them.

As soon as they saw me arrive they smiled and shook my hand. One of the students handed me a bottle of a tart, strong liquor and I took a long drink, savoring it with a greed I had completely suppressed, and suddenly felt better. Everyone wanted to talk to me at once. They asked me about the situation in the Hospital of San Pedro and San Pablo and sympathized that I had to endure the torture of being in charge of it. They had nothing good to say about the Yankees: they had set up their own hospitals in some of the city's most luxurious houses and had access to equipment of which we could only dream. They wanted me to go see for myself. They said the Yankee soldiers would bury their dead immediately after simply firing a salute. By contrast we, in our makeshift military hospitals in our own city, had to salvage the bandages of the dead, then pile the bodies one atop the other and burn them, instead of burying them as would have been the Christian thing to do.

One of the nurses reached with a big spoon into the boiling pozole they were making and served me a steaming bowl, while

I licked my chops in anticipation. It burned my tongue, but I took my time, savoring every bit. I added tortilla, bits of onion, chile powder and oregano. I relished a pig's knuckle. I drank another swig of that liquor, and I could feel very clearly it cauterizing my esophagus.

"Now that you've eaten dinner, can you accompany us, Dr. Urruchúa?"

I shouldn't have eaten—it seems that food of all sorts lately hasn't agreed with me—because it had distanced me blissfully from reality, and the sudden return was brutal. The first thing I encountered made my stomach turn: a line of wounded people lying on the ground in the gravel, waiting in the order they arrived, because there was no longer any room in the little hospital. To top it all off, a punishing wind had blown all afternoon, unheard of in September, and ended up infecting the open wounds, since for lack of resources there was no way to bandage them or close them up medically. What are we to do, doctor? they asked, their hands gesturing in desperation.

It was hard to distinguish between the moaning, crying, screaming, sobbing and delirium caused by fever.

They informed me that the corpse of a captain held in highest esteem by the national guardsmen, who fought like a dragon at the front of the ranks, had been found outside the Cathedral without a nose, that's right, without a nose, but also castrated and with a slice of his intestines stuffed in his mouth. The Yankees were exacting their revenge in ways no one, not even their worst enemies, could imagine. Numerous women and girls were found raped and mutilated. Some of them were on the pile of corpses. Did I want to see it with my own eyes? They assured me that they weren't exaggerating. On the contrary, they left out details so that I could keep my dinner down.

Inside the little hospital's tent—with just one kerosene lamp on the ceiling which swung back and forth, projecting long trembling, ghostly shadows—the first patient I saw was a poor soldier with a bandana in his mouth. When they took it out from time to time to allow him to breath more easily, he would roar as much as moan in pain, his eyes fluttering. What could he be seeing in the world right then? Two nurses were trying to hold him in place while one of our surgeons amputated his leg. The surgeon was sweating profusely while another nurse tried to keep the sweat out of his face as he sawed mercilessly.

Why "mercilessly," I wonder, right after I have written it. Should it not be, contrary to what one might suppose, that no matter how good physicians are, they become more and more sensitive to human suffering? So what happens to that hyper-sensitivity in extreme conditions? Do people fade away or go into convulsions when they see a drop of blood, which is what happened to that nurse I had? Maybe that explains what happened to me after going past the first few rows of wounded patients.

"What's the matter, doctor? Did the soup disagree with you?"

I had made a valiant effort to hold back, but I finally excused myself and ran to an empty bucket in the corner. I vomited loudly, retching so strongly my whole body shook. I was completely wrung, and my hands were shaking uncontrollably.

I took the bucket outside myself and emptied it in the shrubbery. I stayed outside a few minutes, breathing in the fresh air and mopping the sweat off my forehead with a bandana smelling of rubbing alcohol that a nurse lent me.

"I'm fine now. Don't worry. This often happens to me when I eat pozole for dinner. I actually like it a lot. It was so good that I couldn't resist asking for seconds, as you saw."

"You seem very pale, doctor."

I asked for another drink of the liquor they had offered me and I lit a cigar—my last one—and returned to the tent. I felt a tingling sensation in my legs and everything around me seemed like it was submerged in some type of peach marmalade. I took another swig of liquor.

After asking me far too many questions about my well-being, the physicians informed me about the rest of the wounded and something unusual that had just happened: a Yankee soldier had come to them with a bullet lodged in his abdomen. He was undoubtedly wounded nearby and his companions did not rescue him. When he saw the white flag of the hospital, he dragged himself there as best he could. What should they do with him?

He was wailing in the fetal position, both hands clutching the side of the bedroll he lay upon. His appearance was so forlorn and he emanated such tremendous anguish that, I thought, he'd shame anyone able to look at him. He held his clenched hand out to me and said something, a request or a lament, in rough-sounding English. His shirt was unbuttoned and his abdomen was bleeding profusely.

He had freckles everywhere and wavy, light brown hair. His facial characteristics had sharpened, there were wrinkles on his forehead, and when he wasn't crying his teeth chattered. I asked the physician making the rounds with me to prepare to operate. The Yankee must have understood my gestures because he called me over, forced me to sit down next to him on the floor and said to me some new incomprehensible words. His eyes were sliding around like mercury in their orbits. As he spoke, a narrow thread of transparent saliva started to form and hang from his bottom lip, like a spider web.

He kept talking and squeezing my arm and I didn't dare stand, or maybe I tried and was unable.

"Please," I asked, but he gripped my arm even harder.

His English was becoming increasingly garbled—I didn't understand a single word—talking about something obviously extremely important to him. His words were growing and piling up, to no avail. Did he realize he was dying? Was he trying to make a final confession? The Yankee was obviously aware that I couldn't understand—my eyes undoubtedly showed it—but he kept on talking nonetheless. Brandishing his scalpel, my colleague signaled to me to hurry up. The Yankee finally gave me a faint smile of sorts and said "thanks," the only word I managed to understand. I also smiled; what other option did I have? He took out a pocket watch, opened it, and showed me on the inside of the gold cover a small blurry photograph of a woman. Who was she? Who was he? What had he been telling me? When he looked at the portrait he sighed and his formless neck and shoulders started to tremble in futile earnest. A breath of air *escaped in a difficult rattle, and once again he tried to look at me with his glassy eyes. This living corpse of a Yankee was still trying to tell me something, and he muttered some final words which were really just puffs of air escaping from his cheeks. His respiration then became so irregular that he seemed more like a fish out of water, his mouth shaped like a funnel. With his lips in that shape and holding the watch in his hand, he fell backwards onto the bedroll and closed his eyes, almost as if he were anesthetizing himself.*

We felt the need to operate on him even though we needed the bandages, thread and medicines for our own soldiers. We later learned that some Yankee doctors had done the same for Mexican soldiers in similar situations.

He lost consciousness almost exactly at the same time as the first incision of the scalpel. With tongs I was able to reach inside him and remove a small bullet. We bandaged him. The next day he was better. Two days later he walked away.

VIII

When I turned around, about two to three hundred yards
from the headquarters I saw a little Mexican woman who
was taking water to the wounded of both armies. I saw
her, very clearly, lift the head of an unfortunate Yankee to
give him water. Suddenly I heard a shot ring out and saw
her fall dead. I turned my eyes heavenward and thought:
"My God, need war be like this?"

ANONYMOUS STORY
NILES NATIONAL REGISTER, AUGUST 1847

"WELL, I THINK that your Father Jarauta, whom you
admire so very much, was a fanatic and only came to
our country to further complicate our lives," my wife says as
she adds white cheese and *guajillo* chiles to the soup.

"Didn't you say that you weren't going to read any more of
what I'm writing unless Isabel makes her way back into it?"

"I went into your study to make sure that they had done a
good job washing the windows and couldn't help but see the
papers on your desk."

After seeing how the episode with Isabel affected her, I
have been much more careful about leaving my work out and
writing things which could get me into trouble.

"So do you think we should *not* have put up any resistance
to the Yankees when they invaded us?"

"What was the point? When all was said and done they took
what they wanted and stayed here as long as they darn well
pleased, didn't they? So many of the believers in your Father
Jarauta shed their blood for no particular reason. Like that
wounded soldier you helped get to the makeshift hospital who
asked you why there was so much suffering. What good did it
do him?"

"You read that part also?"

"The page was right next to one about Father Jarauta."

"With that attitude, what should we do now if the United States wants to take another piece of territory from us?"

"If they want to take something from us, they will take it whether we put up resistance or not, even if we have ten Father Jarautas come to organize guerilla warfare in the mountains of Veracruz, and you know it. And if they decide they don't want Porfirio Díaz in power they will throw him out and someone will arrive whom they support. That's how it will be with every president we ever have in this country, until the sun stops shining and this planet goes back to the Nothingness from which it came."

"What a horrible vision of the world. I prefer Father Jarauta's philosophy, even if you call him a fanatic."

"Even with that useless suffering he caused?"

"Yes."

"Well, you aren't much of a human being, and you are part sadist, as I have always suspected. I prefer for people to steer clear of suffering however they can, which is why I like that Russian writer so much."

"Tolstoy."

"What was the name of that movement?"

"Passive resistance."

"I even like the name. You resist, but passively. Don't you see the difference? If there were a war right here, outside my home, I would sit on a stool between the opposing sides. You would see that neither side would dare touch me and it might even pacify them a bit."

"I think they'd probably march right over you, depending on the type of soldiers they were. Don't be so certain of yourself."

"As human beings we all have a chord of sensitivity which leads us to acts of compassion, and all it takes is for someone to know how to activate it, mark my word."

"I wish you had seen how the Yankees were flogging people in the middle of the Plaza de Santo Domingo."

"It's their own fault for getting them riled up when they arrived."

That final weekend of September 1847 there were indeed still a few areas of resistance near the Ciudadela, along with intermittent acts in other parts of the city during the ensuing days, but they died down very quickly. Small white flags started to appear on the rooftops and in the windows of homes all over the city.

The city government, recognizing evidence of defeat, and having been abandoned by the President of the Republic, the Supreme Court of Justice, the governor of the District, and above all by the armed forces, issued a new statement which, as I think about it, almost sounded like it could have been written by my wife (when I read it to her she agreed: "I would have hung a white flag outside our house, whether you would have wanted or not").

To those who continue to fight against American forces, recognize that you are irresponsible and unpatriotic, and that your suicidal attitude will drag many innocent lives into harm's way.

Lay down your arms and we will once again consider you patriots.

To those who have decided to accept the presence of American troops here as inevitable, strengthen your resolve and make it known to your friends and relatives.

To those who have placed a white flag outside your houses, place another next to it.

Sure enough, two and three white flags immediately appeared outside many houses.

Attempt passive resistance in light of what happened afterwards? Remain calm, control the blood boiling in our veins, get used to the idea that nothing could be done about it, and look for the bright side?

Once the Americans had the city completely secured, they exacted their revenge by beating and even executing anyone they suspected of insurrection. Reports circulated that they accused and punished people who merely looked at them cross-eyed or made strange gestures. They would invade family homes to search for weapons and as long as they were there they would steal whatever they wanted and rape women and girls. Innumerable reports of this type were filed. (The Americans, on the other hand, could not eat at Mexican establishments because several soldiers found rat poison in the meals they had ordered.) They traveled throughout the city, poking around in every nook and cranny, knocking on doors and windows with their sabers, letting people know they were present and terrifying them with their curt orders.

That same Thursday, in the Plaza de Santo Domingo, they began to carry out public floggings to demonstrate the implacable harshness which they intended to impose on the city. Crowds formed to witness them with an eagerness which I had previously only seen in people waiting for parades.

A giant Yankee soldier was leading us curious onlookers with an authoritarian gesture that consisted of holding his hand over his head, then pointing where we were to go and moving it that direction.

They would strip the shirt or blouse off the guilty party, in the presence of hundreds of impoverished Mexicans and a group of Yankee soldiers. The one whose turn it was to inflict the punishment would revel in choosing a staff from several which an underling would display to him.

He would test it in the air in sudden movements, producing cobra-like whistles.

The rest of the soldiers and the underling would take several steps back. People in the crowd would murmur, whisper, complain quietly or openly insult the Yankees, taking precautions to maintain their anonymity. They knew that if they were identified they would be flogged as well.

I saw a woman make obscene gestures as she shouted, "Yankee son of a whore, go beat your own mother!"

In an instant a huge hand fell on her as if from the sky, grabbed her by the hair and dragged her away.

After that, when people issued insults they did so quietly, as if they were just whispering to the people next to them.

The Yankee soldier would apply the first blows of the punishment with great force, each time producing the sound of a snapping whip, and would continue even after the accused would stumble. Sometimes the very effort of applying the punishment would cause the soldier to pause to catch his breath, and then he would raise the stick into the air and continue with even more fury than before.

The American soldiers would sing out the number of blows:

"One, two, three, four, five ..."

Before reaching ten, blood would appear on the backs of the prisoners.

After the first few whacks many of them would fall to their knees, wrap their arms around the legs of their tormentor and beg forgiveness. This seemed to fire up the eyes of the soldier, who'd shake them off by kicking them in the face, and then he would carry out the rest of the sentence with even more severity. But many others, particularly women, would endure without ever uttering a word the ten, twenty, even thirty blows, in accordance with the severity of their alleged crime.

IX

While we were astonished by the number of presses con-
fiscated for printing counterfeit money, we were assured
that at least twice that many are still in use in Mexico,
but since they belong to highly distinguished political figures, the government is afraid to prosecute.

MARQUESA CALDERÓN DE LA BARCA

ESPITE THE PUNISHMENTS (or perhaps thanks to them)
and occasional conflicts, some of which were intense, little by little the city returned to a state of apparent normality
(tragedy was not allowed to surface during those days). Establishments once again opened their doors, among them the-
aters, businesses, restaurants, boarding houses, cafés, bars and
bullfighting venues. (The Yankees became huge bullfighting
fans. One afternoon one of them, quite drunk, spontaneously
jumped into the arena and with noteworthy valor fought a particularly fierce bull. The crowd demanded that he circle the
arena to the cries of loud acclamation.) The streets filled once
again with office workers, beggars, dandies and women in the
finest attire, devout Catholics going to mass at the Cathedral,
young people looking for places to have fun, vendors of water,
chicken and coal. The air filled with sales pitches for all kinds
of products, including clothing, birds, candy, chestnuts, fried
plantains, haircuts and myriad trinkets. Mule-drawn streetcars
emerged from Dolores Street and dispersed to every part of
the city. Sunday traffic in the Alameda returned, with its fine
carriages, coaches, extravagant livery and Mexican cowboys
donning wide sombreros and filigreed jackets. And the aromas
and vibrant colors of flowers and fruits came back as well.

The city returned to apparent normality, but according to
many people—especially the rich and foreign business owners,

as one would expect—things were better than ever for the city's residents, with the streets safer and a flow of money as never seen before.

American troops effectively isolated the city from the rest of the country, it is true, but at the same time it stopped the flow of people into the city from rural areas and provincial cities, in other words Indians and beggars, which pleased many people who had openly stated they'd become rather fed up with that problem.

"Imagine if this beautiful city of palaces never grew to more than the two hundred thousand inhabitants who currently live here! I hope the Yankees build a big wall and keep things forever the way they are. Admit it! Wouldn't that have its advantages?"

"Wouldn't it be great to have the police force continue the way it is right now?"

"We were really in a rut—we had become accustomed to the almost invariable routine of military uprisings and conspiracies!"

Once the representatives of national power departed for Querétaro, Mexico City's government was forced to deal with its own demands and needs, to resolve its own problems, and do so well, and do it quickly, because the invaders were looming and allowing it to operate with precious little tolerance for error.

I heard a woman at the Alameda comment, "You can say whatever you want, but the Yankees have put people to work, and the city looks better than ever."

In contrast to the oppressive tyranny of the prior national authorities, the American authorities turned out to be, in the view of "decent" folk, more flexible and even more "humane," even though they imposed a stricter work regimen. And "since their local administration has had the widest scope of any we have known," according to Suárez Iriarte, the city government's liaison to the Americans through the Municipal Assembly, local citizens had finally become more involved in city matters, offering suggestions that ranged from cleanliness and public safety to increased efficiency in the mail system, an issue which had never previously been examined.

The solid organization of the government turned out to be advantageous for the invaders as well as for the representatives of the vanquished, since in the end the same issues concerned both parties. The chaos of the first few days, coupled with the general confusion and disorder into which idle troops could fall, necessitated not only public shows of punishment—like the floggings in the Plaza de Santo Domingo and executions of common people for the slightest offence—but an all-encompassing short-term restoration project. This was particularly true because the United States needed—and immediately—to recover the onerous expenses of the war, even if it meant finding new forms of financial compensation, and to accomplish it they had to reorganize the city and make it more productive.

As Suárez Iriarte also said, "From now on we will be measured by the 'pressing law of necessity'" (United States "necessity," naturally). Hence, after conducting an inventory of its scarce resources, the Municipal Assembly decided to reorganize the financial system as a first step. It immediately administered a census—the best the city had ever conducted—of the number of people and amount of capital per household, for the purpose of establishing a more effective system of taxation. Very few people dodged the system. Even water sellers paid their taxes, because floggings in the Plaza de Santo Domingo were also administered to anyone late in payment.

President Polk issued a presidential order to the military and naval commanders who were overseeing Mexican cities and ports to levy special taxes "by virtue of the right of conquest."

According to President Polk, as Mexicans, we were, at that time, subject to "temporary vassalage."

Temporary?

The Municipal Assembly intervened in the "administration of justice," marking the end of the era of influences, special privileges for friends and greasing the wheels with money under the table. It even saw an abatement of our endemic curse of runaway bureaucracy. The Plaza de Santo Domingo was the scene of floggings such as the one administered to the director of a government office for acting with negligence in some petty topic—in his case to the tune of twenty blows.

On one occasion I asked, "And why did they flog that other bureaucrat?"

"Apparently he accepted a bribe."

The important thing, it seemed, was to continue with the public floggings, which had yielded such positive results for public safety and the new labor efficiency. The crowds became bigger and bigger as time went on, especially when the offender hailed from the common poor, the group which received the most punishment. "Decent" folks had a fail-safe argument to justify this situation which seemed so unjust: that it was the poor who had provoked such disorder in the city when the Americans entered. Those "decent" folk would dress up in their formal wear and try to establish friendships with high-ranking military officers. They treated common soldiers, even though they were Yankees, as if they hailed from the classes of the common poor, which was actually quite right.

The Americans published their own newspaper, *The American Star*. In its first edition, dated Monday, the twentieth of that tragic September, General Scott published a clear proclamation of victory, one which left no room for doubt. If honor falls to the invader, all that is left for the invaded is shame. God was on the side of the powerful, and as the vanquished all we could do was be quiet and obey, period. Warnings were not ignored as bluffs. The newspaper included paid inserts sponsored by various groups which declared their allegiance to the invaders. For example, in one of the first editions there was an insert signed by "several Mexicans" who "wanted only the security of the people and their property" and said in one of its most substantive sections, "If General Scott has the strength and courage to overthrow the monster in our midst known as Judicial Power, he deserves the crown of victory." It did not surprise us, then, that those same Mexicans nominated General Scott as the Civil and Military Governor of Mexico, instead of General Quitman, who was ultimately appointed. General Scott's actual title was absolutely insignificant, for he could do with our city whatever he pleased. Furthermore, he drew praise in the public opinion for acting democratically, as was published in *The American Star*: "Punishment to be administered to John Garvey, a soldier, for lack of military discipline: walk without stopping for three consecutive days and nights, carrying a thirty-six-pound weight, with only one-hour breaks for breakfast and one-hour breaks for dinner." Several Yankee soldiers even received floggings in the Plaza de Santo Domingo, administered by their own companions.

Scott's democratic fame was consolidated when an editorial was published in which the reappearance of *El Monitor Republicano* was celebrated as a venue for "free thinking and free expression." It finished with the message: "Welcome to the new Mexico City."

Recruiting from the ranks of the famous regiment of riflemen, the most organized, best-trained, but also the most "hardened" of the American army, the Municipal Assembly organized an exceptional body of around five hundred policemen, who were relentless in their duties. If they encountered people "whom they didn't like," they would stop them for the flimsiest reason, rough them up, find out where they were going via a sort of sign language and spit on them. Personally, all it took was for one of those Yankee policemen to give me a little push to send me running to my house for several days, where I would cower even in my dreams.

But such disdain for the Mexican people had its advantages for other groups of people, especially the ones who favored the use of a "heavy hand" and thought that anything was justified in the name of increased peace and security. The military authorities lightened up on the nightly curfew, changing it first from ten to eleven, and then eventually to midnight. People were able to go without fear for their safety to social events, take leisurely walks, eat out or see a play. Thieves, pickpockets and troublesome drunkards—who had formerly owned certain parts of the city, especially at night—disappeared as if by magic. Also as if by magic, almost every morning the corpse of one of those "hardened" Yankee policemen was found stabbed, castrated or with his head crushed by a flower pot dropped from the top of a building. This circumstance greatly increased the number of floggings administered to the dozens of possible culprits, detained at random from among the city's most humble classes.

Some of the city's eternal problems, like water delivery and sewage treatment, found noteworthy improvements as the Assembly called upon the expertise of the American corps of engineers who had no particular mission at the time. Suárez Iriarte proposed that the water level of lakes in the valley be raised, which was immediately accomplished with all due diligence. Construction of the aqueduct of San Cosme was initiated. With two levels of arches, the upper one was to carry water from Santa Fe, known as "thin" water because of its purity, and on the lower level "thick" water was to flow, which was to come from the fountains in Chapultepec Park—during the rainy season it was cloudy at best.

The Americans were big supporters of not only bullfights but also theater. There were even plays written specifically for them, like *A Painful Love*, by Juan José Pérez Doblado, which featured a tormented relationship between a Yankee soldier and a young woman of the Mexican aristocracy. At one point in the play the soldier said to his future father-in-law:

In my own humble way, I labor on behalf of a richer humanity; this annoys people like you, who want to pigeonhole people because of their nationality or physical attributes. When it comes to race or culture, love breaks down established patterns and opens an array of unexpected variations, exceptions, new options and nuances. In order to capture the ultimate and unmistakable human reality, in this arena, as is the case in all arenas, a person has to abandon the flock—whether it be Mexican or American—and in the process discover a tumultuous vision replete with freedom in the highest sense. This freedom can only reach its zenith in the sphere of love, that warm and indivisible homeland.

How did that Yankee soldier learn Spanish? Elementary, explained the young woman in love:

Our love taught it to him.

With great regularity the Americans also frequented cock fights—where they left a fair amount of gold coins—restaurants, cafés, Sunday strolls, and above all else, the bar of the Hotel Bella Unión on Tlapaleros Street, where exiled by poverty our women of the streets provided sexual entertainment to the invaders. There was something disgraceful about watching the giant Yankees dance with our tiny women to the live music of a piano, and then shamelessly start to make love to them. Someone composed a song, which became very popular, based on these scenes.

Our women of the evening
Now understand English
Yankees ask them: "Do you love me?"
And they answer: "Oh, yes!
Me understand money
And you are muy cute!"

Here is another:

If our hot little ladies
Were only made of sweets,
I don't know the limits
Of how many I would eat.
But they are made of fingernails
And they scratch you like cats;
But when the Yankees come along
They don't even give us a chance.

As far as I was concerned, I hardly ever left my house. I spent all day long reading and writing. My anguish died down—there's nothing like confronting a ghost to exorcise it— I started to sleep better, the lights in the sky were scared off— I had seen them land, to my horror, on Earth—but some kind of physical and mental disorientation came over me which when

I mentioned it to Dr. Urruchúa, he diagnosed as even more dangerous than my previous ills.

"But I don't feel anguish the way I did before."

"That may be the worst symptom of all, Abelardo my friend. Besides, I am afraid this ailment has no treatment."

"So what should I do?"

"We would have to ask the physicians at San Hipólito."

"But that's an insane asylum!"

"Maybe they have a similar case or something not as severe. Don't be so afraid of insane asylums, my friend. Sometimes I've gone there and felt like I wasn't the visitor, that they were looking at me as if I were the strange one, and perhaps they were right."

What is certain is that some mornings as I got out of bed, I had the *clear* sensation of being so infinitesimally small that I could have fallen into the shoe I was about to put on. Tying the laces was like torture.

On the other hand, some mornings I felt taller than the door I needed to go through and I would bend over to avoid hitting my head, to the great surprise of my servants.

At times I believed that *someone* invisible was getting closer and closer to me, but I would withdraw to avoid a confrontation. Regarding this condition, Dr. Urruchúa made a very insightful comment which calmed me:

"Perhaps you are simply trying to become reconciled with your shadow."

But the worst (or the best, if you want to attribute some kind of spiritual transcendence to it) was that at times I felt like I'd stopped being myself and had instead turned into a type of passageway. It was a passageway through which strange forces and visitors, in this case visible, would come (although later, after the crisis, I couldn't even remember their faces).

One of my servants helped me to see what was happening one day when she was clearing the plates after dinner:

"Are you all right, sir?"

"Why do you ask?"

"Because you were talking to yourself."

Those periods of disorientation could happen during walks through the city, as I sat in my courtyard or read a newspaper. Inside me, or perhaps outside, a sudden inconceivable capacity to receive would make reality real, so to speak, and something would open up, would become as porous as a sponge. Anything could enter me.

There were moments—luminous or horrific, depending on how you looked at them—when everything around me stopped being what it was, or I stopped being who I was, or who I thought I was.

I was in that terrain where words can only be late and imperfect in describing what is happening.

It was a world in which things, facts and beings would have different names, meanings and identifying traits. Once, to the astonishment of my servants, I received a letter with a red seal at the exact instant there was a peal of thunder and I suddenly perceived the smell of burning coffee. I wasn't sure whether this trio of events had anything whatsoever to do with each other, but just to be certain I screamed, threw the letter into the air and ran outside into the rain.

"He is simply happy, don't read too much into it," I heard my driver say to another servant during one of my unusual moments.

But it would be through that absurd triangle of apparently coincidental things—letter, thunder, coffee—that something or someone would stealthily enter through me, an *other*, which would reveal an inconceivable deception or happiness, the true meaning of some act committed five years earlier, or the assurance that in the near future—perhaps as early as the next day—some foreordained event of which I had an inkling would take place.

It was a simple intuition regarding that thing we call "tomorrow," that monster with a covered face which denies its own existence and power.

In most cases, the eruption of this unknown world was no more than a horribly brief, fleeting sensation—for which my staff was grateful—but it was sufficient to leave me with the assurance that everything has a hidden side—Every Thing—a door to another reality which is opened by the most trivial and common of occurrences, but which sadly we are incapable of opening, or even looking through.

"I feel like I am on the precipice of a horrible happiness or jubilant horror," I told Dr. Urruchúa when he asked me to give him a detailed description of my emotional state, and then he scribbled some notes in a notebook.

One morning my intuition was right on target when I heard a pair of knocks on the door and I said to my servant that it was Doña Isabel. And it was her.

She was wearing the same black veil she wore the previous time she visited to discuss with me her daughter's serious condition, but this time her long fingers, like birds, twitched nervously and her lovely eyes wore the shadows of even deeper rings around them.

"My daughter told me what you wrote about me," she said with a look in which suffering and anger throbbed simultaneously. The cup of hot chocolate she was holding made clinking noises on the saucer, and her voice broke into an incomprehensible stammer. "The problem is that she also told her father. Can you imagine the effect this has had on our family? She accused me of having an affair with you, her own fiancé. My husband's first reaction was ..."—she put the cup of hot chocolate on the side table and took out a lace handkerchief to contain the sobbing which was starting to overflow—"the first consequence was that my husband insulted me as soon as we were alone, he insulted me as he had never insulted me before, and then he gave me the silent treatment. He hasn't said a word to me since. Father and daughter have conspired against me with silence ... and my other children don't dare get involved. They talk to me, but only when absolutely necessary ... My home has been a veritable hell of ice ..."

And then she added point-blank:

"My husband swears that the next time he sees you, wherever it may be, he'll kill you. I know him well, and he isn't joking."

✖

Poor child of poverty, product of the masses, you are born on a bed, you live there, reproduce there and die there as well.

ÁNGEL DEL CAMPO

I T STARTED WITH *a sharp pain at the top of my stomach, a cold sweat in my hands, an unbearable sense of weight on my knees and a dizziness which would only go away if I would lie down in bed. Under these conditions I cannot go to the hospital.*

Abelardo visited me and I told him about the burning acidity which goes up and down my esophagus, the substance which stops at my glottis and fills my palate with bitter tastes, saliva which I can't swallow, continual spasms in a zigzag pattern in the area of my colon, diarrhea occasionally tinged with blood and burning in my stomach. The pain is so intense that I double up continually. I have begun a drastic diet—I told him when I saw his worried face. I drink only tea, atole and donkey milk, and take certain salts. I told him he needn't worry and assured him that I would soon be better.

After we talked about my health he told me about Father Jarauta.

"After the enemy quelled our heroic popular insurrection on the fourteenth and fifteenth of September, Father Jarauta and the guerrillas who were still alive—I hear that they number more than a hundred—had to go into hiding in towns and cities not far from Mexico City, where they continue the fight. Even the Mexican army is now after Father Jarauta, but it would seem that he is everywhere, because just when they think they have him trapped in one place he suddenly appears in another, and then vanishes like smoke. One day he is in Pachuca and

the next in Querétaro, or he pirates a convoy of supplies enter-
ing Mexico City near the Guadalupe sentinel. They recently
detained a poor man in San Juan Teotihuacán, thinking he
was Father Jarauta, and hurriedly executed him. They pro-
claimed the news of his death far and wide until the real Father
Jarauta organized a riot near the Peralvillo military installa-
tion and left a mocking note. Word has it that he or his people
are responsible for the nocturnal deaths of Yankee soldiers
whose bodies show up in the mornings. They are undoubtedly
in the city, because I can find no other logical explanation for
the sudden appearance of this notice on every street corner of
the city:

Residents of Mexico City, awake from your dangerous lethargy. Look at how your religion and homeland are immersed in
their greatest disgrace, awaiting the day when their valiant servants decide to avenge the affront afflicted by those ambitious,
cruel invaders so lacking in morals. Arise in mass, let us be
unified, and with one voice let us call out: Long live the Mexican Republic! Long live her Catholic religion! Long live Christ
our King! Long live the Holy Pope! In the name of saving their
country and their religion, may the people once again rise up
against the Yankees, even if their only weapons are their bare
hands! Death is better than the apparent peace imposed on
us, and the ambition for spoils and the diabolical pride of the
occupiers simply grows by the day. This is the only way to save
our country, Catholicism and ourselves from the shackles of
foul slavery. We would rather die killing Americans and their
puppets than surrender to their powerful arms, their false gods
such as money and "progress," and their hypocritical offers of
democracy.

Signed: Celedonio Domeco de Jarauta.

"Who posted all those notices everywhere in the city while
avoiding the constant rounds of Yankee soldiers and the relent-
less police force?"

"Isn't it possible that Father Jarauta is actually the one who
has made a deal with the devil?" I immediately felt bad for say-
ing that.

Abelardo simply clucked his tongue, and, continuing to speak with caution, said:

"I wouldn't put that past him, if he thought it would help him to put an end to the lethargy and counterfeit peace, with its counterfeit gods, the Yankees are imposing on us. The night he stayed in my home, he told me, 'If I could, I would pour vinegar and salt onto the hearts of the inhabitants of Mexico City to keep them from finding any rest or solace in the presence of their invaders.' It seems that, at least for now, he has an infinite ability to create chaos. Recently he got The American Star and El Monitor into a fight, if you can believe it, because the first accused the second of being in cahoots with Father Jarauta, which could get it shut down. Listen to this note: 'Where did El Monitor get the news that eight hundred American soldiers had left Pachuca to go to Tulancingo in search of Father Jarauta? With our superior information, we know that only ninety soldiers went, and that Father Jarauta became terribly frightened, because he is actually a cowardly, hypocritical priest who only knows how to attack from the shadows. Father Jarauta and his three hundred companions, who are just as criminal as he is, fled immediately. Does El Monitor maintain correspondence with Jarauta? We call upon authorities to find out in short order. Because their relationship seems very close and they seem to be in collusion.' El Monitor, in an editorial written by its publisher, a courageous man, Vicente García Torres, responded to The American Star the very next day and spared no words in the process: 'We ask our colleagues, who claim to care about being democratic and faithful to the truth, to show us the proof upon which they have based their statements that our newspaper has a close relationship with Father Jarauta and is colluding with him. The truth is that both our newspapers have the same information, but our rivals build up or minimize stories in accordance with their personal and national interests.' As you can see, Doctor, there is still a flicker of hope at the end of the long, dark tunnel which our city is experiencing at this time."

I confessed that we might not make it to the end of the tunnel. I charged him, if that should turn out to be the case, to contact my niece Irene so that she could have my meager belongings. I told him that I wanted my medical equipment to go to the hospital, and that he was to have the notes I had written regarding the Yankee invasion, in addition to some reflections—I hoped I wasn't imposing—I had made about his nervous condition and its treatment.

This all seemed to bother Abelardo, and it got worse when I gave him a gold watch in which was encased a small, fuzzy photograph of a woman. Who was she? I was never able to find out because I couldn't understand the Yankee who gave it to me after I removed a bullet from his body, brought him back to health and then sent on his way.

As soon as Abelardo left I started to write these lines. They are almost assuredly my final lines. Today it is becoming clear to me that I was born for this, that my entire life can be seen as preparation for this final moment, that every prior experience, whether peaceful or agitated, buoyant or disheartening, takes on meaning and comes into focus here, slipping away but within a powerful clarity, running headlong toward an inevitable place, finding at the last moment my destiny.

✕ I

The great danger is that the Americans will bring us not just Protestantism as the official religion, but also the associated sense of money and industrial productivity which fly in the face of the most basic teachings of Jesus Christ.

JUAN JOSÉ PÉREZ DOBLADO

"I'M DISAPPOINTED IN YOUR chronicle," says my wife. "First you talk about Father Jarauta. Give me a break with that yarn about his guerrilla warfare and his proclivity for tilting at windmills. And then you leave the story of Doña Isabel hanging after she visited you. Poor woman, you destroyed her life. Her husband insulted her as he had never done before; her daughter is giving her the silent treatment, and justly so after what you wrote about the two of you flirting in the theater. I would have liked to meet Doña Isabel to talk with her, woman to woman, and warn her about you."

"Let me try to explain this to you. I *wrote* that we had flirted in the theater, but that didn't really happen."

"It didn't really happen?" she asked, her eyebrows arched high in astonishment.

"It was all in my imagination. She swore to me that she was completely oblivious to what I thought we were experiencing. She was absolutely unaware of moving her arm close to mine or mine moving close to hers, or of breathing the same burning, sensual air. She said she was far too worried about her daughter's critical condition to pay attention to whether I was transmitting my animal magnetic fluid, as Dr. Urruchúa would have said, quoting Mesmer."

"Poor woman. Another of your victims. To think that I ever felt jealous over her! And your morbid fantasies about stabbing yourself in the chest!"

"Isn't it possible that you are the morbid one, and that's why you are so keen on having me write everything that happened with Isabel and her mother?"

"That could be. I would love to have the Negretes, the Miers and the Ayalas read your own accounts of your indecent behavior. And if you publish it, I would like to see it become a public scandal. I would be delighted to give a copy, each one personally signed by you, to each and every one of my friends. Given the dull life we lead under Porfirio Díaz in this country, almost anything would be a welcome relief. The other night when we were visiting the Prietos, what did you call this period of tranquility we are experiencing?"

"Peace with heavy eyelids."

"That's awful! Peace with heavy eyelids. Could there be anything worse? So the idea is to look everywhere for something to shake us up and force open our eyes."

"Aren't you the fanatical pacifist who argued on behalf of Tolstoy-style peaceful resistance and against doing anything that could in any way hurt a fellow human being?"

"Yes, but you're driving me so crazy with your lights and your fears that I might change my stance and become a rabid supporter of war."

Doña Isabel had told her husband that she was going to visit her sister in Mixcoac in order to visit me, she said, wiping a tear from her cheek with a lace handkerchief. And it didn't matter because lately no one in her house seemed to care what she wanted to do or stop doing. She said her driver was completely of confidence, perhaps the only person at her house whom she could trust. While I was listening to her, I couldn't keep my eyes off the door: at any moment Don Vicente could come through it, his boots sharply striking the floor and a gun pointed directly at my chest. Or worse, it might be Isabel in a rage, pointing her fingernails at my face. How could I, at that moment, in those circumstances, focus on the lightning flashes in Doña Isabel's eyes, which made me blush the first time I saw them? How could I entertain the memory of the time she was lying on that very sofa because of the dizzy spell she had, with the air of a young woman from the previous century who had fallen asleep and then awakened for me, just for me, with the top button of her black dress unbuttoned—I undid it myself—when I discovered that she had around her neck, in the throbbing veins, born in the warmth beneath her neckline, something like the shadow of an old desire, perhaps at the point of wilting and kept secret from the world until that moment? How could I possibly be brave enough to tell her that after the night together in the theater I dreamed about her again and again, that I would open my eyes at midnight and could almost see her in the darkness, covered by a sheet, under which I could see the outlines of her body, which time had not managed to alter—her silhouette was still lovely—the light hiding the grey in her silky dark hair falling to her shoulders? How could I comfort her, ask her forgiveness, explain that it was all just a literary misunderstanding, because when I write I invent things, I imagine things, I alter things to the point that they become unlikely or impossible? Perhaps because of that very feeling of anxiety which invaded and overran me, I suddenly found myself weeping, having embraced her, stammering, falling down, trying to express my sorrow for having hurt so deeply the two women I had loved the most in my life, telling her how their faces would merge into one when I was with one or the other, that when I was with her I could speak with an honesty I had never experienced with anyone else. I told her how miserable and forlorn I felt, because in the end I wasn't going to have either one of them, that I had lost them and nothing could be done about it, and who would fill the void that they would leave in my life? I told her that I understood that sometimes young people commit suicide over desperate love—and in my case it was two desperate loves—or they go to the ends of the earth or become monks, but how could I ever start to undo the damage that I had done? And only then, finally, did I understand, because Doña Isabel, in a surprising gesture, took my chin and raised my face to look me squarely in the eye and then asked me to seek out Isabel one more time to clarify what had happened; that is what I could do to make at least partial restitution, emphasize that it was a novelized chronicle and that what I was writing was nothing but fiction and that she, Isabel's mother, had no idea, of course, in the theater when her arm came near mine or mine went near hers and she certainly did not feel anything because of breathing the same burning, sensual air which surrounded us, that Isabel had to believe that because she loved me, she kept on loving me even though at the moment she was furious with me because of the misunderstanding—writers are always such liars, someone had assured her—but she was certain, and a mother's instinct never fails when her daughter was in the circumstances in which Isabel, so naïve, so sensitive, and so nervous, the poor thing, found herself, so confused, believing that I was a serious man, and with that brutal father of hers, incapable of believing that a woman could have her own ideas and feelings.

I mustered the courage to ask her a question, looking directly into her eyes:

"I will find Isabel and convince her that everything I wrote is a product of my imagination, but only if you answer just one question with absolute honesty, Doña Isabel—is it really true that everything I wrote was merely the product of my imagination?"

Her eyes lit up with one more flash of lightning even more intense, and they told me everything I hoped they would tell me from the moment we gazed into each other's eyes when she awoke from the dizzy spell she suffered beside me. I even thought she was about to start crying, without any need of lace handkerchiefs or reservations, to throw herself at me and bare her soul, but as I could no longer trust my imagination for once I decided to pay attention only to her words, which took a completely different path than her eyes:

"I swear to you on a stack of holy Bibles that I never felt nor never had any inkling of what, according to my daughter, you wrote."

"Not even right now, at this moment?"

The expression in her eyes didn't change, but she responded, without an ounce of hesitation:

"Not even at this moment."

XII

It wasn't just the sadness from having lost half our national territory, or from the dishonorable invasion of our city, or from having so many casualties throughout the country; above all the sadness came from having discovered our true faces, as Mexicans, reflected in that mirror.

JUAN JOSÉ PÉREZ DOBLADO

THE WAKE FOR Dr. Urruchúa was held in the drawing room of his own home. His housekeeper washed his body, fixed his hair and dressed him in a tuxedo with a bow tie. She had worked for him for over thirty years and was the person who cried most, at times convulsively. She told me how peacefully he had died, how much she loved him, what a good person he was, so kind and so unattached to his meager material possessions, how difficult it was for her to take care of everything, including all the arrangements to have him buried that next morning, how nothing is so complex as dressing the dead, how she could have used some aromatic vinegar.

Several physicians from the hospital attended, along with a small group of students, one of his nieces and her children, and very few of our friends from the Progreso Café. The thick aroma of funeral flowers along with the smell of melting, crackling candles makes me dizzy, but I managed to stay almost until dawn.

On one wall was a large metal crucifix, the arched body throwing a horrific shadow on the back of the room.

I was moved by the attitude of his housekeeper. She stood for hours next to the casket, occasionally kneeling to pray or peeking through the casket's small window to look at him, talk to him and say goodbye over and over.

From the moment she found him deceased in his bed, the corpse belonged to her and no one else. In fact, she waited several hours to notify his colleagues at the hospital and his niece of his death.

I imagined her closing his eyes, shedding the first tears, contemplating at length his inert figure, exhausted, and the way the respected and loved features of his face slowly became sharper, perhaps speaking to him aloud.

I recalled the time that Dr. Urruchúa had spoken to me about overcoming my fear of death. Hadn't I ever experienced the desire to give my life for someone or something? That alone can save us. He had that type of relationship with his patients, in a very palpable way. Perhaps I experienced something of the sort with my writing. Death then becomes inconsequential. We think that we are our bodies. But lo and behold, before long that illusion, that mirage vanishes. When you have a patient seriously ill in the hospital or a friend in great danger, you run to help and leave little bits of your body along the way, like clothing you can no longer use. You trade places with your friend or with your patient when you undertake the activity and really give it your all, and you don't have the sensation of losing anything as a result. Ironically, when you make a supposed sacrifice—which really never happens— you finally discover who you really are. The danger your friend was in not only destroyed your body, but also your concern for your body.

I mentioned something to him about my fear of pain at the threshold of death, and he added:

"I have certainly seen my share of people flee from fear and the idea of death, and it is only natural for humans to be terrified of it ahead of time. But rest assured, my dear friend: I have never seen anyone frightened who is *truly* dying."

At one point, perhaps due to a slight disturbance in the air, the flames trembled slightly around each wick, producing ever so slightly more smoke, and the shadows gloomily lengthened over the walls. I felt the presence of Dr. Urruchúa even more vividly at that moment.

With that thin little voice of his, almost a purr, he said, "I have never seen anyone frightened who is *truly* dying."

When it was almost dawn, there was a heavy silence, occasionally broken by the awful sighs of someone who had fallen asleep ... then awakened and remembered.

The next day they buried him in a cemetery close to the Hospital of San Pedro and San Pablo. Considerably more people were there, particularly physicians, students and patients with whom he had worked. It was a cemetery which almost seemed like a potter's field—you had to take into account the situation of the city at that moment—given the coagulated geometry of the anonymous tombstones, with more crosses than houses in that part of the city. "This city is going to be full of dead people," Dr. Urruchúa himself had told me. How long ago was that?

A priest pronounced a few brief words, one of the physicians spoke on behalf of all of them in even fewer words, the housekeeper wept inconsolably, the doctor's niece, whose name was Irene, felt dizzy, so they administered camphor aroma treatments and took her to her carriage. After shovels pressed the soil down and they made a little hill covered with stones, they placed a very simple, unadorned cross on it, two crosspieces which carried only the doctor's name, the date of his birth and the date of his death.

A thousand memories, pleasant and painful alike, started to circulate in my mind, doing somersaults, engaging each other in combat, and knocking each other down. And when my state of awareness stumbled under the weight of unbearable anguish, I felt a mixture of shouting and wailing make its way up my throat. I sobbed without shedding tears, which is the worst way to cry.

I think that it was there, at that moment, when something that I had seen—or of which I had seen images—that *other*, or the way those little lights in the sky had winked at me, took on a definitive form. It was the final count from the inventory, from the report, from the retelling, from the chronicle of the United States invasion itself. It was a final balance, but with

no associated words or concrete actions: it was a simple ceremonial completion, a clean break from the past, a descent into
silence and emptiness.

XIII

As Mexicans, we are now in a period of maturity and dignity which allows us to respond in the same tone with which others speak to us, and with a smirk at the threats which used to make us tremble in fear.

IGNACIO MANUEL ALTAMIRANO

WITH A LITTLE FURROW between her brows, my wife asks, "Get to the point. To the point! What happened with the daughter of Doña Isabel? Did you find her?"

"I sought her out, but she refused to see me. The servant with white gloves kept bowing to me as he explained that Señorita Isabel was not in a position to receive me at that moment. The same thing the next day. I wrote her a letter and she responded curtly, saying that she never wanted to see me again, that I was a swine, and that she knew I was trying to contact her only because her mother had gone to my house to request it. Later on I learned that she went for a long time with her parents to Cuba, or something like that."

"In other words, you destroyed the family."

"I suppose so, in a sense."

"None of this 'in a sense.' You destroyed it."

"Fine. I can accept that. I destroyed the family. But I really loved them."

"That's no excuse."

"That's why I didn't want to write the chronicle—I knew I would have to come to grips with the irreparable harm I caused them. Merely thinking about things, bringing them back to life in your memory, or even repenting of them—these don't compare with writing them down."

"So you figure that if you have any hope of redemption, it is because you committed your memories of them to writing?"

"Precisely! In my opinion, the most significant paragraph of the chronicle, by far, does not refer to historical events, to the turbulence of those days, to my visions or nightmares or the moment I stabbed a Yankee in the chest, but the one in which I say that confessions like the one I made attest to the fact that in every religious faith the vast majority of people have an anguishing need to *render an accounting*. To whom? I don't know. Perhaps to everyone and to no one in particular. But might it not be related, in an involuntary way, to anticipating that meeting with He who gave us our souls and who could take them back whenever He pleases? Anything that could temper that meeting cannot be considered trivial, especially if, as I have always thought, it is through writing that the meeting becomes possible. Do you remember that page?"

"Yes, I hope it does help you at the hour you 'render an accounting,' as you call it, and which I prefer to call a type of temporary purgatory which prepares us for the next life, as Fourier says. Did you know that he calculated that every human soul will transmigrate about eight hundred and ten times between Earth and other planets before becoming one with the Clear Light? Since I'm a lousy Catholic, I don't believe in either hell or its opposite. I do believe in purgatory, or a state in which the soul is purified no matter how sickly it has become. Although your sins may be scarlet, in purgatory they shall become white as snow."

"Perhaps for that very reason, the invasion itself may have helped me to start to purge myself. In those days of misery, when I no longer had the company of Dr. Urruchúa, I thought a lot about the Christians of Abyssinia, who saw in the plague they were suffering a divine way to get to Heaven. Might that not apply to me, since the invasion we suffered was not so different from a plague? The Christians of Abyssinia who had not previously been exposed wrapped themselves in sheets contaminated with the plague to ensure their own deaths. I could have done the same thing by putting on the filthy uniform of a Yankee soldier and asking to be buried alive in it. What do you think?"

"I think it's disgusting!"

"I didn't leave my house again until June 12, 1848, when the Yankees departed, at least after a fashion. I went to the Zócalo to witness the ceremony, which was even more degrading than the one on September 13 of the prior year. The United States flag was lowered and ours was raised in the presence of authorities and soldiers from both countries, with everyone standing at strict attention. Can you imagine anything more ridiculous? They played both national anthems, presented arms, then fired a twenty-one-gun salute followed by thirty cannon shots. At that moment I desperately missed Father Jarauta and wished he had been there to shoot the Yankee soldier who was lowering the stars and stripes. It would have been quite a scene if at that moment the poor had revolted, and Próspero Pérez, standing on a bench, had once again asked, 'Are there no men here? Aren't the very rocks from all these buildings calling to us to fight?' But no, everything happened ceremoniously and tranquilly, as if nothing had actually happened. 'The Devil's biggest trick is to make us believe that he doesn't exist.' Remember that!"

"Speaking of the Devil, whatever happened to Father Jarauta?" Magdalena must have been concerned about the look on my face because she immediately softened her stance. "The truth is that I don't agree with his methods, as I already told you, but I like his stubbornness and I admire his unfailing faith. But you do have to admit that anyone who would come to Mexico from Spain to give his life because we had been invaded by the Yankee infidels has to be a little bit crazy, don't you?"

"As you can imagine, he opposed the Treaty of Guadalupe Hidalgo, which was signed in February of 1848, because we were ceding to our conquerors the territories of Texas, New Mexico and New California, two million four hundred thousand square kilometers—more than half of Mexico's territory. The United States gave Mexico fifteen million *pesos* as supposed payment. You can easily understand why Lucas Alemán responded, 'Unless Europe soon intervenes to help us, we will be lost without any recourse.'"

"And that's why Europe sent us Father Jarauta?"

"He issued another manifesto which, once again, appeared on every street in the city. Let me read you part of it: 'Mexicans! The wicked, traitorous work which began in 1845 has recently reached completion. More than half of the Republic has been sold to the invading enemy, to the worst enemy of humanity, to the devil himself, for a despicable amount, more despicable than coins tossed at the feet of a beggar. The rest of the territory will be occupied by American soldiers, now serving as guardians of the traitor to sustain the most horrific crime the centuries have ever seen. The actions of Count Julián come to mind, the way he sold his homeland over a personal resentment. But this horrible action really has nothing to do with that evil one, because Count Julián was blinded by anger, which caused him to allow the Moors into Spain, but the situation in Mexico was fueled by pure self-interest, self-comfort, and "progress," which are the preferred refuges of the devil.' Do you see how Father Jarauta had a very clear vision of where the devil lurks?"

"How ironic to hear that from you, since you've lived off rent from your parents' properties your entire life."

"That is the cross I have had to bear."

"It's a cross that plenty of people would love to bear, that's for sure. What else did the manifesto say?"

"It again called Mexicans to arms, urged them not to recognize the Mexican government for betraying the country, and even to condemn the Catholic priests who were in favor of the Treaty of Guadalupe Hidalgo. He went to Guanajuato to continue directing the guerrilla warfare, but now it was directed against the Mexican government, which caused *El Monitor*, which had previously praised him, to start to speak ill of him. Listen to what an editorial from the month of June said: 'Jarauta was received in Mexico by a hospitable country. It treated him as one of its own children, providing him with arms to defend against the invader. Now Jarauta is turning those arms on the very country which granted him asylum. In defense of his adopted country, Jarauta went beyond simply acting valiantly before God and men, and achieved the status of hero in defense of humanity. As Jarauta promotes a revolution in Mexico, he degrades that honor, he becomes an apostate and deserves excommunication before God, the Church, and men. Death to Jarauta.'"

"I think *El Monitor* was quite correct."

"What else could Father Jarauta do since he always said that we should fight against the Americans as well as Mexicans who were in favor of them? Both symbolized the same thing: Evil, the demon to which you were referring."

"They caught him, I assume. No one gets down from a cross alive."

"Right in Guanajuato, in July of that same year. General Anastasio de Bustamante, a man I happened to meet years later, personally presided over the firing squad. I was particularly impressed with his teeth, which reminded me of a mastiff's—large, yellow and carnivorous."

"Demonic, once again."

"Especially because it's said that the final words of Father Jarauta were the same ones repeated so many times here in Mexico City: 'Long live Christ our King, and death to the Yankees.'"

"And you agree with that sentiment, don't you?"

"Without a shadow of a doubt. We should ceaselessly repeat that refrain until, as you like to say, the sun stops shining and our planet returns to its original state of chaos."

"I'm glad you're too old and have no desire to visit the United States, because if you publish your chronicle, I'm sure they wouldn't let you in anyway."

But I did not want to publish it, and I decided to set it aside and have Magdalena do with it whatever she wants after I die. So I decided to include a dedication to her in the final lines of the final pages.

My love, since readers of this book—if there ever actually are any—may find it strange that I am dedicating it to you, one of its central characters, and that I am doing so in its final lines rather than at the beginning—as is the custom—it seems right

to give my reasoning here. Above all else, it is because without you I would never have written anything, and I would have
been entirely incapable of getting to the end, not just because
of your helpful comments and corrections, but also because
of the motivation it provided to hear you—on multiple occasions and especially at night, when you thought that I was
asleep—looking around in my desk, going through my papers
and notes to see whether I had written anything else, and then
when you found something the way you would read with interest and curiosity. Without your curiosity, do you think I would
have dared to write in such detail, for example, of my amorous
relationship with Isabel? But I knew that your eyes were there,
pursuing me, encouraging me to make a complete confession,
whatever the cost or result. Finally, as you know, I was writing
it for you, and consequently for that Other, or the Mirror, or
the King of Death, or Universal Conscience, or God, or whatever you want to call it. What difference can its name make if
ultimately we believe in the same thing? Sitting in our house,
happily resigned to our odd manner of loving each other, as
you say that Fourier says, reading and occasionally writing, we
haven't exactly been the rose window of a Gothic cathedral, I
think you'll agree, but simply the sudden and ephemeral rose
of a small kaleidoscope. Unfortunately, it has been impossible
for us to share the world of the proud, important poets who
surround us, or of the sad writers of sad things, who are even
more abundant. Just the two of us here, even more alone since
our children left home, convinced that only in this way would
we manage to approach that decisive moment of life (and
death) which together we have glimpsed in a musical chord,
in a poem, in a work of art, or in a mad desire to achieve saint-
liness. At our age that kind of faith has its advantages, don't
you think? If there is *something* after death, what will show up
in our kaleidoscope? What combinations of colors, cold and
warm humor, lunatic and mercurial dreams, discoveries and
disagreements, await us there? Today I believe more than ever
what I have always sensed: that dating back before a distant
past which may not have even existed, I loved you and awaited

you before even seeing you for the first time. My love for you has always been like a hidden heart beating beneath all my happiness and sorrows. It goes back so far that I don't even know during which of my existences it began. And tomorrow, when I am no longer at your side, and you feel that you, too, are about to expire, like the leafless structure of a flower, I will return, so that we can be together at that final moment, just like yesterday, today, and forever.

∾

EPIGRAPH
AUTHOR BIOGRAPHIES

JOHN QUINCY ADAMS (1767–1848)
American politician. Son of the second president of the United States, John Adams, and himself the sixth president from 1825–1829. As Secretary of State negotiated the Adams-Onis Treaty, which forced Spain to cede the Florida peninsula to the US. Inspiration for the famous Monroe Doctrine.

LUCAS ALAMÁN (1792–1853)
Mexican businessman, conservative politician and historian. Minister of Foreign Relations in the cabinet of Anastasio Bustamante; negotiated a border treaty with the United States before the War of Intervention. Died shortly after having occupied the same post in the last administration of Antonio López de Santa Anna.

JUAN NEPOMUCENO ALMONTE (1803–1869)
Mexican general, politician and diplomat. Illegitimate son of José María Morelos y Pavón. Officer in the army of Antonio López de Santa Anna during Texas's War of Independence. Participated in the Battles of the Alamo and San Jacinto and in the Mexican-American War. Charged with finding a European sovereign for the Mexican Crown. Occupied the Regency of the Empire from 1863–1864 and named lieutenant of the Empire with the duty of receiving Maximilian and Carlota.

IGNACIO MANUEL ALTAMIRANO (1834–1893)

Mexican writer, teacher, journalist and liberal politician of indigenous origin. Considered the father of Mexican literature and the romantic movement in Mexico. The disciple of Ignacio Ramírez, "El Nigromante" ("The Sorcerer"). Elected as a representative to congress in 1861. Fought in 1865 during the French invasion, reaching the rank of colonel. President of the Supreme Court of Justice and founder of the publications *El Correo de México* and *El Renacimiento*. Author of the novels *Navidad en las Montañas, Clemencia* and *El Zarco*.

MANUEL BALBONTÍN (1824–1894)

Mexican military officer and historian. As an artillery lieutenant fought in the Battle of Churubsuco. Author of *La invasión Americana, 1846 a 1848*. Reached the rank of colonel and joined Porfirio Díaz during the Revolution of Tuxtepec in 1876.

MARQUISE CALDERÓN DE LA BARCA (1804–1882)

Scottish-born writer who emigrated to the United States; real name was Frances Erskine Inglis. In 1838 married Ángel Calderón de la Barca, named Spanish representative to the Republic of Mexico in 1839. The couple remained in Mexico until 1842. Widowed in 1861 and given the title of marquise by Alphonse de Borbon in 1876. Known for her book *Life in Mexico during a Residency of Two Years in That Country*.

MANUEL CARPIO (1791–1869)

Mexican doctor, conservative politician, and esteemed religious and *costumbrista* poet. President of the Chamber of Deputies in 1824, and deputy again in 1846 and 1848. Translator of Hypocrites into Spanish.

HENRY CLAY (1777–1852)

US politician. Senator, member of the House of Representatives and presidential candidate on several occasions. Known for his diplomatic skills; resolved several political conflicts, earning the nickname of "the Great Peacemaker."

CARLOS MARÍA DE BUSTAMANTE (1774–1848)
Mexican chronicler, journalist, historian and politician. Named by José María Morelos y Pavón editor of *El Correo del Sur*, a publication of the *independentista* cause. Member of congress from Chilpancingo, where he wrote the September 14, 1813 inaugural address of Morelos. Collaborated on the editing of the first Act of Independence of Mexico. Elected deputy from Oaxaca in 1822.

JOSÉ TOMÁS DE CUÉLLAR (1830–1894)
Mexican writer, journalist, politician and diplomat. Known by his pseudonym Facundo. Fought against the American invasion in 1847 and later served as a diplomat in the United States. Novelist in the romantic style of Manuel Payno. In 1869, founded the weekly which he directed, *La Ilustración Potosina*, and also collaborated on *El Siglo XIX*, *La Ilustración Mexicana* and *El federalista*. Author of *La linterna mágica* (1889–1892, 24 volumes).

ÁNGEL DEL CAMPO (1868–1908)
Mexican writer, journalist and educator. Student of Ignacio Manuel Altamirano at the National Preparatory School. As a journalist used the pseudonyms Micrós and Tick Tack. Author of *Ocios y apuntes* (1890), *Cosas vistas* (1894), *Cartones* (1897) and the serialized novel *La Rumba* (1890–1891).

EL SIGLO XIX
Newspaper founded in 1841 by Juan B. Morales and Mariano Otero. Championed the free press in reaction to Antonio López de Santa Anna's severe restrictions. Morales, who published a series of satirical anti-government columns, was eventually imprisoned for his writings.

JOSÉ MARÍA ESTEVA (1818–1904)

Mexican writer and conservative politician. Senator who also served as prefect and Minister of State during the French invasion and the empire. After the fall of Maximilian was exiled to Cuba, returning to Mexico in 1871.

SAM HOUSTON (1793–1863)

United States politician and soldier. President of the Republic of Texas, senator and governor of the state of Texas after it was integrated into the United States, several years after gaining its independence from Mexico.

MANUEL PAYNO (1810–1894)

Mexican writer and politician. Minister of Finance in the cabinets of José Joaquín de Herrera and Ignacio Comonfort. A representative and senator, also served as Mexico's consul general in Spain. Author of the novels *El Fistol del Diablo* (1846) and *Los bandidos de Río Frío* (1891).

JAMES K. POLK (1795–1849)

United States politician elected to the House of Representatives as a Democrat in 1825, leaving that position in 1839 to become governor of Tennessee. Eleventh president of the nation (1845–1849), the period of the Mexican-American War.

GUILLERMO PRIETO (1818–1897)

Mexican writer, journalist and liberal. Served as a representative in congress several times and formed part of the Constituent Congress of 1857. Served as Minister of Finance in the cabinets of Mariano Arista, Juan Álvarez and Benito Juárez.

WINFIELD SCOTT (1786–1866)

United States general and diplomat. Nicknamed "Old Fuss and Feathers." Considered the most gifted military mind of his times. In his fifty-year career participated in the War of 1812, the US intervention in Mexico, the Black Hawk War, the Seminole Wars and the Civil War. Presidential candidate in 1852.

BARBARA A. TENENBAUM

American historian (PhD, Harvard University). Specialist in Mexican culture at the Hispanic Division of the Library of Congress since 1992. Editor-in-chief of the *Encyclopedia of Latin American History and Culture* (five volumes), and author of *México en la época de los agiostias, 1821–1857*.

GUADALUPE VICTORIANA (1786–1843)

Mexican military officer and politician. First president of an independent Mexico from 1824–1829. Real name José Miguel Ramón Adaucto Fernández y Félix, but in 1811 adopted the name Guadalupe Victoriana in honor of the Virgin of Guadalupe. Member of the insurgent army of José María Morelos y Pavón.

FRANCISCO ZARCO (1829–1869)

Mexican journalist, liberal politician and historian. Editor-in-chief of the newspaper *El Siglo XIX*. Served as Minister of State and Foreign Relations in the cabinet of Benito Juárez.

UNITED STATES

TERRITORIO DE BAJA CALIFORNIA

SONORA

CHIHUAH

SINALOA

DURA

USA

Mexico

Baja
California

Sonora

Baja
California
Sur

Chihuahua

Coahuila

Durango

Aguascalientes

Nayarit

Querétaro

Tlaxcala

(D.F. = Distrito Federal)

Yucatán

Colima

Querétaro

Oaxaca

Chiapas

MEXICO
TODAY

TERRITORY

MEXICO 1857

JA

NUEVO LEON

Y COAHUILA

NGO

ZACATECAS

SAN
LUIS

AGS

POTOSI

GUANAJUATO

QUERETARO

JALISCO

MEXICO

D.F.

TLAX

V
E
R
A
C
R
U
Z

MICHOACAN

OLIMA

PUEBLA

GUERRERO

OAXACA

CHIAPAS

TABASCO

Y
U
C
A
T
A
N

TAMAULIPAS

TRANSLATOR'S
ACKNOWLEDGMENTS

SOME THEORISTS COMPARE translations to play performances: as actors would be silent without written texts,
so would translators be without original texts. The comparison runs deeper, because just as plays require many elements
beyond text and actors, a published translation involves much
more than an original text rendered into another language. I
am deeply grateful for the contributions of many people who
have made *Yankee Invasion* possible. My wife Virginia has been
a constant support for this and myriad projects. Jay Miskowiec
did a painstaking review of the entire text, page by page, paragraph by paragraph, comparing the original Spanish to my
English translation, and then making suggestions. Although
on rare occasion we did not agree on the final product, in the
vast majority of cases I saw that his changes improved the
translation tremendously. Alexei Esikoff has been fundamental in editing this text and has done a great job throughout
the process of preparing it for publication. I am grateful to the
decision-makers at Aliform Publishing and Scarletta Press for
their faith in and backing of this project, as well as to the many
people who have done a superb job with its production. Finally,
in my opinion, Ignacio Solares will go down in history as one
of Mexico's great writers, and this is one of his finest books.
I am grateful for his trust in me to introduce this and other
books to the English-speaking world. As with other texts I have
translated, I sought the opportunity to translate *La invasión*
because I loved reading it and wanted to share it with English-
speaking readers. I hope other readers will enjoy *Yankee Invasion* and other Solares texts as much as I do.

TIMOTHY G. COMPTON

ALIFORM Ⓐ PUBLISHING

Aliform Publishing specializes in the translation of Latin American and world literature by award-winning authors. We're especially proud of our ongoing collaboration with National Medal of the Arts winner Gregory Rabassa and novelists such as Eduardo García Aguilar from Colombia, João de Melo from Portugal, and Ana Clavel from Mexico.

www.aliformgroup.com • aliformgroup@gmail.com

SCARLETTA PRESS

At Scarletta Press, we commit ourselves to absorbing, enlightening, challenging and intriguing our readers by finding new voices and opinions missing from the publishing world. As a small press we can nurture those authors overlooked by bigger companies. Yet through our partnership with PGW/Perseus, we are part of the largest independent distribution group in the United States. Discover why our books win national awards and acclaim. Visit our website to peruse Scarletta's fiction, memoir, political science and how-to titles.

www.scarlettapress.com • editor@scarlettapress.com